Praise for Kathy Brandt's novels

Swimming with the Dead

"A likable, exuberant heroine, the fascinating world of scuba diving, and a fast-paced plot make *Swimming with the Dead* the kind of mystery that takes hold of you and doesn't let go until the last paragraph. A terrific debut for Kathy Brandt." —Margaret Coel, *New York Times* bestselling author of *Killing Raven*

"An impressive debut sure to please the outdoor enthusiasts, *Swimming with the Dead* teems with captivating dive scenes, picture-perfect island settings, and a host of colorful characters. Dive in. The water's great. You won't regret taking the plunge!" —Christine Goff, author of *Death Takes a Gander*

"A very exciting new series. . . . There are many viable suspects who had reason to want the victim dead, so the reader is thoroughly entertained trying to figure out who the killer really is." —*Midwest Book Review*

"Debut author Kathy Brandt sets the stage for a thrilling, fast-paced series featuring Hannah Sampson, head of Denver homicide's Dive & Recovery Team. Hold on to your hats for this one!" —*Roundtable Reviews*

"An intriguing debut." —*Deadly Pleasures*

"This book grabs the reader from the start and never lets go. The pace is quick and sure, and Hannah is a great new character. The island background is clearly described by someone who has spent time there, and is fond of the locale. The underwater action is described in vivid detail. The islanders are all individuals, with quirks unique to those living in this kind of place. I get the feeling the author may have met a few of these people firsthand." —*Romance Reader's Connection* (Mysterious Author of the Month)

continued . . .

"Tough, gutsy Hannah Sampson, head of the Dive and Recovery Team of Denver's homicide division, finds herself in deep in Kathy Brandt's new mystery, *Swimming with the Dead*. . . . Brandt puts a twist on the typical mystery novel. . . . Everyone's a suspect in Sampson's mind, and readers' assumptions are turned backward, somersaulted into suspicion and coaxed into second-guessing. Brandt leads you to the edge and lets you dangle a bit before giving out the secret. Dive in, but with caution. You never know what's lurking beyond the reef."

—*Springs Magazine*

"Suspense builds as Hannah comes closer to the truth in this first-rate thriller. Readers will eagerly anticipate future installments." —*Romantic Times* (Top Pick)

Dark Water Dive

"A compelling whodunit . . . crafting character development, scientific knowledge, and psychological insight that transcend the genre." —*Colorado Springs Gazette*

"Land-locked Coloradoans with a yen for yachting will find their hobby in full sail." —*Rocky Mountain News*

"In a chilling climax, Brandt takes the readers on a hair-raising dive that describes the splendor and the danger of the beautiful Caribbean Sea. This deftly plotted page-turner, a follow-up to *Swimming with the Dead*, is enhanced with a riveting description of the underwater world. A great book—I can't wait for the next installment!" —The Best Reviews

Kathy Brandt

Dangerous Depths

An Underwater Investigation

A SIGNET BOOK

SIGNET
Published by New American Library, a division of
Penguin Group (USA) Inc., 375 Hudson Street,
New York, New York 10014, USA
Penguin Group (Canada), 10 Alcorn Avenue, Toronto,
Ontario M4V 3B2, Canada (a division of Pearson Penguin Canada Inc.)
Penguin Books, Ltd., 80 Strand, London WC2R 0RL, England
Penguin Ireland, 25 St. Stephen's Green, Dublin 2,
Ireland (a division of Penguin Books Ltd.)
Penguin Group (Australia), 250 Camberwell Road, Camberwell, Victoria 3124,
Australia (a division of Pearson Australia Group Pty. Ltd.)
Penguin Books India Pvt. Ltd., 11 Community Centre, Panchsheel Park,
New Delhi - 110 017, India
Penguin Group (NZ), cnr Airborne and Rosedale Roads, Albany,
Auckland 1310, New Zealand (a division of Pearson New Zealand Ltd.)
Penguin Books (South Africa) (Pty.) Ltd., 24 Sturdee Avenue,
Rosebank, Johannesburg 2196, South Africa

Penguin Books Ltd., Registered Offices:
80 Strand, London WC2R 0RL, England

First published by Signet, an imprint of New American Library,
a division of Penguin Group (USA) Inc.

First Printing, May 2005
10 9 8 7 6 5 4 3 2 1

While most of the places in this book are real, both Hermit Cay and Flower Island are fictitious as are all characters and events. At this writing, six of the seven species of marine turtles in the world are listed as endangered or critically endangered, and the outlook is increasingly grim. In some regions, leatherbacks are fast heading for extinction, and the numbers of green and hawksbill turtle have plummeted. Thanks to the efforts of organizations that are working for stricter laws and better enforcement.

ACKNOWLEDGMENTS

Thanks to Shannon Gore for graciously sharing her knowledge about marine turtles and to her turtle monitoring team: Ken Pemberton, Jobe Varlack, Gary Frett, and Dylan Penn of the BVI Conservation and Fisheries for letting me tag along. Special thanks to Jessica Maddox, M.D. for her advice about head injuries and poisoning. All errors are mine.

As always a huge thanks to my agent, Jacky Sach, and to my editor, Martha Bushko.

Most important, thanks to my family for their love and support and especially to my husband, Ron, for seeing me through another one.

Chapter 1

‧◦⊸⊹⊶◦‧

At 12:03 the sea quivered. Then it exploded. The cat, whom I'd graciously allowed to curl at my feet, flew across me, claws extended, fur flying, and hit the ground running. So much for gratitude. I wrestled with a damned tangle of sheets that held me like a mummy. Finally they set me free, and I landed beside the bunk on my ass as the *Sea Bird* pitched up one side of a rolling wave and slammed down the other.

I fought my way to my feet as the boat crashed down onto an ocean that seemed to have turned to concrete. I wanted out of the floating horror house before the thing sank. I clung to anything that was bolted to the floor, pulled myself out of my cabin, into the salon, and made it up the steps to the deck. I didn't like what I saw. This was not what I considered a good start to the week.

The ocean was a confusion of flaming waves. In the middle of it all was the *Caribbe*, Elyse Henry's boat—burning. Flames shot out of the roof, pointing hellish fingers to the sky. I jumped onto the dock and raced toward the heat.

The entire right side of the vessel was already consumed in fire and angry waves crashed against her hull. Where the hell was Elyse? Still inside? No one could survive long in the inferno.

"Elyse! Elyse!" I shouted, frantic and disoriented.

Sadie skirted the edge of the dock, whining, tail between her legs. Neither one of us knew what the hell to do.

The *Caribbe* was a clunky flat-bottomed boat with boxy living quarters perched on top. The fire was concentrated in the galley. Flames flashed out the hatches.

If Elyse was still on board, she could be back in her cabin, trapped, maybe unconscious. I had to get to her before the gas tanks exploded.

I knew better than to spend any time thinking it through. If I did, I might flinch, wait a second too long, and then it would be too late.

"Stay, Sadie," I demanded firmly. She'd be right on my heels otherwise.

I jumped onto the aft section of the *Caribbe*, which was still secured to the cleat on the dock. Just about the time my feet touched the deck, the frayed line broke and the *Caribbe* began to drift out of her slip and away from the dock. At least the *Sea Bird* and the other boats in the marina might be spared the flames.

Then, kaboom! A whoosh of hot air pummeled my face, and a ball of fire roared through the *Caribbe*. The blast hit like a freight train, flinging me off the boat into air and space. I hit the water and was hurled toward the seafloor, tumbling. Finally, my momentum slowed and I fought my way up, arms flailing, feet kicking hard.

Miraculously, I made it to the surface, gasping for breath, but somehow still in one piece. I was surrounded by smoke and patches of flaming oil. I choked up diesel-filled salt water and sought out pockets of air in the burning liquid, trying to see past the smoke through eyes that stung and teared. I was desperate to catch sight of Elyse. I forced my arms and legs into action. Treading water, I whipped around in a circle, searching the darkness and smoky gloom. Nothing.

Then Sadie began barking furiously from the edge of the dock, her fur prickled, her snout pointing at what looked like a rag doll drifting in the water. I swam to the floating mass, my heart pounding, flames licking my arms. I feared what I would find. I knew it was Elyse. By the time I got to the place she'd floated, she had disappeared under the water.

I filled my lungs with hot acrid air and dove. What I wouldn't do for a scuba tank, face mask, and fins now. I went down, arms sweeping, searching, eyes shut tight against the brine. I'd done this before, searched blind in water so mucky it was black. But never without my gear, never in water on fire, and never for a friend who had just gone under before my eyes.

I kicked hard, forcing my body down, hand outstretched, praying to grasp a sleeve, hair, a foot, anything. Nothing but empty water washed through my fingers.

Out of air, I surfaced back into the flames, sucked in another breath, and dove, heading for the bottom. I hit sand and fought to stay under against the powerful ocean forces determined to shoot me back to the surface.

Grasping desperately at the turtle grass that grew along the seafloor, I edged along the bottom, seeking, on automatic now. I swept my free hand back and forth, feeling my way through the water, doing what I'd been trained to do. I brushed against rocks, a conch, a sea cucumber.

God, where the hell was Elyse?

Once more I surfaced, took a hot desperate breath and dove. I knew if I didn't find her this time, I would not find her at all—at least alive. Hell, she might already be dead. I was frantic—panic was setting in. So was exhaustion.

Could I make it to the bottom one last time?

Kicking hard, I pointed my body down. Before I'd even made it back to the seafloor, I swam right into Elyse, suspended a few feet off the bottom. I wrapped my arms tight around her chest. I was not about to lose her. I twisted in the water, anchored my feet on the bottom, and drove them into the sand. Seconds later we were on the surface.

I wrapped an arm around Elyse and side-stroked, pulling her behind me, trying to avoid the pockets of fire still flashing on the surface and at the same time keep Elyse's head above water. I knew by the smell that flames sizzled in my hair.

Finally I made it to the dock, its underside reeking of green algae and dead fish. The owners of the marina, Calvin and Tilda, waited, ready to assist. Their two girls, Rebecca and Daisy, stood back, arms wrapped around Sadie's neck.

Calvin slid his black, muscled arms under Elyse's and pulled her gently out of the water and onto the dock. I climbed wearily onto a slimy wooden rung and Tilda gave me a hand up.

Calvin quickly looked away, embarrassed. It wasn't till that moment that I realized I was topless. I hadn't taken the time to grab a shirt when I raced off my boat. Even in a crisis, Calvin was modest. I didn't have the time or luxury to worry about it. Elyse wasn't breathing.

Frantic, I bent over her and began CPR. Calvin immediately joined me, taking over chest compressions as I began mouth-to-mouth resuscitation.

Over and over, I forced air into Elyse's depleted lungs as Calvin pushed on her sternum. Through a haze, I could see the tension in his face, the perspiration forming on his brow.

Time seemed to stretch out. Christ, how long had we been going now? Was it too late to bring Elyse back? Calvin's face was marked with determination. Neither one of us was about to call it.

"Come on, Elyse, breathe, breathe, breathe," I whispered, and then forced another breath into her.

Finally, a gasp, a shudder. Then water gurgled out of her lungs and down the side of her face, and Elyse took a breath. But she didn't open her eyes.

Calvin and I sat back on our haunches for just an instant trying to regain equilibrium; then he picked her up and we ran toward his van. Tilda tossed me one of Calvin's shirts and I pulled it on as I rushed ahead to open the door and climb in.

Calvin gently handed Elyse in to me. I slid across the seat, and cradled her head in my lap. Once Calvin got behind the wheel, he was a maniac, throwing gravel as he slammed his foot into the gas pedal and swerved the van onto the highway to Road Town. I glanced back to see Tilda, still in her robe, her arms around the girls, Sadie nuzzled into Rebecca's side. Daisy sought comfort from the thumb she was sucking on, her eyes wide. I could see the fear and confusion on their faces.

I felt it too. An hour ago, I'd been sleeping on the *Sea Bird*, my cat keeping my feet warm. Now it was after one in the morning and my best friend was lying in my lap, barely breathing. What the hell had happened?

Chapter 2

⁓

The last time I'd seen Elyse was on Wednesday night, the night we'd encountered a sea turtle nesting on the beach. If I hadn't been with Elyse, I'd never have known it was there. She'd let me in on a miracle, one that was becoming more uncommon with each year as humans brought their hotels and beach umbrellas to these pristine shores.

Once sea turtles had been abundant in the Caribbean. But the story of the sea turtle is the story of the American buffalo. Abundant and easy to catch, turtles became the major food source for the increasing numbers of people who came to colonize the islands. When the slaughter began, some 600 million green turtles were estimated to inhabit the Caribbean. Now a few hundred thousand remain. Elyse and I had gotten lucky when we encountered the turtle nesting around the point.

We'd been over there walking along the beach when Sadie started barking. Elyse spied the tracks, distinct in the light of a full moon. The trail led all the way from the water's edge up the beach and into the bush.

"Those are turtle tracks. She's still up there," Elyse had said, excitement sending her voice an octave higher. "I don't see any tracks coming back. Listen! Do you hear that?"

"Hear what?" All I heard were the waves washing the shore and the sharp sudden call of a distant tern.

"In the shrubs, up on the dune. Shhhh. Listen, Hannah," she insisted, impatient.

Finally, I heard it, the rustling and digging of sand being scattered.

"Let's go look," she said, and scrambled up the gentle incline to the trees. Sadie and I were right on her heels.

"There it is." She briefly shone her flashlight on the female, then clicked it off, unwilling to disturb her or confuse her with the sudden light.

"It's a green," Elyse said. "She must be three feet long."

The turtle looked like a huge boulder nestled in the sand, her shell covered with a few barnacles and strands of algae.

"Jeez, Elyse. Maybe we should let her be."

"She's hardly aware of our presence," Elyse whispered. "The nesting female has only one goal, laying her eggs."

We sat in the sand at a distance that Elyse assured me would not interfere. Sadie stretched out nearby, bored now and ready for a nap. The turtle was clearing away the sand with her powerful front flippers, digging deeper.

In the warm quiet night, the moon illuminating the sand and the shell, we watched the turtle doing what these ancient creatures had done for millions of years.

"She's at least forty, maybe closer to fifty, just at the beginning of her reproductive life," Elyse said. We were sitting, shoulders touching, knees up, arms wrapped around our legs, gazing into the pit. "If she survives the hazards of her environment and the intrusion of humans, if these nesting grounds remain undisturbed and viable, she'll return every two or three years for the next half a century."

"Lots of ifs," I said.

"Yeah," she responded, a touch of wistfulness in her voice.

When the turtle determined she'd dug her pit deep enough, she crawled into the depression.

"She'll start digging the egg chamber now. Look," Elyse said.

About then, the turtle began using her back flippers to excavate a deep hole. In an amazingly rote pattern, she dug, scooping sand with the left leg and kicking it forward with the right, then reversing the process until she had formed the perfectly flask-shaped egg chamber.

Then it happened. She began to lay her eggs. White, glistening balls began to fill the chamber.

"Probably a hundred eggs," Elyse said, breaking through the awe I was feeling.

We watched her bury the eggs in the wet sand and pack it down. Then she filled the body pit and concealed it with loose sand and rubble. Finally, she turned and headed back to the sea. I knew it would be the last contact she had with the offspring she'd fought to shore to produce. Now they would be on their own. When they hatched, they would fight their way out of the nest, and emerge. Small enough to fit in the palm of my hand and vulnerable, they would make the treacherous journey to the sea.

At the water's edge, the exhausted female lifted her head once, craning her long neck and scanning the horizon, perhaps hesitant to abandon her young. Then she slipped into the water, her shell glistening in the moonlight, and disappeared beneath the surface.

I'd felt an overwhelming sadness when she was gone. What was that about? Loss maybe? Fear that she would never return? The realization that I had just experienced a miracle and now it was over? The beach felt empty.

"Come on," Elyse said, recognizing my despair. She put her arm over my shoulder as we walked back down the beach to our boats. "We'll keep tabs on the nest. They'll hatch in about two months."

That evening had been one of the many gifts that Elyse had given me since we'd been friends. She was a sensitive soul, who saw beauty in nature's details. While I crashed through life, Elyse tiptoed. Complete opposites, we'd become instant friends.

*   *   *

Now, Calvin and I were sitting in the waiting room at Pebbles Hospital. We'd been there for an hour, drinking one cup of coffee after another. My anxiety levels were peaking with the caffeine and the fact that we had heard nothing about Elyse's condition.

Finally Tom Hall came out. I wondered if the guy ever went home. He'd been the doctor on duty every time I'd been at the hospital. I'd had my fair share of cuts and bruises needing a few stitches here, a Band-Aid there.

"Hannah, you again," he said. Hall was a tall, skinny guy, eyes sunken, his complexion the color of paste. He was a character right out of Sleepy Hollow.

"Yeah, how is Elyse?"

"She's in critical condition. She has a fractured collar bone and tibia, lots of abrasions. The biggest problem is the head injury. Looks like some swelling. She is not conscious. We've checked her cranial reflexes; her pupils are constricting with light. Her brain stem seems to be undamaged, but I am very concerned. She isn't breathing on her own."

"What are you doing for her?" I asked.

"I've called in a specialist, a neurologist from St. Thomas. He'll be here late in the morning. I've ordered blood tests—electrolytes, blood counts, and cultures, a CT scan of the brain and neck, a toxicology screen, and EEG. We'll know more when we have the results. In the meantime, we've got her hooked up to IVs and a respirator. I'll be setting and casting her leg and we'll be monitoring her condition.

"Let me see those burns," he said turning his attention to the red splotches barely visible under Calvin's shirt. Hall didn't miss anything.

I winced when he lifted the fabric off my shoulder. I'd felt the sting every time I'd surfaced in the fire-slicked ocean. The flames had danced across my back and shoulders until I dove under the water again.

"Come on, Hannah. Those need to be taken care of." He led me into an examining room.

"Take the shirt off and put this on," he said tersely. He handed me a faded blue-and-white hospital gown that opened in the back, then left, pulling the curtain closed behind him.

I stood alone for the first time since the blast had rocked my boat and thrown me into disaster. Finally, I leaned against the examining table. Fatigue swept over me, adrenaline giving way to pain, shock to reality.

I'd directed a steady stream of empty conversation at Elyse all the way to the hospital—kept telling her she was okay, she'd be fine. Right now, I was having a hard time believing it.

I caught a look at myself in the nearby mirror. I didn't like what I saw. I looked like a waif. Calvin's shirt, covered in oil and blood, hung to my knees, the cuffs way past my fingertips. My long chestnut hair stuck out in clumps of singed tangles, but worse were the brown eyes, haunted, fearful. The face was gaunt, high cheekbones sooty, as though brushed with black blush.

Chapter 3

B y the time Hall came back in, Calvin's shirt lay in a
heap on the floor and I'd managed to climb onto the
metal examining table. He was accompanied by a sleepy-
looking nurse who just smiled at my fruitless attempts to
keep vital body parts covered with the skimpy gown. The
two of them went about inspecting the burns on my hand,
shoulders, and back. Then the nurse dabbed salve all over
them and covered them in gauze. Christ, it hurt.

"Could be worse," Hall said after a few minutes. "Just
your right hand and the one spot on your shoulder are second degree. Your back is only slightly red, no worse than a
bad sunburn. Keep the salve on it and change the bandages
tomorrow," he said, handing me the tube of gunk and some
extra gauze. "I want to see you again in a few days."

"Doc, tell me the truth about Elyse." I wanted a straight
answer and the right answer. I wanted him to tell me that my
best friend wasn't lying in there dying. Maybe Hall couldn't
do both.

"It's too soon to tell, Hannah."

"Yeah, but what do you think? Come on, Doc. You've got
to have an opinion."

"It's serious. The breaks and abrasions, those will mend.
And she was fortunate that she wasn't badly burned. But the
head injury—that concerns me, and the fact that she hasn't

regained consciousness. We'll know more when the tests come back."

I couldn't even think about losing Elyse. We'd been friends from the day I'd moved to the British Virgin Islands and we'd become neighbors. She lived in the boat across the dock at Pickering's Landing, where Tilda and Calvin Pickering managed the small marina and about twenty boats.

Elyse's boat, the *Caribbe*, belonged to the Society of Ocean Conservation, a nonprofit environmental group based in London. Elyse was the only employee in the British Virgin Islands. By now, what remained of the *Caribbe* would be lying at the bottom of the bay.

I live on the *Sea Bird*, a thirty-seven-foot Island Packet, outfitted as a live-aboard. It had become home for me and Sadie, a golden retriever–lab mix who has been putting up with me since she was a puppy. A few months back Nomad joined us. She's a red, long-haired tabby that I'd found under a tree, starving and trying to nurse three kittens—all of which were now in the hands of loving families, the Pickerings among them. Rebecca had insisted that I keep Nomad. She'd pleaded, said I was obligated because I'd saved her. What could I say to a six-year-old with tears in her eyes. Nomad had become mine.

I'd first come to the islands on a special assignment, investigating the death of the Denver police commissioner's son, a scientist doing research in the BVI. He'd disappeared while out diving only to be found seventy feet under the water, just off the coast of Tortola, trapped inside a wreck, dive tank empty. The commissioner had been devastated and wanted one of his own people in the Denver PD and an experienced diver checking things out. He'd sent me.

After I'd apprehended the killers, John Dunn, the chief of Tortola police, had asked me to stay and offered me a job, and I'd decided to give it a try. He needed a diver and underwater investigator on his team, and me, well, I'd needed to get away.

*   *   *

Calvin was still in the waiting room, elbow propped on the arm of a chair, when I came back in.

"Hannah, you be doin' okay?" he asked, standing.

"Yeah, nothing serious." Nothing that showed anyway. "Hall says we can go in to see Elyse for a minute."

We went in together. She looked peaceful enough. She was a beautiful Caribbean woman, petite, chiseled fine features, skin the color of caramel, hair in short tight curls. She'd just celebrated her thirtieth birthday, but right now she looked about twelve, small and vulnerable under the white blanket. When I took her hand, it felt cold.

Calvin and I were quiet on the ride back to Pickering's Landing, lost in our own thoughts. I was the first to speak, but I knew Calvin had been asking himself the same questions.

"What do you think happened, Calvin?"

"Dat explosion, I'm guessing it be da propane. Diesel don't be exploding like dat. Don't think der be any leak either. I helped Elyse refuel yesterday afternoon at da dock. I'm real careful about it. So is Elyse."

"Was Elyse having any problems with the boat?"

"Naw, everything was working fine. I'd been over da entire mechanical system a month or so ago. It was da yearly maintenance check. Worked on dat ole stove of hers. Tole her she should be gettin' dat conservation society she works for to be buyin' a new one, da kind with a safety shutoff. It be workin' fine though. I replaced a hose, a couple of gaskets. Checked out da engine, fuel pump, cooling system. Dat boat be in perfect order."

I knew Calvin's work. If he said it was perfect, it was. He had worked on the *Sea Bird* too. Calvin was one of those people who never did anything halfway.

"Did you hear anything at all before the blast?" I asked him.

"No, Tilda and me, da girls, we all be asleep."

"When did you last see Elyse?"

"It was in da afternoon," he replied after giving it some thought.

"Did she say anything?"

"Just da usual. You know Elyse. It always be somethin'. Last week she be talkin' 'bout da coral bleaching over in the shallow water up near Anegada. Yesterday, she be goin' on 'bout da problems over at the gravel pit."

"What problems?"

"All dat sediment runoff into da bay. She said she be goin' to meet with Amos Porter, da man owns the pit. She be wantin' to talk to him 'bout it before she started puttin' on da pressure for some controls."

"Did you see anyone around yesterday?"

"Nobody I don't usually see. Da delivery truck come by bringin' goods for da store. Some of da local farmers stopped with fresh produce. Tilda be spendin' 'bout an hour looking at all dem bananas, mangoes, guavas. You know how picky she be 'bout what she be puttin' in da store."

I knew. I'd come to take the quality for granted at the little marina grocery that Tilda ran.

"Da owner of the *Blue Dancer* was down at da docks real early. He don took his boat out fishing and come back with a couple of small snappers. He be one unhappy man."

"Did you see anyone around the *Caribbe*?"

"No, but I be goin' into town 'bout three. Didn't get back till maybe six, six-thirty."

"What about Tilda?"

"She be busy in the store, stocking the shelves, doin' inventory when I left. Knowing Tilda, she be back dar all afternoon. Dat woman had everything done by da time I got home and she be makin' dinner. Why you askin'? You think dis was no accident?"

"You know me, Calvin. I have to ask."

Calvin swung the van into the gravel at Pickering's Landing and cut the engine. It had to be close to four in the morning.

"I be real worried 'bout Elyse," he said.

"Yeah, me too," I said, touching his arm. "Good night, Calvin."

Sadie saw me coming down the dock. She'd been sitting

on alert anxiously waiting for me. She ran toward me, smelled my bandaged hand and whined.

"Sweet Sadie. It's okay," I whispered. I stood on the dock looking out to where the *Caribbe* had been. The line was still tied to the dock; the other end floated in the water, frayed and blackened. Debris floated nearby, and a few tiny flames still lingered. The island fire trucks would have come and gone. Nothing to do but watch the flames burning. I'd called Dunn, the head of Tortola PD and my boss, from the hospital. He'd have a couple officers and another diver over here at first light.

I wasn't waiting. Until I knew better, I was treating this like a crime scene. By morning, the stuff floating in the water might be drifting halfway to Cuba. I forced exhaustion aside and headed back to the *Sea Bird*. Gathering flashlight, a net, evidence bags and jars, and the boat hook, I loaded it all into in my dinghy. Sadie clambered in next to me. There was no leaving her behind this time.

I untied the dinghy and rowed toward the wreckage, shining the light into the water. Long skinny ballyhoo drifted just below the surface, their silvery bodies reflecting in the beam from my flashlight. I rowed slowly through the litter. There wasn't much worth retrieving—just a lot of ruined pieces of wood, the top from a Styrofoam cooler, a life preserver. Everything Elyse owned was down on the seafloor.

I spotted something orange floating in the water. As I got closer I realized it was Elyse's baseball cap, the one she always wore, orange with the *Society of Ocean Conservation* script encircling a turtle. My breath caught in my throat. I remembered the last time I'd seen her in it. It had been just a couple days ago when we'd sat at the end of the dock laughing. Right now the joke eluded me and I knew it would be a while before I found anything that funny again.

I wondered if she'd had the hat on when the boat exploded. Not likely. It had probably been hanging on the hook where she always left it, with her rose-tinted granny glasses perched on the bill.

I shone the light into the water, looking for anything else that might be important. The beam glanced off a small brown bottle bobbing on the surface near what looked like part of a door. I rowed over, scooped the bottle out of the water and into an evidence jar along with the seawater, and capped it. I could see the label, something called Ambien. It had *SAMPLE* stamped across it and a few white tablets inside. I found nothing else worth retrieving.

"Come on, Sadie, I need some sleep." I rowed back to the *Sea Bird*, tied the dinghy up, and went below. My boat was a mess. Books, broken dishes, and dog food littered the floor—the aftermath of the explosive seas that had tossed the *Sea Bird* like a toy boat.

I was pulling the last of the glass and dog food from under the salon table, when the broom came out with a bright green sticky note attached to a bristle. I recognized the Society of Conservation logo. It was a note from Elyse.

> *Hannah*
> *Come by the Caribbe when you get home tonight.*
> *Doesn't matter how late. I need to talk to you.*
> *Elyse*

Christ. I hadn't seen the note when I'd gotten in last night. I had been out sailing all day with O'Brien. He owns SeaSail, the largest and most successful charter company in the British Virgin Islands. I met him the first time I came to the islands. I'd suspected him in the murder I was down there investigating. He started making passes the day we met. I pride myself on the fact that I was *almost* convinced of his innocence before I jumped into bed with him.

When O'Brien dropped me off at the *Sea Bird*, I'd never turned on the salon lights—just gone straight to bed. Elyse would have stuck the note on the chart table, thinking I wouldn't miss it. And I wouldn't have if I'd turned on the damn lights. What the hell had Elyse wanted to talk about?

Chapter 4

❦

I was assembling my dive gear when the police cruiser, the *Wahoo*, came roaring into the bay, engines cutting back at the last possible instant. The boat slid up to the dock in a spray of water.

"Snyder!"

"Hey dar, Hannah. How you be doin' dis fine day?" Deputy Jimmy Snyder smiled, that damned smile. Jimmy was the youngest member of the Tortola Police Department, just a skinny kid really, with hair in tangled cornrows closely knotted against his scalp.

Stark was with him. He threw me a line and I tied the *Wahoo* to the cleat where the *Caribbe* had once been secured. Stark was a detective in the department and had been for almost ten years. He was big, black, and bald, his shiny head usually sporting a pair of sunglasses. He looked more like a drug dealer than a cop.

Stark and I had clashed in the past, interactions that went from passive aggression to outright hostility. Finally, we'd made peace. Stark was a soft touch. I'd actually talked him into taking one of Nomad's kittens. He'd named her Camille. Old girlfriend, I figured.

Stark helped Snyder climb onto the dock. Jimmy still wasn't a hundred percent. He was hobbling because he'd stepped in front of a bullet meant for me a few months back.

Since Jimmy's brush with death, Chief Dunn had kept

him on a short leash in the office, doing paperwork. He'd
also managed to find some extra funds to send Jimmy to the
local college for training in computers. No one was sure
Jimmy would ever recover completely from his injuries and
even if he did, the kid needed to be kept out of harm's way
for a while. Otherwise he'd never see nineteen. And a little
education never hurt anyone. God knows why Dunn had let
him behind the wheel of the *Wahoo* today.

Edmund Carr was with them. He was a small man, about
thirty-five, balding, with delicate hands but a firm grip.
When he wasn't diving, he could usually be found sitting
behind his desk at Central Bank, dressed in a conservative
business suit.

I remembered the first time I ever dived with Carr. He'd
gone down with me to retrieve the body of a tourist who had
been shot in the head and dumped into the water. Before it
could drift out to sea, the body had gotten caught in the coral
off of a tiny island called Sandy Cay near Jost Van Dyke just
north of Tortola. Carr had helped me secure the underwater
evidence, bag the body, and take it to the surface.

Ever since, Carr had made himself available whenever I
needed help with a recovery. I'd given him some rudimen-
tary training in underwater investigation. I was doing my
best to build a reliable team. Diving alone was foolhardy,
and I trusted Carr by my side at depth. At least now he knew
better than to retrieve anything at all under the water until I
gave him the okay. And he was cool-headed and competent,
not one of those Type A divers out to prove how good they
are.

Carr handed me full tanks and his equipment and stepped
onto the dock. I was already in my wet suit. Getting into it
earlier this morning had been a delicate operation because of
the burns. Tilda had helped with the process when I had
gone up to the marina for assistance—but not before she'd
insisted on cutting my hair.

"It's got to be done," she said. "Some of it's not two

inches long. You can't be going around with short clumps of burned hair all over your head."

She was right. The long hair that I'd been so adept at pulling into a ponytail in the heat and up into sexy wisps for a date with O'Brien had to go. She cut. And cut. Long strands of chestnut hair dropped around my feet as the two girls looked on giggling.

"Done," Tilda said, handing me a mirror. It wasn't bad. She'd cropped my hair to two inches all the way around. A couple of curly strands bounced onto my forehead. The whole effect might be considered sophisticated, if you thought about it the right way.

"Oh Hannah, you look so cute, like a movie star," Rebecca chimed.

"Cute?" I said. Rebecca was jumping around my chair on one foot, singing a song about a hare. Clearly she didn't know the difference between *hare* and my new hairdo.

Tilda rebandaged my hand and the spot on my shoulder with lots of extra tape. Then I'd put on a light Lycra wet suit to keep the bandages in place. My heavier wet suit had slid on more easily over the Lycra but now it irritated my shoulder.

Carr had brought full air tanks, four of them. I clipped one into my buoyancy compensator vest, abbreviated BC in a world full of abbreviations. Then I attached my hoses to the vest and the tank. I twisted the air valve and checked my pressure—3100 psi. Then I breathed through the regulator. I'd done this so many times, I could do it in my sleep—the important preliminaries for a safe dive.

I put on my weight belt, with enough weight to take me to the bottom, sat down on the edge of the dock and pulled on my fins. Stark helped me into my BC. I tried to ignore the pain as the equipment settled onto my burned shoulder. I needed to get into the water where the weight of the tank would be lessened. I spit in my face mask, smeared the saliva over the lens to keep it from fogging, rinsed it in seawater, and snugged it in place. Then I grabbed my underwater camera gear and flashlight and stepped off the dock and into the ocean. Carr followed me.

Once in, I filled my BC with air so I could easily stay on the surface until we were set to descend. Though the shoulder pain had eased, once I hit the salt water the burning on my hand was like hot needles poking me. The water was still slicked with oil and littered with pieces of the *Caribbe*. The smell of diesel was overpowering. We needed to go under.

We gave one another the okay signal—fingertips on top of heads—released air from our BCs, and started down. This would be a shallow dive, just out past the dock in about thirty feet of water.

We could see the *Caribbe* on the bottom. She was tilted on her side. The center section of the starboard side was entirely demolished. The roof and three of the four walls that had enclosed Elyse's living quarters were gone, exposing the interior and a gaping hole in the hull. Most of the port side of the boat was still intact, including the head with the toilet still bolted to the flooring, sink and medicine chest attached to the wall.

In the galley the stove was still affixed to the port side wall. Everything else was a shambles. The refrigeration unit lay in the sand ten feet away. Not far from it were mangled cupboards with pots and pans, scattered and twisted among shards of broken rose-patterned china. Elyse's grandmother had given her the old dishes.

One fine bone china cup lay on its side in the sand a few feet away. I felt sick seeing Elyse's few treasures lying in ruins. I swallowed hard and kept going.

It looked like the explosion had blasted out the bottom and right side of the cabin, demolishing everything in its path. A school of blue tangs were circling the wreck, nibbling on anything edible—a water-laden loaf of bread, a bag of saltines, God knows what else. I took several long-range photos of the boat where it lay; then we moved in for a closer look.

I led, hoping to find some clue as to why the boat had exploded. It didn't take long. The gas stove was a blackened, gaping shell, the oven door hanging by one hinge and swaying in the current. I took photos of the stove—close-ups of the charred interior and the top where the burners had been. The knobs were completely gone.

Then I joined Carr who was busy shining his flashlight into the gaping hole in the floor. The propane, heavier than the air, would have settled down in the bilge. It had been just a matter of time. Eventually the bilge pump would have kicked in. The spark would have ignited the propane, the subsequent explosion blasting through the hull and out the side. That Elyse had survived at all was miraculous. She must have been somewhere on the port side. If she'd been in her bed, I had no doubt she'd be dead.

We continued our search, swimming back to the stern section and locating the hold that contained the propane tanks. The top of the compartment had been destroyed and the interior was a shambles. One of the tanks was still intact, the line screwed tightly down on the valve. The other tank was hanging off the side of the boat, the valve section completely blown away. Clearly, the second explosion—the one that had thrown me into the sea—had occurred when this tank went. I shot photographs and then we swam to the engine compartment. Again I took pictures and we examined the system, which looked intact.

These checks complete, we made our way around the inside of the boat, taking samples of charred wood and fabric. The lab would check for hydrocarbons that would be present if gasoline or kerosene had been splashed inside the boat.

I opened the compartments and drawers that were still intact—flares, tools, rain gear. An empty wine bottle was wedged into a shattered floorboard. I wondered where it had come from. Had someone else been aboard? I had never seen Elyse drink. I worked the bottle out of the splintered wood with my knife and dropped the bottle into an evidence tube that Carr had retrieved from one of the mesh dive bags.

We continued to swim through the salon and started back toward the stern section, our fins brushing against debris. The passageway back into Elyse's cabin was narrowed by the collapsed ceiling and walls of the boat. I took the lead and we made our way into it, our tanks clanging against fiberglass. The hall was a maze of sharp twisted metal and dangling wires. One slice in my regulator hose and my air would be bubbling out into the water instead of into my mouthpiece, and I'd be trying to scramble to the surface before I drowned. I moved slowly, bending back the jagged pieces as I went, so that Carr and I could swim through.

Finally I made it into the open area of Elyse's cabin. Carr came in right behind me. I could see blood seeping from his arm and tinging the water pink. A piece of jagged metal had sliced right through his wet suit. When I motioned to the wound and signaled, he noticed it for the first time, gave me the okay sign, and shrugged his shoulders. He probably hadn't even felt it. He would later though.

Elyse's belongings were strewn all over the place. A potted bird-of-paradise lay broken in her bunk along with several tattered books. In the head, one of her sandals was stuck in the toilet. The cabinet above the commode hung precariously, swaying back and forth slowly in a sluggish current. I opened it. Inside were toothpaste, toothbrush, a hair pick, medication.

While Carr held the evidence containers, I scooped up seawater along with the contents. I didn't really expect these things to tell me much. But I'd learned that thoroughness the first time through a scene paid off. Maybe there was a print, or something that would tell us what had happened on the *Caribbe*. Really, I was just following protocol for lack of anything else to do.

I checked my gauges. We'd been down almost an hour. My air was at 700 psi. Standard procedure was to start back up when the gauge read 500 psi, enough air to safely make it to the surface. But we were finished down here. I signaled to Carr. We were gliding over the sandy bottom when I spotted something black in the sand—one of the stove knobs, perfectly preserved. I scooped it into an evidence container and we headed up.

Stark and Snyder grabbed the evidence bags when we surfaced. Then we handed up our weight belts and climbed out into the sun and onto the warm dock. Carr sat down, breathless from the exertion of making it out of the water with his tank on.

"One of these days I've got to quit smoking," Carr said. Then he leaned back, grabbed his shirt that lay in a puddle of seawater on the dock, and pulled a soggy cigarette out of the pocket.

"How about now?" I taunted. Carr had been talking about quitting since I'd met him.

I picked up the pack of cigarettes and threatened to throw them in the water.

"Come on, Hannah. I'm an injured man. Give me the damned cigarettes."

"These things are going to kill you, Carr," I warned, handing the crumpled package back.

Stark and I helped him out of his wet suit as Jimmy went to retrieve the first-aid kit from the *Wahoo*. The cut in Carr's upper arm was deep but thin. I dabbed disinfect onto it and then Jimmy put a butterfly bandage over it to keep it closed.

"Well, you going to get around to telling us what you found down there?" Stark asked.

I described the stove, told him that it looked like the explosion had been caused by propane collecting in the bilge.

"How would that happen?" Jimmy asked, incredulous.

"It's pretty obvious," Carr said, his tone reflecting an amazement that the kid could be so stupid. "She left the gas on."

"I never be knowin' Elyse to be dat careless," Jimmy said.

"Come on. Happens all the time. Most people smell the stuff before it explodes. Elyse probably passed out drinking that bottle of wine," he said, indicating the bottle we'd retrieved.

"Elyse does not drink, and I don't need your opinion, Ed. We will be treating this like a crime scene," I said, pissed that Carr was so eager to blame the explosion on Elyse. But Carr was not in charge here. Christ, he wasn't even a cop. He was a damned banker along to help with the dive.

I could hear the anger and defensiveness in my voice. I was thinking about the sticky note that I'd discovered under the salon table. Maybe if I'd seen it when I'd gotten in last night, Elyse wouldn't be fighting for her life right now.

"Sorry," I said a moment later. I didn't need to take my frustration and fear for Elyse out on Carr.

"It's okay," Stark said. "We know how close you and Elyse are. Let's get this stuff to the lab, have them check for accelerants, prints on that stove knob, the other stuff you've collected."

We loaded the gear and evidence containers into the *Wahoo* and I handed Stark the three rolls of film I'd shot as well as the pill bottle I'd pulled out of the water last night.

"You coming?" he asked.

"Naw, I'll take the Rambler. I want to stop in at the hospital."

When I got there, Mary was sitting in Elyse's room, reading poetry to her—Pablo Neruda.

"Can't hurt," she said. "People say that hearing and awareness can be acute, even though a person is unconscious. I'm reading the uplifting material and maybe I'm keeping her brain waves active."

"Makes sense to me," I said, bending to give her a quick hug. "How long have you been here?" By the tired eyes and rumpled clothes I'd guess hours.

I'd met Mary the day Elyse had dragged me up to Mary's home in the hills to look at the black '65 Rambler that Mary was selling. It was typical Elyse, convinced she knew what was best for everyone around her. Mary had a car to sell; I needed one. To Elyse, it was obvious. And she'd been right. It was the perfect car, a boxy old convertible in mint condition. It was only later that I realized the car had been only part of Elyse's motivation. The other part was introducing me to Mary.

Mary was the psychiatrist who had helped Elyse through a hard time some eight years back. She'd diagnosed Elyse with bipolar disorder, helped Elyse come to terms with the illness, and managed her medication. They'd been close friends ever since. In fact, Mary was more a mother to Elyse than a friend.

"How's she doing?" I asked.

"No change. The neurologist is supposed to be getting in anytime."

Just then Dr. Hall and another man walked in.

"Mary, Hannah, this is Dr. Marks."

"Good day, ladies. Please excuse my appearance. Just stepped off the ferry from Red Hook. Kind of a salty wet day out there."

Dr. Marks was probably fifty, with salt-and-pepper hair and a hard New York accent. Hall had said he was one of the best, a high-powered doctor who had decided to retreat from the city to a more reasonable lifestyle in the Virgin Islands. He had given up a lucrative practice to do it. I had to admire the guy.

"I'll be examining Elyse, going over the charts, running a few more tests. It will probably be tomorrow before I have a complete picture unless something unexpected occurs."

"Like what?" I asked.

"You never know with head injuries. Sometimes the patient just comes around," he said.

Or dies. He didn't say it, but the unspoken hung in the air.

When Mary and I entered the brightly lit waiting room, Chief Dunn was there, sitting in the corner, head buried in the *Island News*. As usual, he wore a suit, white shirt, and dark tie. Dunn's idea of casual was to remove the jacket. He was big—a good two-sixty, six-three. He was always struggling to keep the weight down—difficult with a wife who could cook like Julia Child. His hair was close-cropped and peppered with gray. No one messed with Dunn. He carried himself with the dignity and authority of a man who was used to being in charge. He was my boss and head of the Tortola Police Department.

"Hi, Chief."

"Hannah, Stark said you'd be here. Hello, Mary. How is Elyse?"

"Same. Still comatose."

"I talked to Carr and Stark," Dunn said, turning to me. "They told me what you found on the *Caribbe*."

I knew what was coming. Dunn and I had been agreeing to disagree since I'd started in the department.

Chapter 5

❧

"What makes you think a crime was involved here?" Dunn asked. He knew I was treating the explosion as an attempted murder.

"What makes you think it wasn't?"

"Come on, Hannah. That propane stove of hers was ancient."

"Calvin said he'd just gone through the thing last week. It was working fine."

"What about that empty bottle you found down there? It seems possible she decided on a glass or two before dinner, fell asleep with the burner still on."

"Jeez, you sound like Carr." I told Dunn about the note Elyse had left on the *Sea Bird*, that she'd wanted me to come by the *Caribbe*, no matter how late.

"You're making something out of nothing, Hannah," Dunn said. "She probably wanted to talk about her love life or some violation involving dead sea creatures. Besides, why would anyone want to hurt her?"

"Come on. You know Elyse. She's always in someone's face about something."

"Okay, let's go through it. What was she up to this last week or two?" Dunn asked, turning to Mary.

"Nothing out of the ordinary. We had lunch a few days ago," Mary said. "She was up to her usual, monitoring water quality over near Simpson's Bay, collecting data at the dive and snorkeling sites. Actually, Elyse has been feeling very optimistic about the state of the reef. Of course that doesn't mean she doesn't find her battles."

"What about her personal life?"

"She's been dating Alex Reidman. He owns the Callilou, out at Burt Point," I said.

"Sure, I know Reidman. Nice restaurant, pricey. Were they having any problems?"

"No. Elyse likes Reidman but she's not serious about him. He's been pursuing her, but he's not someone she could really care about."

"What do you mean?"

"He's ambitious, an entrepreneur, into fast cars and money. That's not Elyse. She could care less. Her values lean toward the esoteric. You know that. Besides, Reidman is extremely self-centered. When he thinks about the world, he thinks about it in terms of how it relates to him. When things happen, they happen to him. He'd never be there for Elyse if she needed him."

"Doesn't sound like you like him much," Dunn said. "Why would Elyse be seeing him if he's such a jerk?"

"Oh, he's charming, good-looking, and they have a good time together, but she told me she was going to break it off with him."

"You seeing that as a motive, Hannah, spurned lover? Doesn't seem too likely."

I knew Dunn was right. Reidman could never be that wrapped up in any woman. He was too wrapped up in himself.

"Come on, Chief. I'm not saying it was personal. But dammit, this whole thing reeks of foul play."

"What else was she involved in?" he asked, looking at me like I was hopeless.

"There is one other thing," Mary said. "I'd asked Elyse for some help with one of the kids I've been working with. You know her, Hannah. Jillian Ingram."

"Sure. She comes over to visit Elyse, hangs out on the boat." Elyse had told me about Jilli.

"Jilli has been into drugs," Mary explained to Dunn, "not just marijuana, but heavy stuff—speed, acid. I'm sure that the drug use is just a symptom and that Jilli is running from something.

"I knew Elyse would understand this. She used illegal drugs herself when she was struggling to control her mania and depression without a diagnosis or doctor's care.

"Elyse has been a tremendous support," Mary said. "Jilli doesn't get any help from her parents. They are in total denial that Jilli has a problem. They believe it's just a phase, that she is getting involved with the wrong kids. They resent Elyse's involvement. Jilli is only fourteen and extremely angry at her parents. Elyse has been good for her. She's helped her through some very rough stuff."

"What kind of stuff?"

"Jilli was picked up over on St. Thomas last month. She'd been caught trying to buy narcotics from an undercover cop," Mary explained.

"So she's got a record?"

"Not yet. She was lucky that she was picked up by the police before she got involved with someone who would really hurt her, or ended up overdosing in an alley. They arrested her and she called Elyse. Elyse called her parents and went with them to St. Thomas to explain the situation to the cops. They released Jilli to her folks with an agreement she'd get into a drug abuse program. That hasn't happened."

"How does any of this even remotely relate to the explosion?" Dunn asked. "Nothing indicates that this was anything but an unfortunate accident."

About then Hall and Marks walked into the waiting room. Hall stood for a moment thumbing through Elyse's chart.

"We've gotten the head and neck scans back. There is a small epidural hematoma, causing edema on the right side of her brain. It shows up as white density. I've started mannitol, which will help to absorb some of the fluid. The big factor will be whether the bleeding continues. For now, we'll monitor her closely, do another CT tomorrow. If it shows continued or increased bleeding, we'll have to do surgery to release the pressure or there will be increased brain damage."

"Have you been able to assess the damage to this point?" I asked. Christ, the thought of Elyse being paralyzed or having brain damage. I mean, talk about unfair.

"It's just too soon to tell," Marks said. "But I must be frank. There is always the chance of physical and mental impairment. The hematoma is small, but I am concerned that she may have microscopic axonal injuries not detected in the CT scan."

"This simply cannot happen to Elyse. She's had enough trauma in her life," I insisted, hands on hips, as though I could demand that it not be so.

"What else have you found?" Mary asked.

Hall flipped through the sheets on the chart, running a bony finger down the page. "We did a complete drug screen also. No alcohol, barbiturates, THC. But there was one thing—she was positive for benzodiazepine."

"What's benzodiazepine?" Dunn and I asked in unison.

"It's a sleep aid," Mary said. "Ambien."

Chapter 6

❧

I remembered the medicine bottle I'd pulled out of the ocean the night before.

"Elyse had a bout of insomnia," Mary said. "It must have been eight months ago now. It's important that she get enough sleep to maintain equilibrium. I insisted on giving her a sample of the Ambien and told her to take it if she needed it. But as far as I knew, she never did. What was her blood level?"

"Minimal. I'd guess two or three tablets, just enough for a 'dead to the world' night's sleep," Hall said.

Dunn summarized the scenario as we stood outside Elyse's door. He had it all worked out. Elyse had taken a couple of sleeping pills, then fallen asleep with the stove on. The flame had gone out, the fumes filled the cabin, the gas had settled in the bottom of the boat and exploded.

I didn't want to hear it and headed for the door before he could finish.

"Hannah, stop!" Mary demanded, catching me by the wrist.

"Let me go, Mary. I need to get into some air that doesn't smell like death and disinfectant."

"Hannah, listen to me. I'm sure Dunn is right."

"Dunn is dead wrong. Come on. The only reason Elyse even had those sleeping pills was to humor you. The only thing Elyse ever took to help her sleep was chamomile tea, for chrissakes."

"What are you suggesting, Hannah?"

"Someone slipped her the pills, turned the damned gas on, and left her to die." It seemed obvious to me.

"You don't need to find a scapegoat here, Hannah," Mary said. "It's not your fault that you didn't stop over at the *Caribbe* last night."

The psychoanalysis bullshit really pissed me off. I didn't want to hear it, especially because I knew she could be right.

"Dammit, I think Elyse needed my help. I should have seen that note, Mary. She wouldn't be lying in that hospital bed now if I had."

"Come on, Hannah. If it hadn't been for you, she'd be dead right now."

"Yeah." I pushed the door open and walked quickly into the heat and sun.

Dunn caught up with me at my car. "Detective Sampson."

So I was Detective Sampson again. A sure sign he was about to get on my case.

"I don't want you trying to make anything else out of this thing with Elyse. It's pretty clear what happened."

"Hey, Chief, no problem."

"I mean it. I don't want you going off on some half-baked notion about murder. We've got enough on our hands."

"Okay, Chief." I climbed into the Rambler.

"I want you to get back to the office, Detective. Stark needs help running down those reports about boats being broken into," he said as he pushed my car door closed.

I'd go back to the office. But I decided to make a stop first. It was on the way . . . sort of.

I knew where the Ingrams' lived. Elyse and I had dropped Jilli off there just last week. The house was hidden behind a row of dense frangipani, the ground beneath littered with fragrant pink and white blossoms. The only way you'd know the house was back there was the sign that read "Ingram" in unobtrusive lettering on a wooden post. I had the feeling the Ingrams didn't really want visitors wandering down there. I turned in anyway.

The driveway was paved and lined with more frangipani as well as mango and rubber trees and ended at a circular drive, the center exploding in color—orchids, birds-of-paradise, and more. All around the exterior of the house, hibiscus, oleander, and red ginger flourished, obviously tended by a loving hand. In spite of the beauty and fragrance of the gardens, the structure itself felt a bit forbidding. It was an old, Spanish-style stucco, the windows closed tight against the heat.

I'd asked Elyse once about Jilli's parents. She'd said they were originally from London but had lived on Tortola for years. He was a lawyer and involved in offshore banking. Clearly, he'd done well.

I walked up the front steps and lifted the brass knocker. I could hear it echoing through the interior, then the sound of footsteps. Finally, a tall thin woman answered the door. She wore a tennis outfit, one of those white, short things with a racket embroidered on the pocket. The look was complemented with red lips and long red fingernails. She was in her mid-forties, hair in one of those Dorothy Hamill styles popular about twenty-five years ago.

"Mrs. Ingram?"

"That's right. And you are?"

"Detective Hannah Sampson, Tortola PD."

"What's she done now?" she asked.

"She?"

"Jillian, my daughter."

"What makes you think this is about Jillian?"

"You mean it's not?" she asked, hopeful.

"Well, marginally, I suppose. Do you know Elyse Henry?"

"Of course, she's been meddling in our affairs with Jilli

for months now. I heard she's been hurt. So, this *is* about Jilli."

"Do you mind if I come in?" I asked.

"Might as well," she sighed.

The house was as opulent on the inside as out. Thick spongy carpeting muffled our steps as she led me into the living room. The room was dark, drapes pulled against the sun—blood wine chairs, a cherry table and a sofa of tapestry, colors picking up the hue of the chairs. The walls were covered with art, reproductions of the masters. Dark brooding faces stared out from the canvases. A Rembrandt, *The Man in the Golden Helmet*, glared at me. Sure, they were works of art but jeez, better left in a museum. I'd go for one of Gauguin's oils of Tahitians lounging in the shade any day.

"Please, sit down," she said, indicating the couch. The thing was hard as a rock. I couldn't see a fourteen-year-old kid slouching on it.

"Can I get you a drink?" She already had one. It looked like straight bourbon—no ice.

"No, thanks."

She poured another couple of inches into her glass and sat across from me, crossing her legs.

"How can I help you, Detective?"

I decided to get right to the point. She was already on the defensive anyway. "You know where Jillian was last night?"

"Like every night. She was out with her friends. There's nothing we can do short of locking her up to keep her home."

I could see why. The place was a mausoleum, the chairs designed for the short-term guest—five minutes and they'd be out of there.

"I heard that she and Elyse were friends."

"Some friend," she said, taking a drink. "She's an interfering bitch." Jeez, the woman didn't mince words.

"She was always talking to Jilli about seeing Mary King, getting to the cause of her drug use. The cause is that she's a teenager who's gotten into drugs and the wrong crowd.

We're her parents. We can take care of things ourselves. We're going to put her into a very strict school in the States, one that guarantees to straighten kids out.

"You know Elyse actually came here." Rita Ingram was on a rant now. "She told us that school was the worst thing for Jillian. Said she needed to be in a drug abuse program and in therapy. What does she know? Jilli had too much freedom in that prep school in London. She'd only been there a year and she was in trouble. We took her to school a sweet little girl. We picked her up and she looks like a devil-worshipping punk rocker. We've searched her room. I don't know where she gets the stuff. We cut off her allowance."

"How's she doing?" I asked.

"Well, she's been very quiet lately. Joel, my husband, is sure it's because she can't find anyone who will give her drugs on credit."

I didn't mention that there were other things her daughter could exchange for drugs if she really wanted them.

"You know, it's a nice change," she said. "You'd hardly know Jillian is around."

Yeah, I bet it was. Rita Ingram didn't need to face the problem, just play tennis, drink her bourbon and pretend her daughter was fine now that they'd pulled her out of school and cut off any funds.

About then Jillian came in. She was a pretty girl, small-boned. Her hair was spiked, dyed pitch black, and highlighted with purple streaks. She wore a pair of baggy pants that hung on her hips, sandals, and a tight shirt, short enough to show her navel, which was pierced and decorated with a gold ring. She looked a lot older than her fourteen years.

"Hi, Jilli. How you doing?" I asked. The last time I'd seen her had been a couple weeks ago, walking through town with Elyse. We'd gone for ice cream. At the time, I could see she was wired, probably on speed. Elyse knew it too. This was a different kid. Affect flat, blue eyes unfocused. I'd guess she'd gotten into Rita's Valium.

"I'm okay. I heard about Elyse. Will she be all right?"

"The doctor doesn't know."

"I don't think we can help you any further, Detective," Rita said. "Jilli darling, would you show Ms. Sampson to the door? I'm going to shower." She filled her glass again and staggered up the stairs.

"Sorry about Mom. I guess I'm kind of a burden."

She walked outside with me, sat down on the steps, pulled a cigarette from hiding inside her bra and lit it. I sat next to her on the upwind side.

"Your mom's having a tough time, huh?"

"Yeah. Guess I can't blame her. I'm not the sweet innocent daughter they had hoped for. Dad's just pissed. I know what they're thinking. All I need is some hard discipline."

"What do you think?"

"I think I'm a bad person. Elyse says I'm not, but she doesn't really know me."

"Your mom doesn't seem to like your seeing her."

"Well, you know. Mom wants to be the one I turn to. I've tried to talk to her. The trouble is she doesn't have a clue. And Dad, he's so sure of himself. He's a 'take control' kind of guy who thinks he's always right. I know he's disappointed in me. He can't understand why I'm not just like my brother. He's got this great new job in a famous London law office. Dad can't understand why I'm different and he really gets angry that he can't control me. Mom doesn't have much to say about things."

"What's your dad think about Elyse?"

"Same as Mom. Doesn't want me going near her. He's sure she's about the worst thing for me."

"When did you see Elyse last?"

"A couple of days ago, I guess."

"You two have an argument or anything?"

"No," she said, averting her eyes. The kid was hiding something.

"Here's my card. You need anything, I want you to call me."

"Sure," she said. Like right, in another life.

I left her sitting on the steps, elbows crossed on her knees, forehead resting on her arms, gazing at the cement. She was so god-awful alone, the pain palpable. What had happened to this kid?

Chapter 7

❦

By the time I got back to the office it was almost four. Thank God Dunn wasn't around. The first thing I did was pick up the phone and call Mary. Her voice mail answered. I left a message asking her to find some way to check on Jillian, parents or not. I was worried about the kid. Then I called the hospital and talked to Hall.

"Hey, Sampson, nice of you to show up." Stark was standing behind me when I hung up the phone. "How's Elyse doing?"

"No change. Still unconscious."

"Damn." That was all Stark had to say about it. Typical Stark. But I knew he was upset too. He'd known Elyse since they were kids, getting into trouble together doing things like freeing hermit crabs from local pet stores.

His way to deal with his concern was not to deal with it. He got down to business.

"I could use a little help here," he said, throwing a stack of papers on my desk. "We've got reports about break-ins on boats from all over the islands."

The detective unit in our small office across from the library did all the investigative work and handled island-wide crime. Other ancillary offices scattered around the islands handled local disturbances. Our unit was composed of three detectives—Stark, Alvin Mahler, and me. Jimmy Snyder was a deputy but he often talked Dunn into letting him accompany one of us. Usually it ended up being me. He was a smart kid and ambitious, but still too damned young. Seven street cops also worked out of our office, as well as Dunn's secretary.

Stark and I spent the next hour going over the complaints. Not surprisingly, the break-ins were occurring in the most popular anchorages, places where there were a lot of boats, mostly charterers down for a week or two of sailing. Few people ever locked their boats or homes in the islands. The BVI were known to be a "law and order" type place where the crime rate was low.

Lately, though, there had been a rash of reports. Four boats had been broken into over at Cane Garden Bay two nights ago. It was the night of the full moon, which meant dozens of boaters headed up to the Bomba Shack for the full moon party. They'd left their boats unattended—no lights, no dinghy, all sure indications that no one was aboard.

Whoever had boarded had gotten on and off quickly, rummaging through chart tables and cabinets. It was amazing what people left right out in plain sight—binoculars, GPS units, high-tech cameras, expensive jewelry, fanny packs with cash and credit cards.

Other reports had come from Soper's Hole, the next major harbor to the south. Nothing had occurred in the more remote anchorages or on the islands that were sparsely populated. Peter Island, Cooper, Jost Van Dyke had reported no thefts. A few reports had come from the Baths on Virgin Gorda, and several from North Sound, near Saba Rock and the Bitter End. We split up the duty and would start checking things out tomorrow. Stark would talk to the yachters who'd been at Cane Garden Bay and Soper's Hole. I'd motor up to Virgin Gorda, talk to the resort and restaurant owners, and the people who ran the grocery store.

"Chief wants Snyder to go with you. I've got Mahler."

"Snyder? I thought he had desk duty and classes."

"Yeah, well, he's on semester break, and to tell you the

truth I think he's driving the chief crazy. Kid can't stand being in the office."

"Hey, how 'bout you take Snyder?" I pleaded.

"Not a chance. I mean, I like you, Sampson, but not that much! Besides, you and Snyder have a history. And you know how he loves the *Wahoo*. You'll need to take it to North Sound."

It wasn't that I didn't like Snyder. I mean, the kid had saved my life. It was just his damned eighteen-year-old hormones. And the fact that in his eyes I was old, for chrissakes. Besides, I worried about Snyder getting hurt again.

When I got home, Sadie pounded down the docks, overcome with the joy of seeing me. Nothing like a dog.

"Hey, Sadie." I knelt and scratched her behind the ears. "I missed you too."

She jumped onto the *Sea Bird* after me and followed me down below. Nomad was curled up on the salon table. She was obviously pissed that I'd been gone all day. She lifted her head, gave me the look, jumped off the table, and headed for my bed. She couldn't ignore the sound of the can opener though. The minute she heard it she was at my feet, rubbing against my leg.

"Yeah, all is forgiven when it comes to food, huh?" I picked her up and stroked her soft fur. She'd turned into a beautiful animal once she'd recovered from starvation. In spite of her haughty nature, she was a sweet cat. Now she couldn't get enough attention and had forgiven me for being gone all day.

Animals fed, I went down the dock to shore and spent a half hour throwing the Frisbee for Sadie while Nomad looked on from the shade of a coconut tree. Sadie never got enough of the game. No matter how far I threw it out into the water, she'd be back with it and ready to do it again.

"Enough, Sadie." I lay down in the sand. She came over and stood by me whining with the Frisbee in her mouth until she realized it was futile. Then she shook, throwing water and sand all over me, and lay down by my side. Finally, Nomad sauntered over and curled up on my belly. I lay with one hand under my head, absently scratching Nomad and watching the palms swaying in the breeze, their fronds rustling against each other. A laughing gull flew overhead.

When I rose, the sun was just touching the water. People who spend a lot of time on the ocean talk about the green flash. They say that when conditions are just right, the sun will hit the water and an instantaneous green flash will color the sky. I'd believe when I saw it, but I always found myself waiting.

Right now, rays of orange, purple, and pink shot into the clouds and down into the glassy water reflecting all the way to shore. Fish were jumping, forming designs of liquid in overlapping rings that reflected the colored light. A couple of pelicans were fishing in the bay, swooping down on their unsuspecting prey. They dove straight into the water, came up with dinner in their pouch, tilted their heads back, and swallowed.

After a year, I was beginning to feel at home in the islands. And I was being accepted as a part of island life, even by Stark, who had put me to the test, made sure I was someone who could care about his islands and his people before he quit giving me the cold shoulder. I'd finally met with his approval when I sat vigil in the hospital with Snyder's family until word came that he would live.

I had come to the islands for reasons that were entirely selfish. I'd wanted to escape, leave the violence of life on the Denver police force behind—and forget the horrible conditions of police-diving in the polluted black water, where I found bodies tangled in shopping carts or caught in barbed wire. Visibility was so horrible that I once swam right into a huge industrial dryer. How the hell it had gotten there is anybody's guess.

Mack, my old partner on the force, had told me I was kidding myself to think I could escape. He'd said that I'd never find a place without evil. In one sense he'd been right. I'd not found paradise. Plenty of evil existed in these islands. But I loved the people and the pace—island time, people called it. Locals wondered at the rush that those who were not from the islands seemed to be in. "What's the hurry?" they'd ask, and few could come up with an answer that made any sense, even to themselves. Something I had never expected, though, was that I would find real peace and serenity diving under the tropical waters.

I lay back down in the sand and watched the constellations take shape in the darkening sky, and thought about Elyse. No matter what Dunn said, I was sure this was no accident. I'd learned a long time ago to follow my instincts. Sometimes I was wrong, but I was right often enough. And I knew Elyse.

She and I had connected from the day we met. It was one of those friendships that was immediate. We were alike in a lot of ways. She was as stubborn about her work as I was mine. Just last month, I'd gone with her to save a ray that she'd found tangled in a net.

And Elyse was no dummy. She'd been around boats most of her life and living on the *Caribbe* for a couple of years. She was careful, paid attention to details. She'd never leave that stove on. And she would not have left a note asking me to come over no matter the time if it hadn't been important. I'd be damned if I was going to let this go.

I headed for the shower. I'd forgotten about the burns until hot water hit them like sharp needles. I leapt out from under the heat and bent over, hands on knees, and waited for the pain to subside. Then I stepped halfway back in and tried to wash the sand away from one limb after another. This was definitely not my idea of a hot shower. I'd been known to stand under rushing water for half an hour, letting the stream of liquid carry tension down the drain.

Washing my hair was an exercise in creative problem solving, leaning in sideways, trying to lather my scalp with one hand. Having a short haircut suddenly didn't seem so bad. I got out, dabbed at my wounds, smeared the damned

salve all over my shoulder and hand, and covered them with
fresh bandages.

I was meeting O'Brien for dinner. I hadn't seen him since
we'd been sailing on Sunday. He'd visited Elyse at the hospital earlier that day but had left before I got there. I needed
him now. Dinner was kind of secondary on my priority list
at the moment. I was more interested in the comfort of a
warm body next to mine—O'Brien's body in particular.

I rummaged through my closet, looking for something
sexy. It had to be the black dress, formfitting and just bare
enough to show a little cleavage. I pulled it on and analyzed
the effect in the mirror. Good. At thirty-seven, I had to admit
that I still looked pretty damned good in a short, tight dress.
Right now though, the dress, accented with gauze and white
tape at the shoulder, was not exactly a fashion statement.

I dug through my drawer, finding and rejecting a sweater
and a silk overshirt. I was not about to change into anything
less revealing. I didn't have that many options anyway. My
entire wardrobe consisted of two dresses formal enough for
dinner at the Sea Scape, where O'Brien had wanted to meet.
Finally I found a sheer black scarf with silver threads accented with blues and purples. Just right. I draped it around
my neck and across the bandages and headed into town.

I was late. O'Brien was already there with the Freemans.
I'd forgotten all about that part of the plan. O'Brien had
been determined that I meet them.

He'd told me all about the Freemans. Neville Freeman
was campaigning for chief minister, head of the territorial
government, and O'Brien was supporting him. He thought
Freeman was the man for the office and had made a sizable
contribution to the campaign. O'Brien could afford it.

"Hannah, you look ravishing!" O'Brien stood and pulled
a chair out for me.

"You look pretty good yourself," I said, heart rate picking up a notch.

He was actually wearing a jacket and tie. No matter what
O'Brien wore, though, he managed to look like he'd just

stepped off a boat, and I'd bet he didn't have any socks on with the boat shoes he always wore.

"Neville, Sylvia Freeman, this is Hannah Sampson," O'Brien said.

Sylvia nodded and smiled, but there wasn't anything friendly behind it. I got the feeling she disliked me already. Maybe it was because Neville practically knocked his chair over to stand and gush about how wonderful it was to finally meet me. The guy was a flirt.

The Freemans were a perfectly matched pair, both in their early fifties, dress understated but expensive. He was wearing a lightweight beige linen suit with a shirt, open at the collar, in subtle tones of olive. Sylvia wore an elegant off-white dress with a jacket, pearl necklace, matching earrings, the colors perfectly complementing Neville.

They were both born in the BVI and were well-placed on the island. Neville came from old money and I knew he was very influential in all parts of the community. He'd been campaigning hard for chief minister. His campaign promises included a commitment to improvements in education and more stringent environmental regulations, all while improving the economy. In fact, he argued that these reforms went hand in hand—that an improved economy required that islanders be better educated and the environment protected for tourism. It all made a lot of sense.

The other candidate, Bertram Abernathy, was much more of an extremist in terms of the environment. He was arguing strongly against any development that had an adverse and long-term impact on the environment, no matter what the economic advantages were. Abernathy felt that it was important to keep the islands unspoiled and argued that doing so would inevitably keep tourism strong. Of course, Elyse had been campaigning for him, but many people wanted the more balanced approach that Freeman offered, O'Brien included. I was still riding the fence.

Freeman's campaign was making a big deal of his family's long history on the islands and the fact that he came from a family of slaves. His great-great-grandfather was brought from Africa to work on the cane plantations. When freedom came, the family had been savvy, becoming landed and powerful. Neville Freeman had inherited it all and owned several pieces of land in the islands, including Flower Island, a beautiful little place with a couple of deserted white-sand beaches lined with palms.

Members of Freeman's family had resided on Flower Island off and on for almost two centuries, in a little enclave that was once the retreat for the plantation owner. The original house was still there, along with the outbuilding where the house slaves had lived.

The place was empty most of the time these days. The Freemans lived on an estate over near Carrot Bay, using the home on Flower for occasional weekends away. The place was off-limits. "No Trespassing" signs were scattered over the entire perimeter of the island.

"What happened to your hand?" O'Brien asked, noticing the bandages for the first time. I filled him and the Freemans in on the details: the explosions, pulling Elyse out of the water, and taking her to the hospital. I skipped the part about being topless. Neville would have loved to hear about it.

Dinner conversation revolved around politics, tourism, and the charter boat industry. O'Brien was all for some regulations on boating: requiring holding tanks on all boats, fines for dumping waste or garbage, the building of pump-out stations. It was a costly proposition for the islands and many of the locals felt the big boating companies should foot the bill. O'Brien wasn't opposed to companies like his taking on some financial responsibility but also felt that taxes should pay a part. Freeman wasn't committing one way or the other. I could tell O'Brien was frustrated that Freeman wouldn't take a clear stand.

At some point, Sylvia lost interest and pulled me into conversation about a women's social group that I really should consider joining. I was amazed she'd even mention it. I'd fit in like a whore in church. She was going on about all the wonderful things the group was doing for the children on the island, while O'Brien, seemingly engaged in his own debate with Freeman, discovered my foot under the table and wrapped his foot around my ankle.

Hours later, O'Brien followed me home. Although he had a beautiful villa overlooking the harbor above the marina, there were few places he'd rather sleep than on a sailboat, especially mine.

Chapter 8

❧

The morning light was pink and muted, the *Sea Bird* absolutely still in the quiet water. I could hear a gull complaining from its perch somewhere in the harbor and O'Brien breathing softly beside me. I lay for a while, trying to absorb the calm for the day ahead. I was determined to find the person responsible for the explosion on Elyse's boat. When Dunn found out what I was up to—and I had little doubt that he would find out—he'd be pissed and chewing me out in that damned level tone of his. Dunn never raised his voice.

Finally, I slipped out from under O'Brien's arm, careful not to awaken him. By the time I jumped onto the dock the sun was blasting over the hills. Coconut palms were bathed in rose-colored light and the water was a sheet of silver reflecting gold. I stood on the dock filling my lungs with the scents of the morning. For a moment I was confused by the open water where the *Caribbe* was supposed to be. Then I was angry.

Ten minutes later, I pulled up in front of the Society of Ocean Conservation office—Elyse's office. I figured a quick look around wouldn't hurt. I wanted to know what Elyse had been working on that might have gotten her into trouble. The front door was locked. I walked around the side, peering into the window. Through the slatted venetian blinds I could see little, but the place had that empty feel. I tried the door in back. Unlocked. Typical Elyse.

The back room was filled with supplies—chemicals, test tubes, one of those short boxy refrigerators where Elyse kept her samples. A microscope was set up in the corner on a table, a carton of glass slides opened nearby. Elyse's bike leaned against a wall. It was an old Schwinn: bulky tires, wide fenders, a metal basket attached to the handlebars.

Elyse's office was in the front. It was way too small to hold what it did—a desk, file cabinets, overflowing bookshelves, studies and reports stacked on chairs. I started with the desk. It was littered with another stack of reports, memos, notes, and pages of data. I piled the folders that were strewn on the desk chair onto the floor, sat, and began to look through the material.

There was a detailed report about sediment runoff into Simpson's Bay from the gravel pit near the airport. It contained several pages of tables: GPS coordinates, with corresponding data on water temperature, visibility, bottom conditions, and sea life. Elyse's written report followed. In it, she discussed her findings: the smothering of nearshore reef communities, an increase in water turbidity that was also associated with decreases in coral growth and productivity, and more sediment accumulation in mangroves.

Calvin had said that Elyse was complaining about the runoff the Sunday morning when he helped her refuel the boat. I jotted down the address of the gravel pit and the owner's name, Amos Porter.

Next was a report on rat eradication on Hermit Cay. It was a summary of the successful efforts written by La-Plante, the chief scientist who had conducted the project. Elyse had taken part. She had camped out at the cay for a week, helping to maintain bait stations and monitor conditions in terms of safety for other wildlife, especially any birds and other vertebrates that might ingest the poison.

Another folder was earmarked for Tom Shields and Liam Richards. Tom and Liam were two semiretired oceanographers who were in the islands as volunteers, counting and tagging turtles. Inside the folder marked with their names I found an old report about sea turtles along with a map of habitats and nesting grounds.

Other loose sheets of paper scattered around the desk included everything from coral bleaching to the repopulation of black urchins, which had been almost completely wiped out of the Caribbean some twenty years ago, to an e-mail from a guy over at Brandywine Bay about someone leaving bags of garbage onshore. When I turned the fax machine on, a message from the coast guard spewed out about the prosecution of the fishermen whose boat we'd found last month loaded down with shark fins.

I found Elyse's appointment book in the top desk drawer. It was filled with notations and appointments: dinner dates with Reidman, support group meetings, an appointment to meet with Abernathy, the candidate for chief minister. She had penciled in an appointment with LaPlante for Monday that she'd obviously missed. I wondered if LaPlante knew that Elyse was in the hospital.

I tossed the folders and appointment book into a shopping bag Elyse had stashed under the desk. I'd pass the old turtle survey on to Tom and Liam and go through the rest of the material back at the office. I shut down the fax machine and was just placing a finger on the light switch when a shadow appeared at the front door. Someone turned the knob and pushed on the door, then peered in the window. The shadow moved away and I could hear footsteps crunching along the side of the building. I stepped into the back room and waited, pressed against the wall behind the door.

Who the hell would be snooping around Elyse's office at this time of the morning? Someone looking for something? Kids looking for a place to hang out instead of being at school? I waited. Whoever it was hesitated at the back door. Finally, the knob turned, the door slowly opened, and one foot wearing an expensive, hand-tooled cowboy boot crossed the threshold. Then a man's fingers, big, soft, and manicured, wrapped around the edge of the door and eased it open. Obviously trying to remain soundless, he pushed on the door and stepped inside, where he stopped again, hesitant. Then he moved into the room.

"Hold it right there," I said, slamming the door shut as I pulled my gun. I hoped the guy would be cooperative. I hate pointing guns at people, much less firing.

"What the hell?" The man turned. "Hannah, jeezus, you scared the shit out of me."

"Alex, what are you doing sneaking in here?" Alex Reidman, Elyse's boyfriend. I lowered the gun.

"I was on my way to the bank. I saw the light on. I thought I should check. Make sure everything was okay. What are *you* doing here?" he asked, glancing nervously at the gun I held by my side.

"Checking on a few things."

"Like what?"

"Like what Elyse has been up to the last few weeks."

"Doesn't seem as though you should be rifling through her stuff," he said, noticing the shopping bag I held.

"Look, Alex. I'm just not buying this accident theory. I think someone tried to kill her."

"Who would want to hurt Elyse?"

"I'm betting she was into something that threatened someone."

"You really think anyone would try to kill her over the environment? I seriously doubt it," he said.

"People kill for all kinds of reasons," I said. "Did Elyse talk to you about anything she was up to?"

"You know Elyse. She's always fighting one cause or another. Lately it was a lot of talk about that kid, Jillian."

"What did she tell you?" I asked.

"Elyse was concerned about Jillian's parents sending her to that school. She said she was going to talk to them about it. Certainly nothing so extreme that they would feel threatened. Though I suppose they might have worried that Jillian would simply take off if Elyse convinced her to. I know she spent a night on Elyse's boat one night. She'd had a fight with her folks. I guess a parent could get pretty upset about their kid being gone all night."

I remembered the night Jilli had stayed with Elyse. She'd come over there on the verge of tears. We fixed dinner together. By the time we'd finished eating, Elyse and I had found a way to make Jilli laugh.

"You're way off base here snooping around her office, and there is nothing more I can tell you," Reidman said.

"I want to know what Elyse was doing. I don't think she'd object to my being in her office."

"You need to let it go, Hannah," he said. I wondered why he cared.

"What difference does it make to you, Alex?"

"None at all," he said. "Is Dunn going along with this?"

"I'm not letting this go until I find out what happened on the *Caribbe*." I avoided the question about Dunn.

We walked out together, Reidman making a point of engaging the lock and pulling the door closed behind us. Kind of proprietary, I thought. Maybe a bit too protective. Fine. I had what I needed. Besides, I could get back in if I wanted.

Reidman was heading down the sidewalk as I climbed into the Rambler. When I passed the bank a block down from Elyse's office, Edmund Carr was just opening it up for the day and holding the door for Reidman and a few other anxious customers. I honked and waved. Carr smiled and waved back. Reidman ignored me.

Chapter 9

It was almost ten by the time I snuck into my office. I hoped Dunn wouldn't notice. Fat chance.

"Good morning, Detective." He stood at the door, hands on his hips.

"Morning, Chief. Sorry I'm late. Kind of a long day yesterday. I overslept."

"No need to be making excuses. Alex Reidman called. He said he ran into you at Elyse Henry's office."

Christ, he must have called Dunn the minute he'd walked into the bank.

"What's his problem?" I asked.

"I believe he was concerned that you were trespassing, Detective."

"Jeez, I knew the guy was a control freak but this is silly. Elyse is a friend."

"I know, Hannah, and I know what you were doing. Let it go. Snyder has been chomping at the bit to get out of the office. I want you to focus on those thefts. Stark and Mahler have already gone over to the west end, but they can't conduct their investigation without help. Snyder's waiting for you down at the dock."

I tried not to blame Dunn for being so shortsighted. We were notoriously understaffed in the department, and he'd been getting a lot of pressure about the boat thefts. People were worried about the effects on tourism. But dammit, why couldn't he see that there could be someone out to get Elyse? I'd help investigate the thefts, but I wasn't about to let it interfere with finding out who had sabotaged the *Caribbe*. Besides, I was sick of being told to "let it go."

When I got down to the docks, Snyder had the *Wahoo* gassed up and was hobbling around on deck cleaning the damned boat. He didn't see me coming. He was reaching for something down in the hold when he suddenly stood up and bent over, held onto his side, and grimaced.

"Snyder," I said, stepping onto the boat, "you need to take it easy, for chrissakes."

"I be doin' fine. Just a bit a' pain in da belly. Probably something I had for breakfast. You know my mama. Food be da cure for all dat ails. She be stuffing me with conch stew and potatoes every chance she gets."

Snyder had put on some weight, his gangly body filling in. He was looking less like a kid, some of the innocence gone. Nothing like almost dying to throw you out of childhood. It was sad but inevitable. I was sorry that I had played a part in the transition though. But in spite of everything, Snyder's eyes were still full of the devil. Thank God. I hoped it stuck into old age.

Snyder fired up the engine and before I could object, he was behind the wheel and accelerating the *Wahoo* out of the slip.

"Snyder," I warned, "let's keep it below warp speed, okay?"

"No problem," he said, as though it was a given and he always watched his rpms. Then he gave me that damned smile and pushed the throttle forward. A local fisherman in his small boat waved with one hand, holding on for dear life with the other, as our wake hit his boat. The locals knew Jimmy and his lust for speed.

We headed out of Road Harbor and into the Sir Francis Drake Channel. It was crowded with sailboats, tipped on their sides, sails filled. It was a perfect sailing day. Just the right amount of wind. It would have been a perfect day to be out on the water with O'Brien. He'd be analyzing the wind, tightening sail, adjusting the arc in the mainsail, then five minutes later doing it all over again. O'Brien couldn't sit still on a sailboat. He was always searching for perfection.

Snyder and I motored east along the southern side of Tortola, past Paraquita and Fat Hogs Bay, then Beef Island and the airport. An American Eagle flight from San Juan swooped down to the runway and disappeared. It would be dropping off and picking up the sailboat charterers who made up the bulk of tourism on the islands. Across the channel, near Salt Island, a dozen sailboats and dive boats were anchored at the Wreck of the Rhone, one of the best dive sites in the Caribbean.

Virgin Gorda was the westernmost island in the British Virgin Islands, with Anegada directly north. Then it was open water west all the way to St. Martin. Snyder headed the *Wahoo* through the Dogs between West Dog and Great Dog, past George Dog and then the Seal Dogs. The names hardly conjured up beauty but beautiful they were. Protected by the National Park Trust system, the little islands were surrounded by spectacular snorkeling and diving. Fortunately some mooring balls had been installed to protect the delicate sea life from the damage caused by anchors being dropped on the coral and wiping out hundred-year-old colonies.

Still, the hapless, or those who just didn't care, had managed to do some damage. Right now I could see a big fifty-foot catamaran circling in the day anchorage at George Dog. All of the moorings were full. Instead of going elsewhere, the skipper was easing the boat into the bay. A fat guy, stomach hanging over a skimpy spandex swimsuit, was standing in the bow, getting ready to drop the anchor.

Snyder turned into the bay before I'd suggested it myself. Elyse had indoctrinated Snyder and everyone else about ocean conservation. She never let anyone get away with wanton destruction when she encountered it, and she conducted an ongoing campaign to make sure that charter boat captains, police, dive shop operators, anyone who made a livelihood in or near the water did the same. Everyone understood that destroying the reef destroyed what made these islands special and that it would affect tourism. But even more important, it would ruin the islands for their children and their children's children.

I'd been diving at the Dogs with O'Brien and Elyse—at Bronco Billy, the Chimney, and the Visibles. We'd swum under arches and ledges blanketed in a rainbow of color, thick with purple and green algae, the oranges, reds, and yellows of sponges, and coral. We'd encountered nurse sharks, spiny lobsters, banded coral shrimp and moray eels, brittle stars and crabs under ledges. Anemone flourished, their pink and purple tentacles swaying in the currents. Fish of every size and hue—queen angels, triggerfish, indigo hamlets, fairy basslets, and stoplight parrots—inhabited these reefs.

Snyder slowed the *Wahoo* and we circled the big boat, called *Catnip*. It carried the logo of the Sail BVI fleet out of Tortola.

"Ahoy on *Catnip*," I yelled. The captain let up on the throttle and put the huge boat into neutral as Snyder expertly maneuvered the *Wahoo* alongside. I threw a couple of bumpers over the side and grabbed onto their rail.

"What's the problem?" the captain asked. He was obviously put out by our intrusion into their vacation.

"You may not drop your anchor here," I said.

"Why the hell not? There's plenty of room." By now, the guy who had been standing on the bow had worked his way to the cockpit.

"You be knowin' what is underneath your boat?" Snyder asked.

"Sure. Bunch of rocks and fish."

"Dem things you be callin' rocks are living coral. You drop your anchor here, you be killing 'em."

"Jeez, what's a few coral?"

"A few coral?" I said. "If every boat that came in here did what you're planning to do, there would be no coral left. You want to get in the water and see the wonder, then you'd

better be protecting it. You see those elkhorn down there?"
The water was so shallow and clear, I could make out several big ones, probably three or four feet tall, their tan
"horns" golden in shafts of sunlight. He could see them too.

"Your damned anchor and anchor chain will break and
crush them." I was getting really angry and sounding more
like Elyse every day. But I figured someone needed to fill in
for her. I knew plenty of others who would too because they
believed in what Elyse was doing. But there would be some
who would be glad she wasn't around to harass them or their
customers.

"I would like you to either find a place to anchor in sand
or find a mooring ball," I said.

Snyder and I watched him as he made his way back out
into the channel. It looked like he was going to the Baths on
the southernmost end of Virgin Gorda. Fine. Hopefully, he
would pick up a mooring over there.

Fifteen minutes later, we were bringing the *Wahoo* into
North Sound. It was a big area of water, protected all the
way around by Virgin Gorda and two smaller islands—
Mosquito Island and Prickly Pear. Just around the bend was
Flower Island, Neville and Sylvia Freeman's little piece of
paradise.

North Sound had a playground feel to it, especially during the height of the season. Several small resorts nestled
against the hillsides. A couple of windsurfers zipped across
the water, their sails brilliantly colored triangles against the
sky. Up near the Bitter End, a tangle of kids in little day sailers managed to veer off just in time to miss ramming others.
Their teacher was in the middle of it, shouting directions
from his own boat. A seaplane was landing over at Leverick
Bay. Nothing like the secluded islands.

In spite of all the activity, the Sound retained its beauty.
Flowers bloomed on hillsides and the turquoise reefs of Eustatia Sound, too shallow for anything but a dinghy, were
well protected and preserved. Saba Rock was perched at the
opening. When I'd first been up to Virgin Gorda, a rickety

wooden bar was practically falling off into the water on the rock. Now a new restaurant with a few ritzy overnight accommodations had been squeezed on the tiny rock.

Snyder and I tied the *Wahoo* to the dock and went into the bar. I let Snyder take the lead. He had a rapport with people, especially the locals. If he didn't know them personally, he knew someone who knew someone who was a relative. I wasn't disappointed.

"Hey dar, Jimmy. What you be doin' way over here in da Sound?"

"Hey, Mr. Chitton. Didn't know you be workin' over dis way."

"Been working here about two months now. Kind of a second job till Cora can get back at work. She don hurt her back trying to move one of dos damn mattresses at the resort. Tole her dat wasn't her job. She spose to clean rooms, not move furniture."

"Dis be Detective Sampson," Jimmy said. "Hannah, dis is my second cousin's husband's brother."

Hum, that would make him related? Maybe. Chitton was an older man, around sixty, bloodshot brown eyes, loose puffy skin sagging underneath.

"Hey dar, Detective. Nice to be meetin' you," he said. "What can I be helpin' you with?"

"You be workin' a couple nights back when dos boats got broken into?" Jimmy asked.

"Yeah, I be here. Busy night. Lotsa boats moored in the harbor. People on shore eating here, over at da Bitter End, down at Biras Creek. Lotsa empty boats. Heard about dem robberies next morning."

"Did you see anyone around who seemed out of place, suspicious that night?" I asked.

"Dat be a hard question. I was real busy, makin' drinks, talkin' to folks at da bar. Some real nice folks in here, wantin' to know all about life on des islands. You know, askin' what it be like for da people who live here. How dey live,

schools, dat kinda thing. Nice when folks be really interested."

Yeah, I thought. It had taken me a while to begin to understand the islanders. I'd learned some things the hard way,
like the fact that failure to greet another when you pass is
considered an insult. It wasn't till O'Brien made this clear
that I'd understood why I was being shunned. But jeez, in
the States, if you said hello to everyone you passed, you'd
be considered a freak. It had been a real lesson in how cul-
tural differences can cause misunderstanding. I was still a
long way from getting things right.

"Da place was real noisy dat night," Chitton was saying.
"Some kids running around on da docks, a few small boats
moving around in da dark water, people going back and
forth to shore. Any one of dem coulda been checkin' for
empty boats or watchin' for people to leave and boarding
them. Dey would need to keep a careful eye out, but it could
be done if dey be gettin' on and off real quick like."

"If you had to guess, who do you think?" Snyder asked.
"You be livin' here 'bouts."

"Well, I sure don't think it be any tourist. Got to be local.
Maybe kids. Dar be a few wild ones around, dem dat da parents aren't takin' care with, watchin' and givin' a whippin'
now and again."

"Maybe," Jimmy said. "The thing is these robberies be
happening back over by Tortola—at Cane Garden Bay and
da like. Were a couple jus' last night. That be a long way for
kids to be going. Be needin' a decent boat."

"Well, dat be a fact."

"Would you give us a call, if you think of anything else?"
I asked.

"I sure will be doin' dat."

"Hope your wife gets better real soon," I said, shaking his
hand.

"Oh, she be up and around in no time. No worry. Da good
Lord be providin'."

This was another thing I'd learned about the islanders.

They seemed to trust in things working out. "No worry. No problem." These were the phrases of everyday conversation, whether it be in response to drought or to the fact that you'd just splattered a jar of tomato sauce all over the supermarket floor. But I could see the worry and fatigue creasing the bartender's face.

Snyder steered the boat the short distance to the docks at the Bitter End. It wasn't even noon. Things were fairly quiet onshore, the restaurant empty. A clerk at the front desk couldn't tell us anything.

We walked down the sidewalk past rows of windsurfers tipped on their sides in the sand and stopped at the sailing school office. We talked to several of the instructors, hoping that they might have noticed someone who seemed out of place on the water paddling around near the boats.

"Hell, Saturday in the harbor. We're just trying to keep our students from crashing into the docks or colliding with a windsurfer. Lots of activity in the Sound. Nothing out of the ordinary."

We made one more stop down at the grocery store. A couple of sailors were inside, trying to figure out what they would need to get them to the next grocery store. They were going to Cooper Island and then around Peter and Norman.

"Won't be findin' no groceries in dos places," the clerk said. "Ice if you're lucky. Less'n the *Libation* be comin' by."

"What's the *Libation*?" one of the sailors asked.

"Dat be da floating supply boat jus started da business. Young folks with a real good idea ya ask me. Usually have bread, some fruit, rum. But you best be gettin' what you need here."

After they grabbed a cart and started down the aisle, we stepped up to the counter.

"Hey dar, ma'am, I be Deputy Snyder over by Road Town. Dis here be Detective Sampson."

"Sure, I'm Karrie Brown. I be livin' next to your uncle over by Spanish Town. He be talkin' about you. How you be gettin' hurt. You lookin' good."

"That be Uncle George. How he be doin'? I got to get over to see dat man," Snyder said. Pleasantries tended to, he got down to business. "We be here checkin' about dos break-ins on da boats two nights ago. That woulda been Saturday night."

"Yeah, everybody in da harbor be talkin' about it."

"You remember who was around on Saturday?" I asked.

"Same's mos' every day. Sailors in for supplies, kids coming in for ice cream. Chef at da restaurant always comin' in here in a panic on Saturdays, running outta one thing or da other on Friday and gotta have more for da Sat-urday crowd. Dis last Saturday, it was eggs, cheese, and ver-mouth. Wanted me to sell him the eggs I had on reserve for da *Libation*.

"Dat man was angry. Told him I wasn't going to sell him da eggs. Dos folks on dat supply boat already got a weekly order in. Nice young couple. They depend on picking up da eggs 'long with da other stuff dey order—da bread, fresh baked goods.

"Dey comes in every Saturday late to pick da stuff up. Spend da night, den motor from boat to boat in da harbor on Sunday morning. Then dey head down to do a circuit round da Baths, Cooper, the Bight next morning. Dey say da fresh croissants be one big hit on Sunday morning in da Sound for folks lounging on dar boats. Guess I be rambling, but any-ways, I tole da chef he'd have to be makin' his sauce with-out dem eggs.

" 'How the hell I supposed to make hollandaise without da eggs?' dat chef be tellin' me. I tells him dat why dey call him chef, ain't it?" When Karrie laughed, her whole body shook.

"You be givin' my greeting to my uncle," Snyder said as we headed out the door.

Snyder and I made the rounds in the harbor, talking to the skippers of the boats that had been robbed. All of them told the same story. They'd been ashore eating dinner and dancing. One of the local steel drum bands had played long into the early morning hours.

None had noticed that things were missing until the next morning. One guy had lost an underwater camera setup worth thousands. Others reported missing binoculars, watches, GPS units, computers. One woman said she had rings, earrings, and necklaces taken, expensive stuff—diamonds, emeralds, fourteen-karat gold. Why she needed that kind of jewelry on a boat was beyond me.

Snyder and I raced a storm back to Road Town and made it into the dock right before the sky opened up with a hard soaking downpour, water coming down in sheets. We ran for shelter under an awning at the dock and watched the ocean turn gunmetal and seething.

Chapter 10

❧

Amos Porter was a big black guy in work boots and new Levis. He was standing in the middle of the gravel pit, wearing a hard hat, leaning on a shovel. He didn't look like he'd been using it though. His shirt was pressed and spotless, not a speck of perspiration on his face. But I could tell Porter was used to hard work. He was brawny, the creases of his hands permanently embedded with dirt and oil.

I'd heard that he was a shrewd businessman, self-made and determined. He'd worked hard to get where he was. He supplied gravel to just about everyone on the island, had the contract for the roads and the new airport construction, and worked with most of the developers. Two backhoes were parked behind a modular unit and another was lifting huge chunks of earth into a dump truck. Another one waited behind the first, exhaust wafting from its stack. This was a major operation, with hundreds of thousands of dollars invested in equipment.

I'd left Snyder back at the office and told him to tell Dunn that I was going for a late lunch and then to have Hall check out the burns on my shoulder. I'd be back in the morning. All lies, but not Jimmy's lies. He would simply be passing on what I'd told him.

The gravel pit was just around the point, a huge scar in the landscape above Simpson's Bay. The sun was already back out, but I could see the effects of the heavy rain. Gullies of water were running through the pit and washing sediment into the bay. A stream of brown was spreading over the turquoise water in an increasingly large arc. It looked even worse than what Elyse had described in her report.

As I walked up, Porter asked, "What can I be doin' for you, ma'am?" confused about what someone who didn't look like she drove a backhoe was doing at his gravel pit.

"I'm Hannah Sampson, Tortola police," I said, offering a hand. He wiped his palms on his jeans, a habit he'd clearly developed and refined over the years. His grasp was firm.

"Police? One of my guys be in trouble?"

"No, nothing like that." I was surprised that was his first thought and wondered what kind of trouble his guys got into.

"Dey be a kinda misbehaving bunch sometime, down at da Dabloon," he explained.

I wasn't at all sure how to begin a conversation about Elyse. Dunn had made it painfully clear that I was not to pursue any investigation into the explosion on her boat. And I didn't know whether Elyse had ever confronted Porter about the runoff. Only one way to find out. I decided on the direct approach.

"Do you know Elyse Henry?"

"Sure, I know her." His voice hardened and he dropped his lighthearted island slang. "She was down here last week. She said she was writing up a report about the effects of the gravel pit on the bay. If she thinks she can shut down my operation, she's mistaken. I've worked hard to get where I am. I'm not going to give it up because she's worried about a few fish and coral in the harbor. What's this got to do with the police?"

"Elyse has been injured. She's in the hospital."

"Well, I be sorry to hear that," he said. He didn't seem surprised though, and he didn't seem sorry.

"Do you know anything about it?"

"Why are you asking me? You think I'd hurt her?"

"Well, you just said she was threatening your livelihood."

"That don't mean I'd hurt her. I'm not into solving my problems that way. Besides, nobody's gonna close me down because of her reports. She can write as many as she wants. Folks on these islands need my gravel. The folk who call the shots down at the government offices know that. Hell, half of 'em are involved in some kind of building themselves or they want better roads to their homes and businesses. That's called progress. And the tourists, they want them fine hotels."

I knew that was only one side of the story. The people who owned property down in the bay, including the owner of the Coral Head resort, had to be complaining to the Conservation and Fisheries Department about the runoff, maybe even to the chief minister.

"What about the effects on that bay down there?" I asked.

"Just one little bay. But I told Elyse I'd be trying to do some work here to keep the water from running down to the sea. I'm in the process of applying for a good-sized loan. I don't need a bad report about my operation from her or anyone else that might threaten the loan. I've been putting in drainage to collection ponds."

"I'd love to see what you've done. How about a tour?" I wanted to know whether Porter was just bullshitting me or whether he was sincere about working on solutions. Maybe all he wanted to do was divert any suspicion by appearing to be taking Elyse's concerns to heart.

"Detective Sampson, I am a busy man and I don't like what I can see you are thinking. Now I need to be getting into town." He turned and walked back to the trailer and slammed the door.

All he'd accomplished was to increase my motivation. Why hadn't he simply put my concerns to rest by showing me the work he was doing to divert runoff. Maybe he wasn't doing anything at all. I intended to find out.

I parked the Rambler down the road at a snack shop and waited, hoping that Porter really was going to head into town. I didn't wait long. Ten minutes and two Bob Marley songs later he drove past, never even glancing my way.

Back at the gravel pit, I pulled off my tank top and squiggled into the tight black dress that still hung in a dry-cleaning bag in the back. Then I fished under the seat and found a pair of shoes I'd kicked off on the beach during a close encounter with O'Brien. I'd tossed them under there and forgotten them till now. The damned things hurt my feet, but they were perfect for this occasion—three-inch heels and red.

I figured a fashion statement for the guys at the gravel pit was low-cut and short and that none of them would take a second look at anything above my neck. Just in case, I put my sunglasses on, wrapped a scarf around my head, and stepped out of the car, a different woman.

I found Porter's supervisor sitting in the office trailer, feet propped on Porter's desk. He quickly dropped them to the floor and stood, eyes glued to cleavage.

"Hello dar, pretty lady. What can I be doing for you?" he asked, like I might be willing to go out back and roll in the weeds with him. I flirted. And lied.

"I'm Martha Cary, from the bank." I sat down, crossed my legs, making sure to show a lot of thigh, and fumbled through my bag. I pulled out my wallet, searched it twice, and looked at him with a helpless shrug.

"Oh, I am so embarrassed. I seem to be out of my cards. I'm here to assess the property for a loan Mr. Porter has applied for. My boss will be furious if I don't take care of this today. Mr. Porter has been pressuring him to get it done."

"Don't be worryin'. What is it you be needin'?"

"Well, I just need to look around your operation. Won't take long. Just a matter of procedure."

"I be at your service."

"Could I have a glass of water before we go out? It's sooo hot." I made a fanning motion across my chest, once again bringing his gaze to cleavage.

"Oh, no problem," he said, smiling.

As soon as he went to the back, I fingered through a stack of papers on the desk. I could hear him clattering through glassware, probably looking for a clean glass. I was looking for anything that might implicate Porter. All I found was a stack of bills, a couple marked overdue.

I heard the water shut off in the back and was sitting casually in the chair, still fanning, when the supervisor came back and handed me what must have been the cleanest glass he could find, lipstick on the rim. I had a feeling this guy had as many female guests as he could get away with when Porter was gone. I took a couple of sips and stood. He held the door for me.

"Now you be watchin' your step," he said, and damned if he didn't take my arm. "What you be needin' to see?"

"The whole layout—the machinery, anything that adds value to the property." I wanted to find out what kind of business Porter ran. Mostly I wanted to know about Porter himself and whether he was really taking measures to reduce the runoff.

We walked the perimeter as he explained in painful detail how they excavated and transported the gravel. He talked about all the accounts they had and made a point of telling me how integral he was to the success of the business.

"What about the environmental impact?" I asked. "Looks like this is creating quite a scar."

"Well, dat be the price of progress," he said. "Got to be able to pave da roads, build da buildings."

"Does it contaminate the seawater?"

"Well, we be workin' real hard to take care of dat. Come on dis way."

We walked down the hillside to a network of ditches. I was just barely maintaining balance on the rocky terrain in the damned shoes.

"Porter been putting dis type of system in place as a kinda catchment. You can see how it keeps da soil and rock from washing down to da sea. Water and sediment runs across da hillside to those ponds that he's put in and soaks in. Don't know why it's such a big deal myself, a little dirt in da harbor. Me, I wouldn't bother. But Porter's gotten complaints. He be trying to make it right."

So Porter *was* making an attempt to protect the harbor. I wondered how much it was costing him.

"Is this an expensive procedure?"

"Well, sure. Adds man-hours for the crew and takes equipment from da jobs we be making money for. Last week, we had a crew and a backhoe tied up for three days. Road department started complaining. about us gettin' behind on da damned road."

"How long have you been working for Porter?"

"Almost a year."

"Is he a good boss?"

"Sure, he's demanding but he be fair."

"Have you ever seen him angry? Threaten anyone?"

"I ain't never seen Porter mad. Da man just don't have much of a temper."

"Did you ever see him arguing with Elyse Henry, the woman from the Society of Ocean Conservation?"

"Dat's kind of a funny question for an assessment."

"Well, we heard there had been some trouble between them. We need to make sure that Porter doesn't have a history of violence. You know, for the loan, that's important." I smiled and bent to remove gravel from my shoe, the dress sliding up in the back, just short of my ass. That did it.

"Guess I saw him arguing with her one time a while back," he said, distracted, eyes glued to my hemline as I stood and readjusted my skirt.

"Did you hear what it was about?"

"Sure, it was about the runoff. Dat's when Porter started putting in da drainage."

"I think that's all I need," I said. I'd seen enough and I didn't want to be around when Porter got back. I'd been there under completely false pretenses and if he complained to Dunn I'd be in deep shit—at best a lecture, worse directing traffic in a damned uniform under a blazing sun. Fortunately I was pretty sure the supervisor would be able to identify me only by my breast and hip measurements.

"Hey, how about we meet for a drink later?" he asked.

"Yeah, let's plan on later," I said, and scurried down the hill to the Rambler before he could fill in the details.

I headed over to the bank to see Edmund Carr. I wanted to know more about Porter's financial situation and whether the improvements he was making at the gravel pit were cutting into his profits. Maybe that's why he needed the loan.

Carr had been at the bank for ten years and had worked his way through the ranks up to vice president in charge of the loan department. He had his own glassed-in office with a view of the bay. I could see him inside now with a customer who was about to lose it.

"Dis weren't never a problem before you took over." The man was leaning over Carr's desk yelling. "Always get a bit behind in my payments dis time of da year. Anderson gave me da extensions. Knew I was a man of my word, never broke a promise to pay."

Carr saw me and motioned me into his office, looking for any excuse to get the guy out of his face.

"Hey, Ed." I stepped into the office. The man gave me a hard look and stomped out.

"Thanks, Hannah. It's been difficult with some of these customers. They need to realize that times are changing and we no longer operate by a handshake and an 'I'm good for it.' People don't pay, we foreclose."

Too bad, I thought. Carr's policy was hard business for a man who was just getting by. I couldn't help feeling sorry for the guy. He was probably desperate to hold on to land that had been in his family for a century.

"What brings you here?" he asked, pulling up a chair for me.

I sat across from him, ignoring his quizzical expression while crossing my legs and trying to shimmy the skirt down over my knees. Thankfully he didn't ask about the dress and red heels so I didn't have to scramble for a good lie.

"How's Elyse?" he asked.

"Same."

"Any chance she'll regain consciousness?"

"Doc's not saying."

"Let me know if there's any change, will you?" Carr asked.

"Absolutely."

"Did anything turn up in that stuff we brought up from the *Caribbe*?" he asked.

"Nothing yet," I said and shifted quickly to the point of my visit. "Ed, I'm wondering if you can help me with some background about Amos Porter's business."

"What's this all about?" he asked.

"Just some minor questions that I need to clarify. Dunn wants to be sure to tie up any loose ends concerning the explosion on the *Caribbe*."

"I thought you said Dunn ruled it an accident."

"He wants to make sure that we haven't overlooked anything." I was getting in deeper and deeper. Dunn would kill me if he knew, and he was bound to find out the next time he ran into Carr. I could only hope that I had some answers before that occurred.

"Well, I can't really reveal information about his finances, Hannah."

"How about a general picture, Ed? You know, the kind of stuff that's discussed between friends over drinks."

"Okay, Hannah, but this better not go farther than my office. I can tell you without even checking that Porter's business is doing very well. He wants to buy a couple more pieces of earthmoving equipment. He told me today that he's just picked up another big job from a developer who is building a resort over on the north shore."

"Just what the island needs," I said, "more concrete."

"It's good for the economy, Hannah. Provides jobs, brings money to the island."

"You're sounding a lot like someone campaigning for Freeman. I'm surprised you're not more concerned about what it's doing to the environment, Ed."

"Sure, I'm concerned, but I think Freeman's got the right idea about responsible development."

"So, you are supporting him."

"Absolutely. He's the man for the future."

"Maybe." I didn't want to get into it with Carr about politics. I had other things on my mind. "Thanks for the information, Ed." I was surprised that he'd been willing to tell me as much as he had.

"Yeah. Well, I hope it helps you put this thing with Elyse to rest. Just remember it didn't come from me."

Chapter 11

❦

I drove back into Road Town to pick up O'Brien at Sea-Sail. We planned to visit Elyse, then drive up to see Liam and Tom, the scientists updating the turtle study. I'd called to tell them about the report that I found earmarked for them in Elyse's office. They were anxious to read it and insisted I come up for dinner and that O'Brien come along.

When I got to the SeaSail marina, O'Brien was down at the docks, lost in a maze of sailboats. O'Brien's fleet was comprised of over a hundred boats, from thirty- to sixty-footers—monohulls and catamarans, even a couple of racing boats. I found him hanging from the top of a mast on Dock C. Louis, his manager, was on the deck, yelling up at him.

"Did you check that block on da halyard?" he shouted.

"Hey dar, Hannah," Louis said as I stepped on board.

Louis had worked for SeaSail since O'Brien's parents had started the company with just one boat. He was more family than employee. He was almost seventy, a sinewy five-eleven with skin the color of chocolate.

"What is O'Brien doing up there?" I asked him.

"You know Peter. Got to be able to get his hands dirty on da boats."

"Yeah." It was one of the things I loved about O'Brien. I'd never tire of seeing him standing at the wheel of a sailboat or pulling up a sail. O'Brien was not the kind to spend his day behind a desk assessing his wealth. All he really cared about was being out on the water.

"Okay, got it!" O'Brien yelled, and lowered himself down to the deck.

"Hannah," he said, smiling like a kid just off a roller coaster. "Just let me wash up and I'll be ready to go."

We were quiet on our way to the hospital. That was one of the other things I loved about O'Brien: He was comfortable with silence. He didn't need to fill the emptiness with words and neither did I. Right now I was lost in worry about Elyse and O'Brien knew it. He left me to ruminate until we pulled into the hospital lot. Then he wrapped his arms around me.

"Elyse is a strong woman," he said. "She'll pull through."

Love you, O'Brien, I found myself thinking. I didn't dare tell him though—too risky. "I hope you're right," I said instead.

The hospital was eerily silent. Our footsteps echoed down the hollow hallway. Elyse's room was dark, a few renegade rays of light filtering through the closed blinds. She was still unconscious. Almost forty-eight hours and nothing at all had changed. Hall had told us it wasn't unusual, that sometimes it just took time.

We sat for a while talking to her, hoping for some sort of recognition, but there was nothing. Not even a twitch. She looked like a china doll under the covers, thick lashes resting on her cheeks.

"Come on, Hannah," O'Brien said almost an hour later, "let's go." He took my arm and guided me out.

I'd tried to cover the fear and suppress the tears behind a tight jaw. But O'Brien knew the signs. I needed to leave before I fell apart.

It was 6:00 by the time we walked out the front door. Snyder was on his way in. He carried a couple of textbooks and a bag from which the aroma of what I'd guess was jerk chicken emanated.

"Hey, Jimmy, thanks for coming." Snyder and I had

agreed to take turns sleeping at the hospital. He knew that I was worried about Elyse's safety. I was afraid that whoever had tried to kill her might come back to finish the job. He'd insisted on helping out for a few days. In spite of his protests, I'd promised I'd find a way to repay him. We'd agreed not to tell Dunn.

"No problem," Snyder said. "Dis be da perfect place for me to work on my studies."

"I can't believe you've got Snyder camping out at the hospital. Do you really think that's necessary?" O'Brien asked as he pushed open the hospital door.

"Yes." That's all I was going to say. I was tired of justifying myself. And I didn't want to talk about Elyse. I mean, what was there to say?

"How did you like Neville and Sylvia Freeman?" O'Brien asked, changing the subject as we drove up toward Tom and Liam's.

"They seem nice enough." I'd hardly given them a thought since we'd had dinner together last night.

"Nice? Come on, Hannah, what does that mean?"

"Well, it's pretty obvious Neville plays around."

"How would you know that?"

"Hey, I'm a cop, remember?"

"Probably has more to do with your gender," O'Brien said.

"Maybe. The signals from Neville Freeman were loud and clear. And his wife saw them too."

"Well, his personal life has nothing to do with his politics as far as I'm concerned. Besides, I think he's just what the islands need. His family has been here for hundreds of years and he's committed to the people. He wants to focus on effective ways to manage growth and protect the environment, wants improvements in education, more pay for teachers, better resources for kids."

Education was one of O'Brien's causes. He'd done a lot for the schools on Tortola and managed to help several kids go on to college. Of course, he was right to believe that an educated population spilled over into all other aspects of island life, and these kids would be tomorrow's leaders.

"Well, I'm sure Freeman will make a great chief minister. You're a good judge of character."

"That's right," he said. "After all, I'm with you, right?"

Liam and Tom's place was a rental nestled in the hills above Road Town. It was a typically Caribbean cottage with a whitewashed exterior, lime green shutters, and purple awnings. I could hear a gecko's distinctive clicking coming from under one of the eaves. Green-throated hummingbirds were buzzing around a hibiscus bush near the porch and zooming past the two men lounging there with their feet propped on the table near a pitcher of margaritas.

"Hello, Hannah, Peter. So glad to see you," Liam said, as he sat up and poured two more glasses of the frothy stuff. He handed them our way as we settled into the two other chairs on the porch.

Both men were in their late sixties and retired from teaching at a small college in Florida. They'd spent most of the last thirty-five years on or near the water, conducting one research study or another. I'd met them just over a month ago, the day they arrived in the islands. They'd been down at the docks outfitting the boat. We'd hit it off right away.

"Looks like you could use a drink," Liam said. He was athletic, broad-chested and compact, hair barely flecked with gray.

"Thanks, Liam," I guess my worry showed.

"How's Elyse?" Tom asked. He was the more serious of the two men. His hair was completely white, his shoulders narrow, just a hint of stomach protruding over the waist of his shorts, bare feet attached to spindly legs.

"She's the same," I said.

We sat on the porch and watched the sun sink behind the hill. Tree frogs began their songs behind the house. Every once in a while Tom went in to stir or chop, refusing any offers of help.

"The kitchen is his domain," Liam said. "There's hell to pay if you step inside his boundaries. I learned that years ago. Even his wife left the cooking to Tom."

"Is she in the States?" I asked, sure that she wasn't. I'd seen the lingering pain in Tom's eyes the first day we met. I hadn't been about to pry—until now.

"No, Tom's wife died. It's been ten years. She had breast cancer. Fought a long hard battle. I know she stayed alive as long as she did for Tom and their kids. Finally she just couldn't do it anymore. Tom never got over her."

"Are you married?" I asked Liam.

"Divorced. Tom and I have been colleagues since our teaching days in Florida. We were both ready to retire and after his wife died, we decided to collaborate and have taken every opportunity to conduct research all over the world. Tom never does seem to be able to get far enough away from home and all the memories."

"Soup's on," Tom said through the screen door.

Dinner was spinach lasagne, salad, and homemade bread—not a speck of meat or seafood on the entire table.

"Tom's a vegetarian," Liam explained.

"It's not so much an ethical concern about killing animals," Tom said. "It's more about the whole picture, the exploitation of our earth. We humans seem to believe that we are the dominant species and have more right to what's here. Instead, we need to be thinking of ourselves as stewards. But we are eating up this earth in every way, decimating rain forests for farming and grazing, logging trees to build more structures, overfishing some species to the point of extinction, raising mass quantities of beef and poultry to feed our increasing population."

"What does that have to do with being a vegetarian?" I asked.

"It has to do with effective use of land. It takes huge amounts of grain to feed the cattle that we eat. Right now the world produces some two billion tons of grain every year. In India that amount would feed ten million people, who eat mostly grain and little meat. But in the U.S. most of the grain goes to livestock and poultry. Our earth's capacity to support the human species is reaching its limit. The competition for water alone is enormous. Either the industrialized world needs to change its eating habits or find a way to increase the yield on productive land. Better yet, of course, we need to stop population growth."

"Tom gets a bit upset about these things," Liam said. "I agree with him, but I keep trying to tell him he's got to take a different tack with people. We both know that much of it is about economics. There just aren't enough people on this earth willing to sacrifice for ethical reasons. Especially if the financial bottom line is threatened by reform."

"Enough," Tom said, clearing plates and returning from the kitchen with steaming mugs of coffee. Talk turned to their turtle surveying as Tom thumbed through the report I'd brought from Elyse's office.

"This is the old survey," Tom explained. "We've come down to do what we can to update it. Our work is very preliminary. We'll collect some data on where the turtles are feeding and nesting. If the funding comes through, a bigger team will be down next year."

"How did you get connected with Elyse?"

"Some of the money for the project will come through the nonprofit she works for, Society of Ocean Conservation," Liam explained. "They put us in touch with her and she's been our liaison down here. She did the background research, collected all the old articles and research on turtles in the BVI at the environmental library in Road Town. Of course, she's familiar enough with the territorial waters to direct us to the places where turtles have been sighted or have reportedly nested. Before we got down here, she did some preliminary marking of sites on the map to help us determine where we should begin."

"What do you hope to accomplish with new data?" O'Brien asked.

"You'd be amazed at how little is actually known about

sea turtles," Tom said. "We have about thirty years of data, when many of these turtles live to over one hundred. Huge gaps exist in understanding their life history. For example, we know very little about what occurs to the hatchlings from the time they reach the water till the time they reappear as juveniles in the feeding grounds near shore. That's a period of almost ten years.

"We want to learn more about longevity, whether they return to the same beaches year after year, how serious the decline in numbers is. The more we know, the better we can protect them. Can you imagine the loss if these ancient creatures become extinct? Their ancestors go back more than 200 million years, to the age of the dinosaurs."

Tom went to get more coffee while Liam continued. "If we can get accurate documentation, we can push for changes in laws. We can also look for potential violations. Right now, it is illegal to take turtle eggs, and turtles may not be disturbed while nesting nor can they be caught within a hundred meters of the shore. It is also illegal to take any green turtle that is less than twenty-four inches and any hawksbill that is under fifteen inches. But the larger turtles can still be harvested from December first to March thirty-first."

I told them about the nesting turtle that Elyse and I had seen last week. "We planned to monitor the nest, maybe give an assist when the eggs hatch by keeping predators at bay as the young make their way to the beach."

"Excellent idea," Tom said, pouring the coffee. "We'd like to help."

"You know," I said, "I see a hawksbill poke its head above the surface almost every day when I'm sitting on my boat in the morning with my coffee. It's hard to believe their populations are so threatened."

"You're probably seeing the same turtle, one that is feeding in the turtle grass in your harbor. I'm sure you've seen the hawksbill that's been hanging out in the hull of the *Rhone* too. But you rarely see more than one, right? Maybe you don't see even that. Years of exploitation have had a huge impact on the sea turtle populations in the BVI. The leatherback is on the verge of being completely eradicated."

"Why do people want to hunt turtles, knowing that their numbers are so limited?" I asked.

"Hannah still wants to believe that people here are better than those she encountered in Denver," O'Brien said. "The simple truth is that a lot of people just don't care. Right now there are five or six restaurants on the island with turtle on the menu. Actually, turtle meat is excellent. And many argue that hunting turtles is part of the culture, tied with tradition."

"And that's just a part of it," Tom said. "A lot of illegal trading goes on in the Caribbean. Hawksbill, or tortoise-shell, is sold all over the world, for jewelry, hair ornaments, and decorations. The shells can sell for about two hundred and twenty-five dollars a kilogram. Green turtles and leatherbacks are sold for oil, cosmetics, leather, perfume. A seven hundred and fifty milliliter bottle of leatherback oil can sell for two hundred and fifty dollars and one leatherback can yield five to ten gallons."

"Just as serious is the destruction of their habitat, mostly because of development," Liam said.

"Why don't you two come out with us tomorrow morning?" Tom asked. "We could use the help. The couple that usually handles the boat is over in St. Thomas all week. We leave at 6:00. We'll have you back by 9:00 at the latest."

"Love to," I said, without hesitation. I knew the chances of Dunn getting in before 9:00 were remote, and I could use a morning out in the ocean looking at the wildlife instead of searching for evidence in diesel-filled water. Besides, I wanted to know everything that Elyse had been involved in during the weeks before the explosion that left her fighting for her life.

As usual, Sadie was waiting for me on the deck, lying on the bow, when O'Brien and I got back to the *Sea Bird*. She heard us coming the minute we stepped onto the dock and raced to greet us, yelping with excitement.

"Hey, Sadie." O'Brien knelt and scratched behind her ears. Then he stood and pulled me to him. The kiss was long and passionate. O'Brien was one of the most tender and loving men I'd ever known.

We strolled arm in arm to the *Sea Bird*, climbed aboard, and walked to the bow. The ocean was still, the night silent. O'Brien sat down, hung his feet over the side, and pulled me down next to him. We could see fish darting through the water at our feet, light shadows moving through the dark water. Our shoulders touched and the warmth of O'Brien's body radiated into mine.

O'Brien began unbuttoning my shirt, slowly, one button, then another. Then he slid his fingers down my neck and over a breast. One thing led to another and soon we were down below in my bed, our naked bodies pressed against each other, his skin smooth against mine. God, I loved having O'Brien in my bed.

"What would you think about moving into the villa with me, Hannah?" O'Brien asked.

Shit. Nothing like putting the brakes on passion. I loved O'Brien but I didn't want to live with him. I liked having my own space, loved living on the *Sea Bird*, and dammit, I was scared to death of the commitment and where such an arrangement would lead. He'd end up wanting to get married or the relationship would fall apart. I liked things just the way they were.

"Come on, O'Brien. You know how I feel about my space," I said, entwining my fingers in his.

"Yeah, I know, Hannah, but for me, if we're going to stay in this relationship, I need it to change and grow."

"Why can't we just let it be what it is?" I was comfortable with things. Seeing O'Brien, spending some nights on the *Sea Bird* or at his home, making love. I treasured him as a lover and a friend. Damn, I didn't want to lose him but I didn't want to move in with him either.

"Just think about it, Hannah. I know you're scared, but sometimes you just have to take a chance."

"Let's talk about it later."

"Just give it some thought," he said again.

"I will." Maybe it would be nice to share a bed with him every night, shuffle around in his kitchen in the morning, make breakfast together. And it might be okay to be able to come home to someone and complain about my lousy day and get a little sympathy. Now all I had was Sadie. She was a good listener, but never gave me the kind of advice O'Brien was so good at.

He was about to continue the discussion when I rolled over on top of him and smothered any further comment.

An hour later I awoke, my head resting on O'Brien's chest, legs entwined. I lay there for a while, happy to be wrapped in O'Brien's body, the boat rocking gently. God, I loved him and these times together. I didn't want it ruined.

Chapter 12

∽◯∾

At dawn the next morning, O'Brien and I were sitting at the end of the dock in Road Town waiting for Tom and Liam and sipping coffee. O'Brien had not mentioned our conversation of the night before, but I knew he was still thinking about it and would not let the subject rest for long. I, however, planned to avoid it as long as possible.

The day was calm, a glassy morning sea. Schools of minnows, hundreds of them, periodically broke the surface, silver blades sparkling in the sun. A bar jack chased them, leaping in a perfect arc and dropping back into the calm.

"Morning, Hannah, Peter," Liam and Tom called as they walked toward us. They'd already pulled on the bottom part of their wet suits; the top portion hung at their waists, the arms of the suits dangling around their legs. They had typical divers' tans—chests and arms pasty and white; hands, faces, necks, and ankles bronzed.

Their boat, a 32 foot aluminum work boat that they were leasing from the marina, was at the end of the dock. Liam led the way, threw his gear into the boat, stepped onto the side and jumped aboard. He did this as easily as he walked. Boats and the sea were clearly second nature after more than a quarter century working on the ocean. O'Brien and I followed. Tom handed us the gear—fins, snorkels, masks, boxes of field equipment—and then he climbed aboard.

As Liam headed the boat out of the harbor, Tom organized the equipment: pens, waterproof markers, tape measure, tags, tagging pliers, tag gun, scalpel, tweezers, vials, binoculars, and a ski rope. He explained the procedure for capturing the turtles as he worked. Tom and I would be the ones in the water, wearing masks, fins, and snorkels. O'Brien would spot and Liam would maneuver the boat. The ski rope would be attached to the boat and Tom and I would be pulled slowly through the water, looking for the turtles.

Once we spotted a turtle, we were to raise a hand and Liam would stop. Then Tom and I were supposed to go capture the thing. This all seemed pretty far-fetched. I've tried to follow turtles before, both snorkeling and diving. They were way too fast for me, not the lumbering beasts one thinks of in the story of the tortoise and the hare. They flew, their flippers like wings. We were going for hawksbills, which Tom assured me were much easier to catch than the greens.

"You need to swim up from behind it with your arms extended," he said, demonstrating. "Grab the shell at the top and the bottom at the same time. You can grab it underneath the flippers but it could snap at your fingers and if it's a big guy, it could really hurt you. Don't grab it on the side of the shell either because it will pull right out of your hands— cutting them as it does."

"Jeez, Tom. This sounds pretty impossible."

"Believe me, it's not. We've done this before. The best time to catch a turtle is when it's resting or feeding. If it sees you, it will swim away. This calls for patience. We'll need to follow until it gets tired and comes up for air."

Liam cut back the engine just off Ginger Island. "We haven't surveyed out here yet but it has been reported as a feeding area. Elyse said she's spotted several hawksbills here. You will definitely see 'em."

I pulled on my wet suit and O'Brien zipped me in. Tom and I sat on the back platform, designed as a staging area and a place to heft turtles into the boat. We strapped on light weights to offset the buoyancy of our wet suits, enabling us to stay under the water more easily. Then we pulled on fins, secured our masks, and jumped in the water.

Tom and I both gazed down into the water, checking out our surroundings and getting our bearings. We were in about thirty feet and hovering over coral. A couple of barracuda had already taken up residence under the boat. Black urchins were nestled in the cracks of rocks, their sharp pointed spines swaying in the water. I dove under and went down for a closer look. Tom was right behind me.

The long antennae of a spiny lobster jutted out of a crevice; dark red spots and a sharp horn protruded over each eye. It was a careful but curious critter. Every time we moved in for a closer look, it inched farther into its hiding place, crawling out again when we backed up.

When we surfaced, O'Brien threw us each a towline. Liam straightened out the boat, took the slack out of the line, and we began to skim over the water, faces down, breathing through our snorkels. A movie played out below us: Sergeant majors guarded their eggs, trumpetfish lurked in soft coral, and lavender moon jellies undulated in the sun's rays.

We both spotted the hawksbill at the same time. It was swimming slowly around some coral feeding on sponges and algae. Tom signaled and the boat stopped. I followed his lead, staying well behind him. He slipped under the water and finned hard but with minimal disturbance toward the turtle. By the time the turtle realized his presence and was about to take off, Tom had a hold of it firmly by the shell, a deep amber with streaks of reds, greens, and browns.

He signaled that he needed help and I grabbed the other side of the shell. We guided the creature to the surface, the turtle providing much of the power. O'Brien and Liam were waiting and pulled the turtle onto the platform, careful to avoid injury either to themselves or the turtle.

By the time Tom and I climbed aboard, Liam had wrapped the turtle's head in a wet towel, which he said would help the turtle stay calm. He had already taken a GPS reading, measured depth and water temperature, and was recording weather and sea conditions and other essential data on the form.

O'Brien and I stayed out of the way and watched as the two men moved quickly. They measured the carapace, length and width; front flipper length; the head; and the underside of the turtle, what they called the plastron.

This turtle had not been tagged before. They attached staple tags to both front flippers between the scales, injected an electromagnetically coded microchip, what they called a PIT tag, into the shoulder muscle, then recorded all the tag numbers on the sheet. Last, they took a tiny bit of tissue for DNA samples, and then O'Brien and I helped them return the turtle to the water. The entire process had taken less than fifteen minutes. The turtle quickly headed beneath the surface and disappeared.

We repeated the entire procedure, capturing two more turtles and taking the data. We were doing the final run when we spotted a turtle struggling below the surface. We swam over to find a green turtle hopelessly tangled in the plastic rings from a six-pack of soda. Its jaw was held closed in one of the loops, its front flipper tangled and torn. The green was too weak to resist us and unable to swim away.

Tom opened a small knife he had attached to his wrist. I held on to the animal as he cut the plastic first from off the flipper, then from around the bill. The minute he'd freed it, it snapped hard. Tom was prepared though. He'd already moved his hand away.

"Okay," he shouted. "Let her go."

The turtle splashed and floundered for a minute, then dove. We watched it head to the bottom and swim out of sight. Then we swam back to the boat and climbed aboard.

"How could that happen?" I wheezed, breathless from the anger that seethed in my chest.

"It's not unusual for turtles to get caught that way," Liam

said. "They feed on jellyfish. Plastic rings, grocery bags—they all look like jellyfish to a turtle."

"It should be okay," Tom said.

"Why didn't we tag it?"

"Too stressed," Tom said. "It needs to be left alone. We'll find it again in a week or two."

Liam started the engine and turned the boat back to Road Harbor. All four of us were huddled up front, protected from spray behind the windshield.

"Did Elyse go out with you on any of these trips?" I asked as we headed into the channel.

"Just one time, last week. She was really worried about whether we knew what we were doing and whether our techniques were hazardous to the turtles. She wanted to see how it was done."

"When was that?"

"Let's see. Must have been Saturday morning," he responded.

"Did you convince her that everything was okay?"

"Sure, we did the same thing we did today. Anything about it worry you?" Liam asked.

"Well, as a matter of fact, yes. I mean all the stapling, injecting, cutting."

"It's completely harmless. The key is to do it correctly."

It was true that nothing Tom and Liam had done seemed to have been harmful. They had been extremely gentle and clearly had a lot of experience handling the turtles. I knew the study was important for the ultimate survival of the species, but still, it seemed such an invasion.

When we pulled into the dock, Edmund Carr was loading up the search and rescue boat and getting ready to go out with one of the other guys, all of whom were volunteers. They were mobilized when there was a distress call. Carr had been on the team since I'd known him.

"Hi, Ed. Is there a problem?"

"Nothing serious. A kid stranded on some rocks over at the Indians. He swam out there and couldn't get back. His folks can't get to him with the current. What were you doing out so early?"

"We went out to help Liam and Tom and learn a little about their surveying," O'Brien said. "The rescue team ought to get involved, Ed. The guys could report sightings."

It was a great idea and typical O'Brien—always looking for ways for islanders to get involved and pull together, no matter the cause.

Tom agreed. "We could really use the help," he said. "We have a lot of area to cover, and we need to check out all the viable nesting grounds over on Peter, Norman, Cooper, Flower."

"You'll need permission to go onto some of those beaches," Carr warned. "Several of them are private. Flower Island is posted no trespassing."

"Surely the Freemans won't object," O'Brien said.

"Maybe, maybe not. But I know Freeman doesn't like anyone going ashore on Flower," Carr said.

Chapter 13

❦

Stark was waiting for me when I got to the office. Today he wore a black T-shirt that stretched tight across his abs and chest. I wondered if he did it on purpose or was simply unable to find shirts large enough. I was pretty sure it was purposeful. Stark usually looked like he'd just as soon tear your head off as say hello.

He filled me in on what he and Mahler had learned about the boat thefts over at Cane Garden Bay and Soper's Hole. No one had noticed anyone suspicious—no kids cruising the harbor in a dinghy, no one who didn't belong, just the usual charterers and fishermen. Snyder had already told him what we had found out at North Sound yesterday.

Stark has asked him to find out who owned the *Libation*, the grocery boat. If it was registered with the Financial Services Commission, Snyder would find the name, address, and schedule of their route around the islands. If not, he'd end up spending the day down at the docks quizzing everyone who came in or out. One way or another, I knew Snyder would have what we needed by the end of the day.

Then we'd talk to them. No one gets to stay a stranger in the islands for long. We needed to learn who these people were and what they might know about the robberies.

"It's got to be the same people involved in all the thefts," Stark reasoned, "not just kids coming out from shore in their little boats. How many has it been? Ten, twelve, in the last week? And it's the same each time, get on and off quickly. It's got to be someone with a fast boat cruising through the anchorages. No one in a dinghy is going to be moving from Tortola all the way up to the Sound. It's probably someone who doesn't look out of place and can scout things out, make sure no one's on board without looking suspicious. Maybe it's a charterer, down here vacationing."

"Doesn't seem likely," I said. I liked to think of this as creative brainstorming, but really Stark and I were grasping at straws. "Guess it could be one of the cruisers that have been sailing these waters for years. The thing is, most are pretty self-sufficient and independent and have enough money and resources that they don't need to risk stealing from other yachters."

"We did get a report of one boat anchored over in Cane Garden Bay for several days, a small yellow-hulled vessel, looking pretty scruffy. The sails were torn and mended and the hull unpainted. There wasn't anyone on board when I went by the boat."

"I remembered seeing the boat just this morning when I went out with Tom and Liam. It was anchored over in Benures Bay and hard to miss. It looked like it was abandoned and ready to sink.

"Guess we should go by and say hello," I suggested.

"What's our rationale?"

"Hell, checking his park pass or something," I said.

"Why don't you and Snyder go?" Stark asked.

"Come on, Stark, a little water won't hurt you, and just your ponderous presence will convince the guy he should fess up. Besides, Snyder's out looking for the *Libation*."

Stark would never admit it, but he was scared shitless of any water over an inch deep unless it was in a glass. I couldn't imagine how someone who had been born and raised in the islands could fear the water and actually be successful at staying out of it. But Stark managed.

I'd once tried to talk him into learning to dive. If I were going to build a skilled recovery team, I needed someone besides Carr, someone in the department, who could accompany me under the surface. And I trusted Stark. But he'd made it clear that he'd never even consider it and that anyone who strapped a tank on her back and went under the water was just plain nuts.

"Christ," he said, grabbing his sunglasses. "Let's go."

I took the wheel and headed the *Wahoo* across the channel and over to Benures Bay on Norman Island. The water was choppy, the wind having picked up in the last hour. The *Wahoo* bounced uncomfortably across the surface, throwing spray up over the bow. Stark sat beside me, trying unsuccessfully to look relaxed.

"Why did you become a cop, Stark?" I asked, hoping to distract him from the horrors of drowning as we reached the channel and deep water.

"My dad and one of my brothers are fishermen. My other brother works for a charter company in Miami. What was I supposed to do? No way I was going work at anything that involved water."

"Is your family still around?" I asked.

"Sure, my mother keeps trying to get me to join my father. She doesn't like my working for the police, thinks it's too dangerous. Me, I say being out on this damn water is what's dangerous. My uncle died out in the Anegada Passage. His boat went down in a storm. We never found him." I could see that Stark was disturbed by the thought of having the sea as his grave.

"You ever been to the States?" I asked.

"Yeah, about six years ago. I decided to live in Miami with my brother. You know, get out of this backward land, find some action. I managed to get a job with Miami PD. Worked my way up to narcotics. It didn't take long. Something about my black skin and accent seemed to make me a good candidate for undercover."

Stark had obviously not lost the look, but getting into undercover narcotics took more than a good cover. He would have needed to be street-smart, savvy, and quick.

"Christ, Stark. Nothing like a death wish."

"Yeah, and me just a simple island boy. I did it for three years and had enough. The pressure got to me, and Miami, well, it's not the BVI. All the people, the pace. I didn't like living that kind of life. I came back to the islands to stay. Got my old job back."

"Smart move," I said. "I'd take these islands any day."

"What about you, Sampson?" Stark asked. "Why did you become a cop?"

"I was living at the edges of a ghetto and working on a degree in literature. Somehow it all became irrelevant when I saw people dying a couple blocks from my dorm. I finished a master's in sociology, interviewed with the Denver Police Department, and never looked back."

"What about the diving?"

"That came later. The department needed someone to fill a slot when they lost one of their divers in a dive accident. I volunteered."

"I'd call that about as stupid as me going into undercover narcotics, Sampson."

"Yeah. I'll tell you what though—it's a much nicer job in the crystal waters of the tropics. Back in the States I was retrieving bodies from icy lakes and brown polluted water. Mostly, diving blind. I'll take this any day."

We were quiet for the rest of the ride and I found myself thinking about the diving I had done in the States. And I thought about losing Jake. He'd been the team leader. It had been a frigid January morning, and we'd been on assignment, diving for a body in an alpine lake.

We'd bagged the body and taken it to the surface, then returned to examine and collect evidence. We were on our way back to the surface when I turned to make sure Jake was behind me. He wasn't. I went back, frantic, searching for him in the dark, icy water. By the time I got to the surface, I was hypothermic and out of air. The team found his body the next day.

Jake and I had lived together for over a year and had finally decided to make the big commitment. The wedding was to be that weekend. Instead, I'd ended up standing in the cemetery, watching the snow falling on his casket. I hadn't heard what the minister said that day. I made a promise back then never to get that close again. It hurt way too much.

I thought I was past the loss, but Christ, my conversation with Stark had brought it all back.

"Sampson, you have a new approach to Benures Bay?" Stark asked. I was so distracted, I had gone right past the entrance. Muttering an apology, I swung the *Wahoo* around and headed back to the bay.

The yellow boat was the only one still anchored in the quiet water. At almost noon, everyone else had moved on. It was a small sloop, maybe twenty-five feet, lines of rust running down the hull from the deck. The vessel looked deserted, no one visible, the boat rocking gently.

As we approached, I saw movement under the tattered bimini that covered the stern section. Then a man stood up and watched as we came alongside. He didn't offer a hand. Stark threw a line over one of his cleats as I maneuvered the *Wahoo* along the rail.

"Don't be scratching the hull," the guy said, surly. Like it would matter. He was thin, dirty hair, at least a week's worth of beard. "What do ya want?"

"Tortola police," Stark said. "Want to see your boat registration and permits."

"What da hell for?" he demanded.

"Because I said so." Stark was standing in the *Wahoo*, hands on hips, glaring at the guy and flexing his jaw muscle.

When the man went below, I stepped aboard and took a quick look around. The boat was a mess: engine parts strewn about, lines tangled on deck, an empty beer can rolling around in the cockpit.

The guy came back up with his papers, torn and smudged with engine grease. The boat was registered in the BVI, owner Timothy Bowen from Tortola.

"Are you Bowen?" I asked.

"Yeah, and I didn't be invitin' you aboard. What's dis all about?"

"Just routine," I said. "What are you doing out here?"

"Jeez, my ole lady and me had a fight. She done trew me out of da house. I been living on da boat till she cools down."

"Where have you been sailing?" Stark asked.

"Stayed over by Cane Garden Bay a coupla nights, then come over here. Like dis quiet place. Only a couple boats ever be here, always leave early."

"Have you been up to North Sound?" I asked.

"Hell no. I ain't going way up dar in dis old scull. Engine ain't even workin'. Came across da channel with my sails. Now dat da winds picked up, I be goin' back across. I figure by dis day dat wife a mine be missin' me real good."

Stark gave me the look. This guy was not our thief. "We've been checking on break-ins on boats in the territory," he said. "There were several over in Cane Garden Bay on Saturday night."

"So dat's what dis all about. Well, it weren't me."

"Yeah, we can see that. Whoever is involved has more moving power than you do. Did you see anything when you were up in Cane Garden Bay?"

Bowen thought for a minute. "Well, dat be da night of da full moon party up by da Bomba Shack. Folks going to shore like crazy and going up dar ta sample dos psilocybin mushrooms. Kinda funny."

"You see anyone cruising the harbor that night?"

"Well, sure, always a dinghy or two motoring into shore or out to a boat. A lotta drunk folks out in dar dinghies dat night."

"Did you notice anyone in a boat with a good-sized engine, a cigarette boat or speedboat of some kind?"

"Probably were a few in and out. Dat dar grocery boat was makin' some deliveries to a couple of da yachts. Coupla fishermen came in late. Hell, I weren't payin' much attention. Have ta admit I just about finished a whole bottle a'-rum myself dat night."

It was something. We'd check out the local fishermen. Hopefully, Snyder had identified the owners of the grocery boat by now. Someone had to have seen something.

"Thanks for your help, Timothy," I said, stepping back on to the *Wahoo*. "Hope your wife has cooled off."

"Oh, she be welcoming me with open arms. Dat's da best part of da fight!"

Stark was tying up the *Wahoo* back in Road Harbor when a nasty-looking guy with fire in his eyes came storming down the dock.

"What's this I hear about you and that deputy harassing one of my customers about anchoring on the reef yesterday near the Dogs? That skipper said hell would have to freeze over before he'd come back down here and rent from me. You need to watch what you do with the tourists, dammit! You are hurting my business."

"Nice to meet you too," I said. I could feel the blood rising to my face when I finally figured out who this jerk was—Fred Jergens, the owner of BVI Sail.

He was a lean guy with chiseled features. Though he didn't look much over fifty, his hair was white, straight, parted on the side and cut precisely around his ears. If he hadn't had so much hate in his face, he might have been attractive. Instead, he was clearly a bully, controlling, domineering and completely unable to keep his emotions in check.

"Cool off, Jergens," Stark said, stepping between us.

"That guy on your cat was about to drop his anchor in the middle of a coral bed," I said. "Aren't you briefing your charterers on where they should and shouldn't anchor? He was about to destroy a bunch of elkhorn."

"I tell them where to anchor, and that's anywhere that doesn't endanger my boats. I'm sick of this damned concern about a few coral. This is my business and I call the shots.

Elyse Henry has been harassing my charterers since I started up, and now you and that kid you call a "deputy." He was almost spitting now, yelling over Stark's shoulder and pushing against his massive frame. I had to admire Stark's composure. "My boats aren't the only ones in the water," he said.

"Maybe it's the fact that yours are the ones causing problems. You need to educate your customers."

"Just quit harassing them." He pointed his finger at me over Stark who was still firmly planted between us. If he could have reached me, it would have been his fist in my face.

"You do it again, I'll be pressing charges," he threatened. He stomped back down the dock, turned once to glare and was gone.

"Jeez, Hannah, is there anyone on the islands that either you or Elyse don't anger?" Stark said.

I wondered the same thing, especially about Elyse.

Chapter 14

~~~∽~~~

When we got back to the department, I told Stark I needed to run an errand and that I'd be back in an hour.

"Right, Sampson. Maybe I should go with you."

Stark saw right through me. I hadn't been subtle. In fact, I'd been on a rant about Jergens all the way to the office. I did manage to avoid any mention of Jergens's connection to Elyse. This was my problem. I did not want Stark involved and in trouble with Dunn.

"I'll be fine, Stark."

I headed out the door before he could argue with me and drove over to BVI Sail. Fred Jergens's charter company was about a half mile east of Road Town.

I was surprised when I got there. I'd expected it to be run-down and ill kept. Instead, a sign, intricately painted in the colors of the BVI flag, graced the entrance. I drove down a gravel drive lined with flamboyant trees that were loaded with blossoms. The office was newly painted in the same colors as the sign. In the back was a small parking lot with only one other car, a white station wagon with Jergens's logo on the side. I parked, walked around the building to the office, and went in, gun tucked under my shirt.

"Good day, ma'am." It was not the greeting I expected. But then it wasn't Jergens standing behind the counter. "How can I be helpin' you?"

"I'm looking for Fred Jergens."

"He not be here right now. I'm da manager. You be interested in a charter?"

"No, just hoping to see Jergens. I'm Detective Sampson, Tortola PD."

"Oh sure, I be knowin' who you are. Seen you in town. I'm William Dobbs."

"You know, this place isn't what I expected. It really looks great."

"I been fixin' it up. Workin' on the boats. Don't think Mr. Jergens be too happy 'bout it though. He chewed me out when he came in. Said I was wasting his money and spending behind his back while he was away. He didn't even notice the boats. Been doin' a lotta work on 'em."

"You'd think he'd appreciate it."

"Yeah, dat's what I thought. Business been slowly picking up with the improvement. Damned I think he going to be firing me after all dis work I been doin'."

"You know when Jergens got back on the island?"

"Couple of weeks ago, I guess. Been in and out most days since."

"How did he know about that catamaran I chased out of the Dogs?" I asked.

"Yeah, that. Jergens was down on the dock when the guy came in on Tuesday afternoon, complaining about the treatment of the local cops. Guess that be you. I been warning the charterers about anchoring in da coral, but Jergens, well, he doesn't care 'bout dat. Da man's down here ta make a quick dollar. He don't care much 'bout da islands."

"You ever see him get into it with Elyse Henry?"

"Well, sure. Ain't too many folks on da island he hasn't butted heads with. Dat Elyse be one determined lady. She came down here last week when she be hearing Jergens back on da island. She warned him to keep his charterers off da reef and told him she'd asked the Park Service to keep an eye on any boats with da BVI Sail logo."

"How did he react?"

"He be real angry. Told her to stay out of his business. If his charterers had any problems, he'd know who to blame. Looked like he be about to grab her when a couple walked in looking for a boat. He be turning into a real gentleman den. Opened the door for her and dat was it."

William walked out with me and was talking to one of the dockhands when I left. Seemingly Jergens had told his employees that he didn't want the faulty gear replaced on any boats until he gave the okay. It sounded like a lot of it was safety equipment.

I could hear William's anger and frustration as he told the guy to go into town and get the replacements. What he hadn't been willing to say about Jergens would probably fill volumes. Jergens was an unethical jerk.

In terms of Elyse—Jergens clearly had reason to hate her. I wondered what would have happened if that couple hadn't interrupted his threats against her that day in his office. From what I knew of Jergens, I couldn't see him letting it go. He'd have needed to finish the argument.

I took Paraquita Bay Road back to the office. It was the long way, maybe four miles instead of three but without the speed bumps that had been installed on Blackburn Highway along the waterfront to prevent fast-moving vehicles from slaughtering chickens, goats, and small children that meandered across the pavement.

I was the only car on the road. I drove slowly, no one behind me trying to make a mad dash past me on a curve. My mind refused to drift though. Instead I obsessed about Elyse and what could have happened on the *Caribbe*. Did it involve Jillian, or Amos Porter, or was the attempt on Elyse all about threats to Jergens's damned charter business?

As I made my way up one twisting turn after the next, the air cooled to a frosty eighty degrees. Cathedrals of red towered above, turning everything underneath a warm pink. The flamboyant trees were littering bloody blossoms across the road. I could hear a gull calling from somewhere up in the limbs, a laughing gull by the sound of it.

I drove higher into moist green. Invisible tree frogs chirped from deep inside the forest. Not quite a rain forest, as there wasn't enough moisture, but the terrain was lush with elephant ear philodendron, tree ferns growing under huge gumbo-limbo trees, and orchids of every hue. Hummingbirds made their way from blossom to blossom.

It felt good to be alone on this tropical road. I was pissed when I heard a car roaring up behind me. I slowed, hoping it would pass quickly and leave me to my solitude, but damned if the guy didn't lay on his horn.

"Shit!"

I glanced in the rearview mirror. It was a Jeep Cherokee; the tinted windshield prevented a view of the interior. The driver was right on my tail. I slowed further and waved him around. He got right up on my bumper, then darted into the other lane. I recognized the driver—damned Jergens. He gave me the finger, cut right in front of me, and disappeared. What the hell was he doing driving up this road? Coincidence? I doubted it. He'd probably seen me leaving his charter company and followed. All for the chance to give me the finger and cut me off?

At the top of the island, I hit Ridge Road and a spectacular view of the north side of the island. I pulled off onto the gravel, got out, and walked to the overlook. Edgy, I kept an eye out for Jergens.

Josiah's Bay lay at the foot of the valley. Surf broke on the point, sending gleaming sprays of water high in the air and down, like diamonds scattering on the rocks. A few sea grape trees tangled along the water's edge; otherwise the beach was empty for miles. Out to sea, the water rippled jade, turquoise, aqua, and then turned deep and black.

I spotted Jergens's Cherokee through the trees, making its way down the winding road toward Road Town. Evidently he'd gotten his thrills for the day. I took a last long look at the view and then climbed into the Rambler and headed back down the steep road into town.

At first, I thought that the wobble in the steering wheel

was due to the idiosyncrasies of the road. I kept going, the momentum of the steep grade carrying me down. As my speed increased, I touched the brakes.

Big mistake. The moment they caught the car veered out of control. I held on, a white-knuckled, finger-stiffening grasp around the wheel, trying to keep the Rambler pointed downhill and on the pavement, but the damn thing was swerving like crazy. I let up on the brake and downshifted, gears protesting.

The car continued on its course downhill, veering from one side of the pavement to the other. One tire hit gravel and the car began sliding and heading for a deep ditch. When I pulled on the emergency brake, the entire right side of the car lifted off the ground, and threatened to roll. If it did, I'd be crushed under the damned cloth top. Back in 1965, no one was too concerned about putting roll bars in convertibles. Shit.

I released the brake, and the tires bounced back to earth. A sharp pop, then another near the front tire, and the Rambler swerved back to the center of the road. The car kept swerving, picking up momentum, and was now headed toward an abrupt curve in the road; one side a rock wall, the other a sharp drop over the edge. I'd never make the turn. The damn car was headed right toward the steep drop-off that ended about 100 feet down in the trees. All I could do was react.

I swung the wheel hard to the right, hoping to slow my momentum and try to turn the car toward the other side of the road. Somehow, hitting a rock surface seemed a better choice than flying off the side of the world. The car, however, refused to change its deadly course, still skidding right toward the drop-off. Christ. I held on, teeth clenched. The car stuttered across the pavement, started slowing slightly, then hit the edge of the road and gravel. I slammed on the brakes, jamming my foot to the floor and grinding the transmission into second gear. Then I closed my eyes and prayed.

I felt the car teeter on the left side for an instant before dropping back on all fours.

When I forced my eyes open I saw that the car had come to an abrupt halt just a couple feet from the edge. I pulled the emergency brake, fear still coursing through me.

Before I realized I'd even opened the car door, I was standing by the Rambler, my legs shaking, my breath coming in short gasps. Another few feet and I would have been tangled down below in the trees. I stumbled to a nearby rock and sat, head in hands, and waited for equilibrium to return. I was drenched in sweat, clothes plastered against my skin. Finally, I regained some control over my body and walked back to the car.

It was still running, engine idling. When I got around to the other side, I understood what the sharp popping had been. The right front wheel was held in place by three lug nuts that had worked their way all the way to the end of the threads. The other two had completely sheared off.

I pulled the lug wrench out of the trunk and tightened the remaining nuts down hard, then checked the other wheels. The bolts on the left front were also loose. What the hell? I admit that I am not one of those meticulous people who do things like rotate the tires at the appropriate time. And I had not thought about replacing them since I bought the car a year ago. But I found it hard to believe that the damned nuts had all worked their way loose at the same time. Anyone could have tampered with them—Jergens included. The Rambler had been out in the lot behind his charter company for a good half an hour while I'd talked with William. Jergens may have been following me to enjoy the effects of his handiwork, then thought better of being so close to the scene of my death.

By the time I got to the police department, the adrenaline rush had worn off. I headed for the bathroom, splashed cold water on my face, went to my office, and dropped into my chair. Finally, I noticed the manila folder sitting on the desk.

I stared at it for a minute, then realized it was the lab reports from the stuff I'd collected from Elyse's boat.

"I told Snyder to leave that report in your office." Dunn had come up behind me, his mass filling the doorway. "I thought I told you that we would not be investigating."

"Sorry, Chief, I forgot that I sent that stuff to the lab." I was lying and Dunn knew me well enough to know it.

"Take a look at it and file it, Hannah. I've already taken a quick look. There's nothing there that indicates foul play. No accelerant in the charred wood and not one print on that stove knob that you and Carr retrieved from the sand. One clear print was lifted from the wine bottle—not Elyse's, but no matches in the database. Could be anyone's, including whoever sold the wine."

"Well, I'm sure that Elyse did not wipe her own prints off that stove," I argued.

"You know as well as I do how hard it can be to get prints from objects that are submerged, especially in salt water— even more unlikely given the fact that the knob had been blown at least forty feet through the water."

"Maybe, but it was pretty much undamaged and in the water less than what, six hours? It seems amazing that there were no prints at all."

"Hannah, you've been retrieving evidence underwater long enough to know better. You know how unpredictable the sea is when it comes to evidence. You need to keep an objective mind instead of looking for anything that would prove this was a murder attempt."

I knew that Dunn was right about the prints. But the fact that no accelerants were present didn't prove anything except that whoever turned the gas on figured, rightfully so, that the propane leak would have been enough to do the job. I wasn't about to give up just because nothing had turned up yet.

"I'm telling you again, Hannah, I want you to drop it," Dunn said, turning to leave. "I don't want to hear from Reidman or anyone else that you are still snooping around on this. And I want a report on my desk by the end of the day on where you are with these boat thefts."

I'd been about to tell him about my near death experience on the road, but realized it would just get me in more trouble—maybe cost me my job. Dunn would want the whole story. I'd have to tell him I considered Jergens a suspect in a case he'd just told me to drop and that I paid a visit to Jergens's charter company on Dunn's time. Until I was sure the lug nut didn't come loose from my own neglect or some juvenile delinquent on a lark, I'd keep the incident to myself. When he was gone, I closed my door and opened the report.

There wasn't much more in it than he'd said. I was working hard to swallow my frustration when Gilbert Dickson knocked on the door. Dickson ran the one-man evidence analysis lab in the office and was an expert with fingerprints. He was a small guy, with a snowy complexion, probably because he spent so much time looking into a microscope. But he was good at what he did, and damned if he didn't ride a Harley.

"Just got a match on a set of prints. That bottle that you found floating in the water, the one labeled Ambien? The prints belong to a Jillian Ingram. They were in the database because of an arrest over at St. Thomas a month ago."

"Jillian?"

"Know her?" he asked, handing me the report.

"Yeah," I said. "Hey, thanks, Gill."

"No problem." He walked out the door whistling something from *Easy Rider*.

I could think of only one way that Jillian's prints could have gotten on that bottle: She had handled it. She could have easily slipped those pills to Elyse if she'd been there that night. The big question was why she would do it. Maybe she'd simply intended to steal them. I needed to talk to the kid.

Dunn didn't see me leave. To hell with his damned report.

Chapter 15

A man with silver hair and a deep tan answered the door. He wore a watch that I was sure cost more than my yearly salary. This was not the butler.

"Mr. Ingram?"

"Yes?" he asked, defensive and suspicious.

"I'm Detective Sampson, Tortola PD. Like to talk with Jilli."

"Jillian is not here," he said, ready to slam the door in my face.

"Who is it, Joel?" a voice called from the living room. "Is it about Jilli?" A mixture of hope and fear laced the voice. Then Rita Ingram appeared behind her husband.

"Detective Sampson. Has something happened to Jilli?" She looked terrible, her hair pulled back with pins, eyes bloodshot and smudged with mascara.

"No, I just came to talk with her. What's the problem?"

"She's run away," she said.

"You might as well come in, Detective," Mr. Ingram said.

The living room was as dark and uninviting as the last time I'd been there, that damned Rembrandt glaring at me through the gloom.

"What did you want to see Jillian about?" Ingram asked. "My wife told me you were already here once asking a lot of questions. If this is more to do with Elyse Henry, I can assure you that Jillian is not involved."

"What makes you so sure?"

"I told her to stay away from her. And I told Elyse the same thing. Jillian doesn't need someone coddling her. She's just a wild kid. She needs to learn some things about life."

"Guess you think that boarding school is the place to learn it."

"Damn straight. They've guaranteed to get my kid on track."

"How long has Jilli been gone?"

"She's been away all night," Rita said. "I'm frantic."

"Why haven't you called the police?"

"The girl is out partying with her friends," Joel Ingram said. "She's showing us she's got the upper hand. She'll be back when she gets hungry. And she is leaving Sunday. I've got her booked on a flight, and she will be on it."

I couldn't believe that they hadn't been out combing the island for her. She was so vulnerable out there alone. I guess it was Joel Ingram's version of tough love.

"I don't know, Joel," Rita said. I could see that she was having a hard time trying to figure out what was best for her daughter.

"Jillian has been so quiet and withdrawn this last week," she said, turning to me. "I'm sure that I heard her sobbing in her room on Monday night, not long after you left. When I knocked on her door, she wouldn't answer."

"You didn't go in?" I remembered how lost the kid had seemed that afternoon when I'd left her sitting on the steps.

"Absolutely not! I would never invade her privacy."

Christ, I'd never been a parent but I'd watched my sister with her kids. She'd have been charging in there, hugging the kid and helping her through the pain. I was sure that Rita had been brainwashed into this hands-off tough parenting style by her husband. No wonder she drank.

"I'll see what I can do to find her," I said, standing.

"We don't need your interference," Ingram said. "We can take care of our daughter ourselves."

"Right."

The first thing I did after I left the Ingrams was find a phone and call Mary.

"Yes, Hannah, Jilli's here. I called her earlier when I got your message about how worried you were. I spoke with her for about five minutes before her father grabbed the phone and told me to mind my own business. Jilli showed up at my door at four o'clock this morning. She's in bad shape."

"What do you mean, bad shape?"

"She found her mother's wallet, took a hundred dollars. Amazing how these kids know just where to go to find drugs. She bought a gram of cocaine. I can't believe some low-life on the island is selling drugs to fourteen-year-olds."

"Believe it, Mary. It happens everywhere, even here."

"She walked all the way up here with the stuff in her pocket, untouched. To tell you the truth, I'm very surprised she came to me instead of finding a place to get high. She was exhausted when she knocked on my door. She started talking and there was no stopping her. God, what happens to our children." Mary's voice cracked. "I think I've seen it all, and then this."

"What, Mary?"

"Jilli was assaulted at boarding school the very first month she was there. By one of her teachers, no less. I suppose it's not surprising knowing Jilli's father. He's a cold bastard who should never have had children, much less a daughter. And Rita, she just goes along. Jilli turned to the first adult male who seemed to care. When it turned sexual, Jilli was too naive to understand until the man raped her. She never reported it or told anyone. She's positive it was all her fault and that she's a bad person. It's no wonder she's smothering her fear and hurt in drugs."

"Where is she now?" I asked, worried more about Mary at the moment. If Jilli had caused the explosion on Elyse's boat, Mary could be next.

"I gave her a sedative and put her to bed. She's been

sleeping most of the day. I've convinced her to go into the hospital—the drug rehab unit. I was about to wake her up and take her there."

"What are you going to tell her parents?"

"Actually, I had hoped you could help me." I knew by her tone that she wasn't giving me any option. "She did have a gram of cocaine in her pocket. A threat from the police of either jail or the hospital might convince them of the necessity of treatment."

"That might work for a couple days, Mary, but the kid's a minor," I said.

"I'll take a few days. This child needs help. She is such a sweet kid, sensitive, smart, caring. God knows how it happened with parents like hers."

"Mary, there's a problem." I told her about Jillian's prints on the empty prescription bottle. Maybe Jilli wasn't the sweet kid that Mary thought.

"Look, let me get her admitted. Once she's in a safe environment, you can ask her about it yourself. Give the kid a break, okay?"

"Okay, but Mary, she could have slipped Elyse the drugs and rigged the boat. You need to be careful."

"Don't be silly," she said and told me to meet her at the hospital in an hour.

When I got to the hospital, I stopped to check on Elyse first. She lay peacefully, same as before. I sat with her for a while, holding her hand and carrying on a stream-of-consciousness monologue. I kept hoping that some word would connect, that Elyse would open her eyes.

"Come on, Elyse," I pleaded, "snap out of it!" But Elyse wasn't listening.

I headed up to the drug rehab unit on the third floor. It was just a couple of rooms at the end of the hallway.

Mary had been responsible for establishing the little unit. She'd convinced a couple of hospital administrators that such facilities were essential even in paradise. A nurse buzzed me in when I identified myself. Mary was at the nurse's station filling out a pile of forms. She looked up and gave a weak smile when she saw me.

"Hannah, let's go talk before you see Jillian," she said, leading me to a conference room and closing the door. "She's still settling in and getting the once-over—blood pressure, temperature, blood drawn. I'm writing up an evaluation and treatment plan."

"Jilli is lucky that there's a doctor like you on this island, Mary. You look really tired. You ought to be at home." I knew I was wasting my breath. Mary would leave when she was good and ready—and that would be when she was sure everything was in order.

"Getting patients into the hospital is always stressful. Often at the last minute they decide they don't want to be hospitalized. I was afraid Jillian would bolt. It is very difficult to admit to a drug problem, much less decide to do something about it. It takes a lot of insight and fortitude, especially for a fourteen-year-old."

"Did you call her parents?"

"Yes. They're on their way. I told them that Jilli didn't want to see them right now but her father wouldn't hear it. I need to be here when they arrive."

"How's Jilli doing?"

"As well as she can be. I think she's feeling relieved that she's in a safe place. But she's scared too. Go gently with her, Hannah," Mary said, concern etching her face.

She walked me to the room and left me there. Jilli was curled up on her bed, on her side, arms wrapped around her knees. Her cheeks were tear-streaked. Christ, she was just a kid.

When she saw me, a mask dropped over her face to disguise the pain. She quickly swiped at her eyes and sat up.

"Hi, Hannah. What are you doing here?"

"Just came to see how you're doing."

"I'm okay. How is Elyse?"

"About the same. You have everything you need?"

"Guess so. I'll probably be out of here in a day or so."

"Give yourself some time. You should stay here till Mary says it's okay to leave."

"Yeah, well, my folks are going to be really mad—especially my dad."

"They'll get over it."

"Maybe."

I took a deep breath. The next part of the conversation wasn't going to be easy. "Jillian, I need to ask you some things about Elyse."

"What about?" she asked. She was listless, closed down.

"Well, when I talked to you on Monday, you said you hadn't seen Elyse for a couple of days. Are you sure you didn't see her Sunday night?"

"No, I didn't," she said, averting her eyes.

"The thing is we found your fingerprints on a vial of her medication."

"I looked through her prescriptions. So what?"

"That particular medication showed up in Elyse's bloodstream when she was tested at the hospital. I thought you might know how that happened." I couldn't figure out how to be any more tactful than this. If this kid hadn't been in such bad shape I would have been pushing a lot harder to trip her up.

"You think I gave her the Ambien?"

"How'd you know it was Ambien?" Okay, so I resorted to one little trick. I am a cop, for chrissakes.

Damned if the kid didn't bend over and start sobbing into her hands. She was rocking back and forth on the edge of the bed when the nurse came in.

"Everything okay in here?" she asked, glaring at me.

"Everything's fine," Jillian said.

I went into the bathroom and pulled a wad of toilet paper off the roll, sat down on the bed next to Jilli, handed it to her and waited.

"I did go to the *Caribbe* that night," she finally said, her voice cracking. "I didn't know where else to go. I'd had a big fight with my dad. Elyse wasn't home. I knew she had a lot of old prescriptions in the medicine cabinet. I found the Ambien and was sitting at the salon table with a glass of water and the vial when Elyse got home. I never opened it.

"Elyse made tea and we talked for a long time with that bottle sitting there between us. She never took it away. Just let it sit, like it was my decision. Finally, she took me home. When she dropped me off, she made me promise that I'd call her if I felt that bad again."

"What happened to the vial?"

"It was still sitting on the table when we left."

"Why did you lie about seeing Elyse that night?"

"I didn't want my parents to find out I'd gone to see her."

I wanted to believe the kid. But the last time I had trusted a teenager, I'd ended up lying on a Denver street with a bullet hole in my shoulder.

Chapter 16

Sadie bounded up the steps, jumped up, put her paws on my shoulders and licked me on the nose. She knew better, but hey, I'd been gone all day. I went below and changed into a pair of old shorts and tennis shoes.

"Come on, girl, let's go for a walk." She scurried down the dock and waited for me in the sand, panting, tongue hanging out the side of her mouth. When I stepped off the dock, she darted down the beach. I followed at a more leisurely pace, stopping to examine the shells that were scattered on the shore. I crouched on my haunches and ran my fingers through the rocky debris, the activity relaxing, a way to clear my head.

The beach was littered with broken pieces of snails, shiny and smooth. I picked up a perfectly preserved shell, white with bands of gold outlined in black. I stuck it in my pocket, stood, and gazed out to sea. Birds were out fishing, graceful forms silhouetted against the setting sun. A warm breeze carried the smell of the ocean—salty and sweet. There were few places I'd rather be than standing in this spot on the edge of the ocean. I regretted that I sometimes got too caught up in things to take the time.

Up ahead, Sadie stood out on the point waiting. We walked inland, through brush teeming with hermit crabs. One was in the process of making the transfer from the shell it had outgrown to another that it could wear more comfortably. I picked a small one up, only to have it instantly retreat into its shell. After a moment it emerged, brave or curious, to explore the palm of my hand, its needle-thin claws tickling my skin. I set it back where I'd found it.

"Let's go swimming, Sadie!" I ran back to the beach with her at my heels and pulled off my shoes. We splashed into the water and then I dove under, fully dressed. When I surfaced, Sadie was right with me. I swam out to deep water and then floated on the surface, watching white billowing clouds move across the deep blue.

O'Brien was rattling around in the galley when I got back to the *Sea Bird*.

"Jeez, what are you doing here?" I regretted it the minute the words were out of my mouth and the hurt crossed his face. It was stupid, thoughtless. But I'd been looking forward to being alone, sitting on the bow with Sadie and Nomad, staring blankly out to sea and eating cold tuna. And I did not want to resume last night's conversation with O'Brien.

"I thought you'd enjoy a decent meal. Guess I was mistaken," he said, anger tingeing his voice.

"I'm sorry O'Brien. Thanks for making dinner."

He had gone all out—red snapper in wine sauce, salad overloaded with fresh spinach, avocado, nuts, and God knows what else. I carried our plates up top to the cockpit table so we could eat under the stars. O'Brien brought up glasses and had a bottle of wine tucked under his arm.

"It's been kind of a bad day," I explained as he poured the wine. I told him about Jillian.

"It's possible that she's lying," I said. "That she dropped those pills in Elyse's tea that night and turned on the gas. Thing is, I can't figure out why."

"Sometimes there is no logical why," O'Brien said. "Just some fool kid, acting on an impulse that she later regrets. Maybe she was high or drunk and Elyse got on her case.

Maybe she'd threatened to go to the girl's parents. Who knows what goes through a kid's mind?"

"Yeah, maybe," I said. But the cop in me wanted logic. I wondered where the logic was in all this? With Jergens?

"What do you know about the guy who owns BVI Sail?" I asked.

"You mean Fred Jergens? Why do you want to know about him?" O'Brien asked.

I told him about my run in with him and the lug nuts coming loose.

"Good God, Hannah, you could have been killed," he said, his voice rising. "What makes you think Jergens was involved?"

"He threatened me today down at the docks. If Stark hadn't gotten between us, I'm sure he would have come after me. Then when I was driving back to the station, he got right on my tail, swerved around, barely missing my bumper."

"I thought Jergens had left the island," O'Brien said between bites of snapper.

"Guess he's back. He was in a rage because I'd confronted one of his charterers about anchoring in the reef over at Great Dog. But it wasn't just me Jergens was pissed at. It was anyone who put environmental concerns above pleasing the tourists."

"That would be Elyse," O'Brien said.

"That would be Elyse." I'd finished eating and had propped my feet up on the cockpit bench. I was leaning against O'Brien and sipping wine. God, he smelled good, like sunscreen and the ocean.

"Well, Jergens is an opportunist and he's ruthless. He knows nothing about sailing or running a charter business. He picked up a few boats cheap and thought he'd exploit the industry down here. I give him maybe another year before he loses everything." O'Brien took a long sip of wine, struggling to keep his anger in check.

"Do you think he'd be desperate enough to go after Elyse?" I asked.

"Desperate, no. More like vengeful. He'd go after Elyse just to get even. You too if you cross him." O'Brien put his arm around me, concern tightening his jaw.

"What do you mean, vengeful?" I asked.

"As far as I can tell, the guy has no conscience. He likes to hurt people as long as he can get away with it. About two years ago when he arrived here and set up the company, some things started happening."

"What kind of things?" I asked.

"One of Blue Water Charters boats burned in the harbor. It was right after an angry charterer had brought a boat back in to Jergens and demanded a refund. The guy was a lawyer and threatened to sue. The engine on the boat had seized up right when the guy was trying to maneuver the thing into a slip. His wife was thrown off the boat trying to grab the dock post and was almost smashed between the dock and the boat. There had been no oil in the engine. He refunded the guy's money, but Jergens was seething. The couple was able to get another boat at Blue Water Charters. Not a week later, a fire started on one of their boats and burned in the harbor."

"You think it was Jergens?"

"At the time, it looked like an accident—a boat with a propane leak. But then about two months later, James Carmichael's dive shop went up in flames. Carmichael was lucky to get out alive."

As casual as O'Brien was trying to be about the whole affair, I could tell he was furious. James Carmichael was a close friend. Finally O'Brien stood, stretched, and gazed out to sea. I stood, wrapped my arms around his waist, and waited.

"A bunch of us got together and helped him rebuild," he finally said. "I cosigned a loan so he could replace his equipment."

"You think it was Jergens?" I asked.

"Yeah, so does Carmichael. He'd been telling anyone

who came into the dive shop and asked about charter companies not to charter a boat from Jergens. We were sure it was Jergens getting his revenge, but there wasn't any proof. The fire had started in the back near the compressor. Dive tanks started blowing up and the structure went up like kindling."

"Does Dunn know about all this?"

"Sure. He questioned Jergens a couple of times, but there was nothing to hold him on. We'd all been keeping an eye on the guy, waiting for him to make a mistake. That's when I added security at SeaSail."

"How come I never heard about any of this?"

"It happened before you came here and Jergens hasn't been on the island for months. Guess he got worried about all the scrutiny. Before he left he turned his operation over to William Dobbs—a good man who actually knows his way around boats. It's too bad that Jergens came back."

"Seems pretty coincidental that Elyse's boat blew up about the time he returned. Sounds like the kind of method he employs against his enemies."

"It is, but Hannah, I know that Dunn doesn't think this was foul play. What makes you so sure it is?" O'Brien asked.

"Call it instinct. I'm not going to ignore it—especially when it involves a friend."

"You don't need to prove that this was a murder attempt to help Elyse. You need to be there when she comes around and help her get back on her feet. That's a hard thing to do, harder than what you're doing now. It takes a huge emotional investment."

"Hell, maybe that's the real fear, O'Brien—that I'm not capable of doing that."

"Oh, you're capable. I've seen you do it. You'll just put your head down and forge ahead. Every day, you'll do what you need to do until it's done."

"It would be easier to find out she didn't need that kind

of help and that she'll come out of this fine—easier to simply solve the case."

"For you, tracking down a killer is easier," O'Brien said,
his tone sarcastic yet tinged with resignation.

O'Brien was right. I was good at the chase. In spite of all
my talk about escaping to these islands to get away from the
violence, it made me who I was. Hell, I needed it. And a
black and white life, one separated into the good guys, and
the bad guys, was easier. Choices were clear, actions de-
fined.

I turned toward O'Brien and slid my hand under his shirt.
I could feel him breathing, his skin warm beneath my fingertips. Since the day I met him, I had been unable to resist
the man.

He pulled me into him, a long embrace, a kiss, and then
I was on top of him, lying on the cockpit bench. I brushed a
strand of hair from his forehead and then pressed my body
against his. God, he felt good. We spent the next half hour
under the stars while Sadie lay at our feet. Then he disen-
tangled himself from the leg I'd wrapped around him and
stood.

"You're leaving?" I asked.

"Yeah. I know you want to be alone tonight."

If I didn't know O'Brien better, I'd think he was manip-
ulating me, using this as a way to pressure me to move in.
But it wasn't O'Brien's style. I knew that he was just trying
to give me some space.

"Come on, O'Brien, let's not do this."

"Hey, it's okay. I'll talk to you tomorrow." The boat
rocked as he jumped to the dock, knocking me off balance.

"Jeez, O'Brien," I whispered to myself as he headed
down the dock to his car. I didn't want him to leave, but
damned if I'd go running after him.

Chapter 17

❧

Dunn was obviously pissed. He was sitting in my office chair, his back erect, arms locked across his chest, feet planted on the floor.

"Morning, Chief," I said, smiling widely. Dunn didn't smile back.

"I got another call this morning," he said, skipping the pleasantries. Bad sign.

"Look," I said, defensive. "I just stopped by to ask Porter a couple of questions." I could only hope that Porter had not discovered I'd returned to the gravel pit posing as a bank official.

"Porter? The call was not from Amos Porter. It was from Joel Ingram. He said you were interfering with his daughter, questioning her at the hospital about Elyse. You've been harassing Porter too?"

"I'd hardly call it harassment."

"Look, Hannah, you've got to stop. I know you've had Jimmy and anyone else you could con into it over at the hospital at all hours watching over Elyse."

"Too much points to attempted murder, Chief." I told him about Jillian's prints and what O'Brien had told me about Jergens.

"None of that means anything. It's all circumstantial."

"I'm not giving it up," I said. I was glaring him down, my hands on my hips, feet firmly planted on the floor in front of him.

"Dammit, Hannah! You are too pigheaded for your own good!" I had never once heard Dunn swear before, and he never lost his temper. He was losing it now, his mass towering above me, fire in his eyes.

"Me? Come on, Chief. Who's the one being pigheaded?" I came back at him, just as angry as he was, and unwilling to back down. "Why can't you see it, for chrissakes?"

"It's you who is blind, Hannah. You've let friendship color your judgment," he said, regaining some of his regal composure. "I want you to drop this."

"I won't do that."

"Then I want your badge and weapon. This is not a police matter. Consider yourself on leave until you can get past this."

"Fine." I slammed the badge on my desk, pulled out my gun, ejected the clip, and handed it to him. No problem. I hated the damned police issue automatic anyway. My .38 was stashed in the galley on the *Sea Bird*.

"And Hannah, I don't want you running around impersonating a police officer," he said, picking up the badge and gun.

I stomped out of the office and sat out in the Rambler for a good half hour cursing and banging my fist against the wheel.

"Dammit!" I muttered. "Dammit, dammit, dammit!" I was as angry at myself as I was at Dunn. I knew he couldn't very well condone one of his detectives doing unofficial investigations on police time. I blamed myself. By now, I should have been able to find enough evidence to convince Dunn that someone had sabotaged Elyse's boat. Maybe I *was* fooling myself about Elyse.

"Shit." I started the car, slammed it in gear, and hit the gas, smashing into a trash can as I swerved out of the lot. Garbage flew across the hood and all over the road. I didn't bother to stop.

*   *   *

I sped down Waterfront Drive, honking and passing any-one who got in my way. When I reached Station Street, the only stop light on the entire island was red. I sat there wait-ing for the thing to turn green, and realized I was out of con-trol, seething. I rested my head on the steering wheel and closed my eyes, the tension easing a fraction.

The car behind me started honking, and when I lifted my head the light was green. It took every ounce of reason and restraint I had to keep myself from giving the guy the finger. Besides, honking was a way of life here. Christ, I needed to get some perspective. Maybe Dunn was right and I'd been on some wild goose chase because I was too stubborn to admit I was wrong.

I turned the Rambler into the SeaSail lot and went look-ing for O'Brien. I found him in his office behind a pile of pa-pers.

"Hannah, what are you doing here?" he asked, then rec-ognized the look on my face. "What happened?"

"Dunn put me on leave," I said. "Doesn't want me back until I'm willing to stop checking into Elyse's accident. I ought to pack my bags and head back to the States." The anger was taking over again.

"Come on, Hannah." O'Brien stood, took my wrist, and led me to the door.

I followed him out without even wondering where we were headed. We walked down the steps and out to the docks as I raged about Dunn and his unwillingness to be-lieve someone slipped those sleeping pills to Elyse.

Before I realized it, we were standing alongside O'Brien's boat, the *Catherine*. She was in a slip on D dock, surrounded by a forest of masts. The boat, named for O'Brien's mother, had been headed for the salvage yard when his parents bought her for almost nothing. She was a classic wooden boat, a single-masted fifty-footer with brass fittings and teak decking. They had made a living taking charterers out on her and the business grew from there.

"What are we doing down here, O'Brien?"

"You need to get out on the water," he said. "And I haven't had the *Catherine* out all month."

I climbed aboard and took a deep breath of ocean air. Then I turned the engine over, took the wheel, and put her in gear as O'Brien untied the lines. He stepped on board as I eased her out of the slip and into the harbor. Once we were clear, O'Brien lifted the mainsail and pulled out one of the headsails. I cut the engine. Any remnants of anger vanished when the wind filled the sails and the *Catherine* picked up speed, cutting silently through the water.

I turned the wheel over to O'Brien, climbed up on deck, and out to the bowsprit. The wind whistled around my ears and blew through my hair. I looked back at O'Brien, standing legs firmly planted on the deck, steering the boat. The sails arched above us, taut, brilliant sheets of white.

We anchored in a quiet cove. O'Brien stripped and jumped naked into the water. I pulled off my clothes and followed him, then swam to the deserted shore. O'Brien pushed me down onto the sand, threw himself on top of me, and smiled, eyes dancing with devilment. He grabbed my arms and locked them over my head, then leaned down, his chest firm against my bare breasts. The kiss was tender and long. Dunn, the job, the last of my anger disappeared. Right now, there was nothing but the feel of O'Brien pressing into me, then the stunning rush, the delirium of lovemaking. Afterward, we lay next to each other, sand stuck to our sweaty bodies.

"Thanks, O'Brien," I said, kissing his belly.

"What for?"

"For getting me out of town."

"What are you going to do now, Hannah?"

"I don't know, maybe Dunn's right. I'll take a few days. Think it through, I guess. I could use some time off anyway."

"Come on, let's head back. You promised to go to that fund-raiser with me this afternoon."

I'd completely forgotten. O'Brien had talked me into

going with him weeks ago. At the time, I had been less than enthusiastic. Now, with all that had happened, I hated the idea of schmoozing with a bunch of political types. "I can't believe Reidman didn't cancel, with Elyse in the hospital."

"Too much invested in the event, I'm sure. And Freeman wouldn't have wanted to cancel," he said. "Besides, what else do you have to do now that you're out of a job? Sitting around worrying about Elyse won't do her—or you—any good."

He grabbed my wrists and pulled me up. We swam to the boat, the warm water washing the sand, sweat, and sex away.

We agreed to meet at the Callilou and I went home to shower. When I got back to Pickering's Landing, Sadie and Rebecca were romping together in the surf while Daisy sat by herself on the beach, intent on building a castle. When Sadie saw me, she raced toward me, stopped, shook sand and water all over me and yelped. Rebecca and Daisy were right behind.

After the explosion on Elyse's boat and the trauma of seeing Elyse hurt, Tilda had gone with the girls to stay with her sister for a few days. I remembered them standing on the dock that night, the water on fire, watching as Calvin had pulled Elyse onto the dock. They'd stood back frightened and silent as we'd done CPR and then rushed Elyse away.

"Hannah, Hannah!" Daisy lifted her arms and I picked her up, twirling her around.

"I'm so glad you're home," I said. "Sadie and I missed you."

"Want to help me build da castle?" Daisy asked.

"Sure but just for a minute though." I kicked off my shoes and sat with her in the sand.

"Make a tower right dar, Hannah," she commanded. I packed a heap of wet sand into a cup and turned it over.

"Perfect! Let's put a flag in it," she said poking a stick into the tower.

"Hi, Hannah." Tilda came out of the store, carrying a pitcher and glasses. "How about some lemonade, girls?"

"Yeah!" they cried, running to the picnic table in the shade.

"I went by for a visit with Elyse today," Tilda said as she poured. "She seems the same. I'm so worried about her. Dr. Hall didn't have anything to say one way or another."

"I know. All he ever says is we have to wait and see. Tilda, do you know what Elyse did Sunday? I never saw her at all that day. O'Brien and I went out sailing early and it was late when I returned. I remember that her boat was dark when I got home."

"She came up to the store for a few things that morning. We were about to leave for church. She said she was going up to North Sound for the day to do a little work."

"How did she seem to you?"

"She was fine. Just like she always is."

"Did you see her when she got back?"

"No. I heard a boat come in around maybe four o'clock. I thought it was Elyse, but I was in the back taking inventory."

"Did you see anyone else around?"

"Just Jillian. I came out to check on the girls. She was helping Daisy build one of her castles. She asked if I knew when Elyse would be back but I didn't. The child seemed upset. I told her she could wait on the *Caribbe*."

"Did you have a good time playing with Jillian?" I asked Daisy.

"Oh yes! She is a ek-spurt at sand castles. She told me so. She made a big, big, tower right in the middle of the castle!"

"You like Jilli, huh?"

"She's my friend. I wish she wasn't so sad, though. I gave her a big hug. But that stupid man came and ruined it all."

"Ruined what?" Tilda asked.

"Jilli's tower. He stepped right on my castle."

"When did you see a man?" I asked.

"Well"—she looked at Tilda and hesitated—"I was 'sposed to be in bed."

"It's okay, Daisy. Tell Hannah what you saw."

"I was lookin' out da window at my beautiful castle. It was so pretty in da moonlight. Then I saw a man on da beach and he stepped right in the middle of our castle!" Daisy turned to her mother. "I'm sorry, Mama. I was only out of bed for a minute."

"Do you know who the man was? Have you seen him before?" I asked.

"I think it was some bad man, 'cause he was mean to step on my castle."

"Are you sure it wasn't Jilli?"

"Oh no, Jilli would never be mean like that."

"What did the man look like?"

"Big, like a monster."

"Everyone looks big to Daisy, especially at night," Tilda explained. "At three, her world is all mixed up in fantasy and reality. There are often monsters about in her imagination. Since the explosion and seeing Elyse hurt, it's been worse."

"Did you see what color the man's hair or skin was or what he was wearing?" I asked.

"He had on a black cape and white, white skin, and he had a long pointy nose!"

"Oh Daisy! She's always making stuff up," Rebecca said.

"Am not! He went away in a car just like Mandy's," Daisy shot back at her sister.

"Mandy?"

"That's her doll," Rebecca explained.

"What does Mandy's car look like?"

Daisy pointed to a little wagon in which her doll sat.

"Did it look like the wagon, Daisy?"

"Yes."

"How did it look like the wagon?" Jeez, questioning a three-year-old was harder than any interrogation I'd ever conducted.

"I don't know," she said, putting her thumb in her mouth. "Was it the same color?"

She brightened. "Yes, it was red, red, red! Just like Mandy's!"

Christ, a white guy with a black cape and pointy nose. If he'd parked under the streetlight, she'd have been able to tell that the car was red. One thing I was sure of, black cape, pointy nose, and red car or not—Daisy had seen someone on the beach that night.

I'd go to O'Brien's damned fund-raiser. Then, one way or another, I was going to track down the guy in the black cape.

Chapter 18

I was late by the time I'd showered and driven to the Callilou. The parking lot was already full. I ended up parking on the road and walking down a dirt path to the restaurant, which was perched out on the point at Nanny Cay. Reidman had bought the place cheap after the last hurricane blasted through the island. It had blown off the roof of the old restaurant and destroyed the interior. He'd torn the old place down and built a five-star restaurant that catered to the tourists. Nothing on the menu went for less than forty dollars unless you ordered a salad.

The restaurant had been designed with Reidman's needs high on the list. His living quarters filled the upper level, some four thousand square feet enclosed behind walls of glass. The guy better pray that another hurricane force wind didn't find its way around the point. I'd never been in his apartment but Elyse had said the view was incredible. All I could see on the second floor as I walked down to the restaurant was reflection, ocean and sun bouncing off the glass.

Reidman had been running the restaurant for a little over a year. Before that, he'd been living in New York and working at one of the big investment companies. Evidently he'd made a bundle, getting out of the market before it collapsed, and then moved down here, returning to New York periodically on business. Elyse had told me that the restaurant was more of a diversion for him than anything else. He liked fine dining and good wine and this gave him the chance to dabble in both.

O'Brien was waiting for me in the restaurant lobby. "Hannah, you look wonderful, even in your clothes," he said, eyes twinkling.

"I like you better naked," I whispered. Then I wrapped my arm around his waist and gave him a surreptitious pinch on the ass. He flinched.

"Sunburn," he said as we were ushered to the Freemans' table in the front.

O'Brien had to be contributing a sizable amount to warrant this kind of attention. Everyone else was already seated. Of course, Alex Reidman had a ringside seat.

I found myself sitting next to Betty Welsh, a reporter for the *Island News*. She was a hefty woman, British, five-ten, probably 200 pounds, with long fake nails painted ruby and shoulder-length hair, dyed black with purple tinges, perfectly coifed and turned up at the ends. Her attire was always garish. Today she'd toned it down a notch. She wore a gray dress with green splotches all over it and green spiked heels.

I had to give her credit though. She had perfected her look and to hell with anyone who didn't like it. I'd gotten to know Betty a few months back when she'd done a piece about a drug smuggling case I'd been involved in. She was fair, reasonable, and a snoop, and above all took her job very seriously.

I recognized several other familiar faces scattered around the room, including Edmund Carr and Amos Porter. The bank probably covered Carr's lunch but I wondered how Porter could afford to attend such an affair. Maybe he couldn't afford not to, given his gravel business.

Waiters were already rushing around, pouring wine and setting food in front of people. For three hundred dollars a plate, we got what Reidman was calling a traditional Caribbean meal—chicken—and a lot of speeches. As soon as silverware stopped clanking and dishes were removed, Reidman introduced Freeman.

Freeman wiped his mouth, set the cloth napkin on the table and rose, acknowledging the applause with a slight bow. He was wearing a black suit with a subtle gray stripe through it, a gray shirt and one of those red power ties that politicians seem to favor. He walked to the podium and waited for a minute before he began, making sure that all eyes were upon him.

"First, I must thank my wife, Sylvia, for putting up with me all these years and for her total support during this campaign."

Sylvia stood, gave the loyal wife smile and a little wave. She too was dressed for the part: conservative brown suit, just a shade lighter than her skin, pearls on her ears and around her neck. She wasn't nearly as comfortable with the attention as her husband was.

Freeman started his rap about how he was in favor of responsible development, better education. He said that if elected, he would get tough on crime and was concerned about the recent spate of robberies in the islands. Without being too blatant, he managed to blame Dunn and the current administration and promised to find the best people to get the situation in hand. I wondered what that meant for the Chief.

He went on to promise to protect the environment for our future generations while still promoting the economy and working to insure more jobs. How he would do this, though, he did not say. It was one of those "feel good" speeches, long on rhetoric, short on details. Lots of laughs, lots of emotional appeals.

Finally, he opened the floor to questions. "Just a couple," he emphasized.

Amos Porter was the first on his feet. "What's your stand on regulating businesses?" he asked. "I know a lot of people think that there should be strict controls, especially where the environment is concerned."

"Amos, I don't think a lot of controls are necessary. We've got a number of very responsible business folks on the islands. I know you're one of 'em."

Amos smiled and sat down. Freeman had told him what he wanted to hear.

"You can't count on everyone being that responsible," a voice called from the back. It was Tom. He and Liam were leaning against the wall.

"So far it's worked. I think you underestimate the folks in these islands." He tried to move on to another question, but Tom wasn't letting him off the hook yet.

"What about a complete moratorium on the taking of turtles in the territory?" he asked.

"Well, Tom, you're kind of an outsider here. For those of us who grew up in these islands, whose families have been here for centuries, the harvesting of turtles is part of the culture. We need to respect that. The season is short enough to protect the turtles."

"Are you saying that you are against a moratorium?"

"I'm against regulating our people from doing something that they have always done. Now don't get me wrong, I don't want to see the wanton killing of turtles and the excessive trading of turtle products."

"What about the fact that turtle is still on the menu in restaurants around the BVI?"

"Those are local folks doing what they've always done."

"Sooner or later, there won't be enough turtles for even the locals to take," Tom said. "And how are you going to reconcile your stand on supporting business and development with the loss of habitat that results from all the growth?"

"I don't think we'll run out of turtles, Tom."

"Don't be so sure of that," Tom said unable to hide his frustration.

"Let's move on to another question," Freeman said, cutting off any further discussion.

"What about the charter boat industry?" Betty asked.

"Everyone knows it's getting out of hand. The anchorages are overcrowded, there's rampant disregard for the reef, and no effective methods for controlling pollution."

"Well, that's a good question and one I plan to address as chief minister. In fact, I've already been talking with a lot of the charter owners here about forming a coalition to study the problem and come up with solutions. Peter O'Brien has offered to head things up. Care to comment, Peter?"

This was the first I'd heard of O'Brien's involvement, but I wasn't surprised. It was just so like him to pull his competitors together for the good of the islands. I could see, though, that he was unprepared and uncomfortable speaking in this political atmosphere. O'Brien was no politician.

"Sure, Neville," he said, standing. "I think most of the charter companies are as concerned as you are, Betty. They understand that eventually, if we don't control growth and address the environmental concerns, conditions will get to the point that sailors will go elsewhere because these sailing grounds will no longer be pristine. I'd rather downsize than see the islands ruined. Of course, there are charter company owners who don't care at all. But I think we can institute changes that they will be forced to abide by."

"What kind of changes?" Betty pressed.

"Limiting fleet size, maintaining moorings, requiring holding tanks, installing pump-out stations, fining companies whose clients act irresponsibly," O'Brien explained.

"What about the expense of running this campaign?" Betty again, directing attention back to Freeman. "You've been outspending your opponent, Bert Abernathy, by thousands. Where is it coming from, and will you be obligated to special interests?"

"You're right, Betty. This campaign's been expensive but if I know you, you've checked into my holdings. Besides, look at all the money I've raised from you all this morning!" He managed to laugh it off, but he hadn't really answered the question.

"What be your plans for Flower Island after you be

elected, Neville? Dat little piece of real estate be worth millions," someone called from the back before Betty could press Freeman further.

"No plans," Freeman said. "Maybe I'll turn it into a preserve some day."

"Sure," the man taunted, his voice skeptical and dripping with sarcasm. "Da day you turn Flower into a park be da day dat folks say hell be freezin' over. And you be sayin' you want to help people with jobs, better wages. How come you ain't doing dat yourself? Payin' wages dat can hardly keep a man and his family alive." The man continued to yell, his voice quavering.

"I pay a fair wage for a fair day's work."

"You sayin' I didn't give you a fair day, Neville? Hell, I be keeping that run-down mansion out dar on Flower together. Weren't for me the damn place woulda fallen to da ground."

He turned to the audience. "Dis man fired me for doin' my job, far's I can see. Didn't want nobody keepin' his daddy's house in shape for da future. Hell, it be a historical landmark. Didn't want nobody on dat island." He was pointing his finger at Neville now and moving toward the front of the room. A burly guy with "Security" on his shirt quickly intercepted him, however, and dragged him out.

Freeman smiled indulgently and made an off-the-cuff joke about disgruntled employees. Then he called a quick end to the luncheon, thanked everyone for coming, and stepped away from the podium.

"Who was that?" I asked O'Brien.

"Caretaker on Flower. Neville said he had to fire him because the guy was stealing from him. Didn't press charges though. I guess the guy has been causing all kinds of trouble for him since."

As we headed out, I noticed that Liam and Tom had Freeman cornered, undoubtedly pinning him down about his environmental stands. I had to feel sorry for the guy. Those two would grill him with questions for an hour if he let them.

Reidman walked with us. The restaurant's staff was busy getting ready for the dinner crowd. One of his stewards was stocking a wine rack that filled an entire wall.

"Quite a collection," O'Brien remarked.

"Kind of an obsession," Reidman replied. "I like keeping an inventory of the best wine in the world in my establishment. A lot of people come here because they've heard about my wines. I've been known to pour a four-hundred-dollar bottle down the drain if I consider it inferior. My personal stock includes only the most exceptional."

As I was contemplating what a pompous asshole Reidman was, O'Brien's cell phone rang.

After O'Brien excused himself to take the call, Reidman corralled me for another five minutes in inane conversation about the merits of a "good Cab." Finally, I escaped and waited for O'Brien in the parking lot.

I found a place in the shade and observed, watching people heading to their cars, Betty Welsh was standing next to her Honda Civic talking with the guy who had caused such a scene inside. I knew she'd get a story from him if there was one.

I recognized Bert Abernathy, Freeman's opponent for chief minister, from his campaign photos. He got into a red Audi. I hadn't seen him at the breakfast. He'd probably been standing in the back, checking out the competition. I was surprised he hadn't taken the opportunity to lambast Freeman. But I'd heard the guy was reserved and didn't go in for dirty politics.

The Freemans walked out arm in arm, a posture that Sylvia seemed uncomfortable with.

"So glad you were able to make it," Freeman said as he approached and shook my hand. "Alex outdid himself on the luncheon didn't he, even though he's been very upset since his girlfriend's unfortunate accident. How is she doing?"

I knew he wasn't interested in Elyse's condition. It was all about campaigning, saying the right things to the right people.

"She's still in a coma," I said and left it at that.

"I'm sorry," he replied, but hardly skipped a beat. "I heard that Dunn suspended you."

"That's right." Word got around fast on the islands but this was ridiculous and I wondered why Freeman even cared.

"I stopped by to see Dunn this morning and check on the state of law and order in our fine community before my speech," he said. "He told me what happened. I hope you can work it out with him. He says you're the only one with the know-how when it comes to examining underwater crime scenes. Me, I like the image—an American who can help smooth things over in terms of tourism, especially with these break-ins on charter boats."

"I'm not much for presenting an image. Dunn will tell you that too, and it's not why he hired me." I stuffed the anger. Freeman was an ass. I couldn't figure out why anyone would support him. And he'd used the boat thefts in his speech to boast his own status at Dunn's expense. I didn't like it.

"Come Ms. Sampson, you must know the effect you have," Freeman said. He was actually leering now. Sylvia stood back, fists clenched. I don't know why she put up with it.

"You are a gorgeous white woman who carries a gun," he continued. "Just what the tourists like. It's as though they've come down here to their own movie set. I very much want you on the force. When I'm elected, I'll make it worth your while. I think a promotion will be in order."

"I am not interested in entertaining the tourists with some James Bond image of a cop in a bikini with a gun slung around her waist," I said. No longer did I even attempt to contain my anger. What the hell was Freeman suggesting? That he could pay me to fulfill his little erotic fantasy?

"You should think about your future," Freeman said, ignoring my tone and giving my hand a squeeze. Sylvia glared at me like it was my fault, then they got in their car and drove away.

Chapter 19

❧

It happened every time—a visceral reaction that I had no control over when O'Brien stepped into my space. I was still standing in the parking lot of the Callilou watching Freeman pull out when O'Brien came out the front door. Lunch stirred in my stomach. He'd finally gotten off the phone and walked toward me now with that damned open, boyish smile. I kept hoping that one of these days I'd get over it—get over O'Brien. It was looking less and less likely.

"That was Louis on the phone," he said. "One of Jergens's boats is out at Eustatia Sound caught on the reef. His base manager, Dobbs, called SeaSail to ask for help. It seems Jergens went out there with his chase boat but with no idea of how to get the charter boat off the reef. Now he's stuck out there too. He tore up his engine in the shallow water. Louis told them we'd assist. Want to come along?"

"Why would you want to do anything to help Jergens?" I asked.

"We can't leave those charterers floundering out there. Besides, William Dobbs is a good man. He'd do the same for us."

"I'd love to spend the rest of the day with you," I said, which was only half of the truth. The other half was Jergens. Was he Daisy's man in the black cape? Maybe.

*   *   *

Louis had the chase boat running when we got to SeaSail.

"Hey dar, Hannah," he said, offering me a hand and helping me onto the boat. If it had been anyone else, I would have declined the help and stepped aboard myself. But I could never refuse Louis's strong grip or kind eyes. Without him, O'Brien would have been lost. He knew the condition of every boat in the fleet and how to fix every possible problem. At almost seventy, his body was hardened by work and the sun. I could see that he was slowing down though.

"Damned arthritis," he said now, showing a slight limp as he moved to the front of the boat. What would O'Brien do when Louis could no longer climb into a boat?

"Hannah, this be William Dobbs," Louis said. "Manages BVI Sail. He be my nephew's wife's sister's son." Louis's wife and his own son had died of meningitis long ago. I'd never realized that Louis had any other family.

"I met William yesterday," I said. "I didn't know you two were related."

"Hello dar, Miz Sampson. Good to see you again," William said, offering me a seat next to him on a wooden platform that ran along the side of the boat.

Louis expertly maneuvered the boat out of the slip and into the harbor. Being at the helm of anything that floated, whether under sail or power, was as natural to Louis as breathing. He lifted his head into the breeze and inhaled deeply. O'Brien was at his side.

"The boat dat's stuck out dar is a forty-two-footer, in the shallows about halfway 'tween Saba Rock and the breakers," William shouted over the engine noise. "There are two couples on board. They just went out this morning. Jergens gave them the briefing."

"What the heck they doing out in dat shallow water?" Louis yelled. "That boat only draws maybe seven feet. The water out dar be less than three feet in places. It be way too shallow for anything but a cat. Unless you really know your way though, you be askin' to be grounded."

I wondered if that was the whole point—a good way for Jergens to collect insurance.

William just shrugged his shoulders.

I had the feeling he wasn't looking forward to seeing his boss. When we got out there, I knew why. Jergens was seething.

"What the hell you doin' with O'Brien and Louis, and that bitch?" he asked. William was clearly embarrassed at Jergens's crass language. I didn't have the chance to tell him I'd been called a whole lot worse.

The people on the sailboat stood on the deck, mouths open, confused. Their boat was tipped at about a forty-five-degree angle and stopped dead in the water. Jergens had his boat tied alongside.

"Sorry, boss, but you asked me to bring help. Didn't know who else to call on." More likely, though, William didn't know anyone else who would be willing to help Jergens.

"Look, do you want help or not?" O'Brien demanded.

"Goddammit, I can handle it. Just leave William here."

"Wait one minute," one of the sailors hollered at Jergens. "You don't let these people help get us off this reef, you'll not receive one penny for this charter."

"Fine," Jergens said.

"What's the situation?" O'Brien hollered.

"He tore up his prop on the coral trying to pull us off," the man shouted back, indicating Jergens's motorboat.

Jergens was fumbling for an excuse for his stupidity when O'Brien took charge. "Okay, let's take a look at the keel on the sailboat," he said. He and William had already pulled on swim suits on the ride over. Now they snugged face masks and fins in place, eased over the side of the chase boat, and swam to the sailboat. It couldn't have been more than five feet deep at the bow. They swam along the side, then disappeared underneath the boat. A minute later, they surfaced.

"Looks okay," O'Brien called back to us. "No serious

damage to the hull. The keel is wedged in pretty tight but we should be able to pull her off."

"Okay, Peter, I be gettin' da lines," Louis shouted.

I took the wheel and kept the boat away from the reef while Louis pulled out a long line, tossing it to O'Brien, who had already climbed onto the grounded sailboat and dropped the mainsail. This was clearly not the first time these two had done this. O'Brien caught the rope and attached it to the halyard while Louis tied the other end securely to a metal bar on the chase boat.

Once they were set up, Louis gave the boat some gas. The line, which was attached to the halyard that ran to the top of the mast, tightened and pulled the boat over on its side so that the keel and rudder were now at enough of an angle to dislodge it from the reef. He kept pulling until the boat slid sideways through the water and over the shallow reef, water washing over the rail.

When it was clear, Louis let up on the engine and the sailboat popped back upright, the keel now free and in deep water. O'Brien wasn't about to let the boat drift back into trouble though. He quickly put the engine in gear and steered the vessel back through the deep areas of Eustatia Sound, around Saba Rock, and into the safety of North Sound.

Louis and I stowed the gear while William tied Jergens's disabled motorboat to our stern. I'd have been tempted to leave him stranded out there.

By the time we got out to the Sound, O'Brien had the charter boat tied to a mooring ball and was standing on the bow. When we pulled alongside, Louis grabbed a chart out of the glove box and handed it up to O'Brien. It was considered an essential piece of information for every charterer who took a boat out. Every shallow area, rock, and reef structure was clearly marked in red as off-limits. The entire area of Eustatia Sound was as red as it got. But Jergens had provided no chart for his clients to navigate by.

The people on the boat thanked us profusely, relieved

that they and the boat were safe and undamaged. They were ready to continue their vacation and were pulling out the champagne when we left.

O'Brien climbed aboard our boat and Louis turned it toward the dock at the Bitter End in North Sound, towing Jergens's boat behind. Jergens was sitting at the wheel, arms crossed and working hard to maintain his dignity. He was out and stomping off the second the boat touched the dock leaving William to take care of things without a word. William jumped out and tied Jergens's boat to a cleat while O'Brien did the same with his. Then Louis and O'Brien headed toward the restaurant for a beer.

"Will you order for me, O'Brien?" I asked. I wasn't about to let this opportunity pass. Right now, Jergens was a captive audience. He'd be heading to the marina repair shop.

O'Brien hesitated.

"It will be fine, O'Brien. I'll get more out of him if you're not around. Me he doesn't like, you he would like to kill." It was pretty obvious that Jergens hated the fact that O'Brien had shown him up and rescued him to boot.

"Well, watch it with him, Hannah."

He and Louis settled at a patio table where they could keep an eye on the repair shop door.

When I got to the shop, Freeman was already gone.

"Da man was real angry when I tole him I couldn't get a new engine from Spanish Town till tomorrow, noon earliest," the mechanic said. "He tole me to just get da damned thing and stormed outta here. I'm pretty sure he be heading to da bar just down the way a bit."

I caught up with Jergens at a sidewalk bar down the quay. He'd already downed half a beer, and an empty shot glass sat on the table. I hoped the drink had taken the edge off his anger. Just in case, I stopped at the bar and picked up another round for him along with a beer for me. It definitely worked. He took one look at the drinks, turned his mouth up in what I thought was the best imitation of a smile he ever managed, and nodded to the other chair at the table.

He tossed the shot down before I even had a chance to get comfortable and shouted to the bartender for another, a double. "Hear you paid a visit to BVI Sail yesterday asking William a lot of questions. You want to know something, you ask me."

"That's why I'm here. When did you get back on the island?"

"Last week. Been over in Puerto Rico for six months."

"Why Puerto Rico?"

"That's where I have my home. This venture down here is strictly on the side. Thought it was about time to get back here and check up on things."

"What were you doing up on Paraquita Bay Road yesterday?" I asked.

"Just a pleasant drive out of the heat." He smirked.

"You know my wheel almost sheared off up there," I said, watching closely for his reaction.

"Well, ain't that too bad. You should take better care of your vehicle," he said, never flinching.

"Seems pretty coincidental—you just happening to be up on the road right before my car went out of control. I'm surprised you didn't hang around for the show." I was taunting him now, pushing for a mistake.

"That would imply I knew what was going to happen."

I let it drop. I needed to get to the real point before he passed out. "Hear you've given Elyse Henry a lot of trouble," I said.

"I'd say it was more the other way around. If that bitch keeps interfering in my business, I'll . . ."

"You'll what?"

"I'll be coming after her."

"What does that mean?"

"It means I'll have my lawyer filing restraining orders."

Right, I thought. I was sure that Jergens never settled his problems through the law. It was too costly, time-consuming, and for him, probably unsatisfying.

"Where were you Sunday night?" I asked him.

"Guess I was over at the Doubloon. Like to settle down there come evening. What's the interest in Sunday?"

"That's the night Elyse's boat blew up."

"Hell, everyone knows that was her own doing," he said, smirking. "Except you, I guess. Hear Dunn suspended you over it."

I ignored the comment. "Someone saw a man down on the beach that night, a white man. That wouldn't have been you, would it?"

"Hell, you're not pinning that on me."

"I hear you like fires," I said, continuing to badger, hoping he'd slip up. I'd caught him off guard. I could see by the look on his face that he knew I was referring to the fires on the boats at Blue Water Charters and at Carmichael's dive shop.

"No one has ever proven those fires were anything more than accidents."

"Like the explosion on Elyse's boat?"

"Yeah, just like."

"That's what I figure too. I'll be watching you, Jergens."

He stood abruptly, fists tight. "You harass me, that boat of yours might accidentally catch on fire too."

"You mean you aren't going to call your lawyer?" I asked.

He took a swing at me, neither my gender nor my sweet nature giving him a moment of pause. But he was a bit too slow to connect. I simply stepped to the side and let his weight carry him past me. He ended up sprawled on the floor, tangled in chair legs. As I walked out the door, he was spewing profanities that even I never used.

Louis was at the helm as we motored past the Dogs on our way back to Road Town. Suddenly a boat was on our tail and gaining fast. Then it shot past us and cut across our bow, drenching us in salt water and forcing Louis to veer off course.

It was the *Libation*, the grocery boat. Jergens stood in the stern section, his middle finger raised. He'd obviously found a ride back and left William to wait for the new motor.

"Damnation!" Louis hollered shaking his fist as they disappeared around the point.

O'Brien just shook his head and threw me a towel. "Jergens is one spiteful and unreasonable son of a bitch. It's amazing that he hasn't ended up in jail by now."

"Yeah, well, if I have anything to do with it, he will," I said.

"Or you'll die trying to put him there," O'Brien said. "You need to watch out for him, Hannah."

Chapter 20

The second Louis touched the bow to the dock, I jumped out, did a quick rope wrap around a cleat and headed to the Rambler.

"Got something I need to do. I'll see you guys later," I called over my shoulder. Jergens and the two people from the *Libation* had already secured their boat and were climbing into a beige minivan in the lot. I intended to follow.

"Wait a minute, Hannah," O'Brien called. "I'm coming with you."

I could tell from the determination in his voice that I wasn't going to get away without him. He got into the passenger side as I watched the van turn out of the marina lot and head east on Waterfront. I pulled out behind them and kept a couple of cars between my vehicle and theirs. I loved the Rambler—a black box with a white convertible top— but it was the only one like it on the island, and very hard to miss.

"Jergens was on his way to complete alcohol saturation when he left North Sound. They're probably going to the Doubloon to continue the party," O'Brien said.

"Yeah, but what's he doing with those two? We've been trying to track them down to question them about the boat thefts. If they're friendly with Jergens, I'd put them in the same category as I put the scum of the earth."

"So what are you implying? That all three of them are in-

volved in those burglaries? More than likely Jergens just
hitched a ride on their boat back to Road Town," O'Brien
said.

"Could be. But maybe he's the one behind all the robberies — saw the delivery boat as the perfect way to bring in
some extra money. It would be a perfect setup. Jergens could
be scoping out his own charterers for viable boats to rob.
Damned if I can figure out what it all has to do with Elyse
though."

"Maybe nothing," O'Brien said.

He was right about where they were headed. The van
turned into the parking lot at the Doubloon.

"Want a beer?" I asked.

We waited a few minutes for Jergens and the other two to
get settled in the bar, then went in. It was dark inside and
smelled of stale beer and cigarettes. Bob Marley blared from
the jukebox and one couple was up on the floor engaged in
what could be called dancing but looked more like sex. The
pirate theme in the Doubloon had long ago lost its luster;
sabers and pirate hats that hung on the walls were covered
in dust. O'Brien and I found a table in the back. Jergens was
too busy flirting with the bartender to notice us.

"Hey guys. Surprised to see you in here this time of da
day." Mona had worked at the Doubloon as a waitress for
years. She wore her makeup layered, mascara so heavy that
her eyes sagged. She did more than just wait tables. She
called herself a masseuse, but her only clients were males
with an extra hundred in their pockets.

"Hi, Mona," I said. "Guess we'll have a couple of beers."
It was either that, flat soda, or the stale coffee that sat on the
burner for hours thickening to sludge. No one ever came in
here for anything that didn't dull the senses.

"Sure thing, honey." She winked at O'Brien on her way
back to the bar.

The couple from the *Libation* were young, maybe late
twenties. She was laden with jewelry — ear cuffs, dangling
orange earrings, a couple dozen bangles on each wrist, and

a tangle of silver chains around her neck. She wore flip-flops, shorts, and a frilly shirt, and obviously spent all day in the sun. Her mate looked hungry—thin, a T-shirt hanging from bony shoulders, tan shorts, and bare feet.

"Businesses like theirs are becoming more and more common in the Caribbean," O'Brien said, referring to the couple. "People selling crafts, jewelry, and clothing from their boats, motoring from one tourist vessel to the next. A number of them are young and come from places like Britain, Australia, France and the U.S. Some of the charterers don't like it at all. Others really enjoy talking to these vendors and looking at their products."

"The island versions of Colorado ski bums, enjoying the environment and barely getting by," I said.

"Yeah, though many of the vendors are islanders trying to make a living through tourism. Those two had a good idea—selling groceries. I've seen them a couple of times recently tied alongside a sailboat and handing up supplies."

O'Brien pulled out his wallet when Mona returned to the table and set overflowing glasses of beer in front of us.

"Have you ever seen that couple in here with that guy before?" I asked her.

"You mean Jergens and the couple from the *Libation*? Sure, all the time. Usually they're arguing. Guess they're having too much fun for that today."

So Jergens did not just encounter the two over at North Sound and talk them into a ride back. He knew them.

"You ever hear what they argue about?" I knew that Mona didn't miss much of what went on in the bar.

"Whenever I get within shouting distance of those three, they clam up. But I've heard them fighting about who deserves the biggest share. Jergens always seems to think it's him. Heard him say more than once that he's the brains."

Right now, all three of them seemed to be best buddies. They were drinking heavily, Jergens and the guy matching each other shot for shot. They stumbled back to the pool room, grabbed pool sticks, and racked up the balls.

"Let's go, O'Brien. We've learned all we're going to. They'll be passing out in another hour and sleeping it off for the rest of the day."

First thing in the morning, Stark and I would be questioning the owners of the *Libation*.

I dropped O'Brien off at SeaSail and went to see Elyse. Mary was pulling into the lot just as I got out of the Rambler. She swung her Miata into the space next to mine.

"Hannah, you're looking a bit bedraggled."

I looked down and realized my shirt was salt stained and still damp from the spray that the *Libation* had sent gushing over our boat on the way back into Road Town. I told her about Jergens.

"I've encountered that man a couple of times. He's got no conscience, feels no remorse, and thinks the world owes him. He's very dangerous." Nothing like a psychiatric perspective.

"Yeah, that's what everyone keeps telling me. But if he's the one who hurt Elyse, well . . ."

"You're still out to find a bad guy to blame this on?"

"I don't know, Mary. I'm not sure what to believe right now, but Jergens is up to something, and I still have plenty of questions about the explosion on Elyse's boat."

"Come on, let's go see how she's doing," Mary said.

Alex Reidman was in the corridor talking with Dr. Hall when we walked in. I was surprised that Reidman had been concerned enough about Elyse to keep visiting. Elyse had told me their relationship wasn't serious. But then, that was her take on it. Reidman had visited a lot. Maybe I'd misjudged the guy.

"Dr. Marks was here this morning," Hall said. "He was very encouraged. The last CT scan shows no enlargement of the hematoma, and less edema. She's responding to stimuli and loud noises. It looks like she'll pull through."

"Thank God." I sat down, rested my head on the back of

the lounge couch, and fought to control the tears that threatened. Mary sat down beside me, her face washed with relief.

"What about brain damage?" I asked, realizing for the first time that even though Elyse might live, she might not be fine.

"It's too soon to know that. Nothing is certain, but Marks has a lot of experience with these injuries. He's guardedly optimistic that she'll be okay."

"Do you think she'll remember what happened?" I asked.

"It's hard to say. It could take a while for things to start falling into place. She'll be pretty confused at first."

I wondered if she'd know who sabotaged the *Caribbe*.

Mary and I went in to see Elyse. She did seem better—some animation in her face, and when I took her hand, she moved her fingers.

"Come on back, Elyse," Mary said.

"I'm worried," I whispered to Mary. "I know you don't think anyone tried to kill her, but what if you're wrong and I'm right? Snyder's spent the past few nights here for me, but the stakes will get a lot higher when the news gets out that Elyse will pull through. If it was Jergens, he could be ruthless enough to come back and finish the job. And what about Jilli? She's just up on the next floor."

"If someone wanted to hurt Elyse it wasn't Jillian. You're grasping at straws, Hannah. Come on. I'm going up to see her. You can give her the news about Elyse and evaluate her reaction for yourself."

Mary punched in her code and we were buzzed into the unit. I sat in the lounge while she spent some time alone with Jilli. The TV was on but no one seemed to be watching it. A couple of patients were sitting in the corner playing chess.

Finally Mary signaled from the hall and I walked with her back to Jillian's room.

"I'll let you two visit while I look in on a couple other patients," she said.

Jillian was sitting cross-legged on the floor near the window, a book opened across her knee. She looked up and smiled when I went in. She looked good. The tension that had marred her face was gone.

"Hi, Jilli. Whatcha reading?" I asked, sitting down beside her and leaning against the wall.

She held up the book so I could see it—*Little Women*. "Mary gave it to me."

"You doing okay here?" I asked.

"Yeah. This is a good place. I feel safe. But my parents want me out. My dad still thinks he's going to have me on a plane to that school on Sunday."

"Do they know you don't want to leave the hospital?"

"Yeah, but my dad says he knows best and that I'm just being coddled and no wonder I want to stay. It's not like that though. We have group sessions every day, and counseling. Sometimes it's real hard to talk about what you're going through. Sometimes I feel totally alone. But at least the people here understand. There's another girl here my age who got abused too. We talk a lot."

Finally, she asked about Elyse.

"Looks like she's going to make it," I said. Her expression turned from one of dread to utter relief. She covered her face with her hands and sighed deeply.

"Wow, that's good," she said. Typical teenage understatement. The kid seemed genuinely relieved. She obviously cared about Elyse. But still, I wondered whether in a moment of drugged confusion she had hurt Elyse. Mary thought she knew the answer. I hoped she was right, because this kid needed a break.

When I stopped at the nurse's station to be released from the unit, Jilli's parents were on their way in. Joel Ingram gave me a nasty look and walked right past me. I knew Mary hadn't told them about the abuse at school. Evidently, it would be up to Jilli to do it. God knows what Ingram's reaction would be.

*　　　*　　　*

I went home, took a swim with Sadie, showered, ate and went to the hospital to spend the night. Snyder had been there the last two nights and he'd started looking a little haggard. Dunn had gotten on his case when he'd fallen asleep at his desk. Besides, if someone had tried to kill her, he—or she—would be back, and I didn't want Jimmy hurt again because of me.

The hospital was like a cavern at night. The day shift was gone and a skeleton crew took over the duties, mostly there to check on patients every few hours and hold down the fort. I'd brought a book and a thermos of coffee and planned to settle in for the night. It would be the green vinyl chair in the corner for me.

An aid came in with a couple of blankets, a pillow, and a cribbage board. "Where dat Jimmy be?" she asked, clearly disappointed.

"Tonight's my night," I said. Now I understood why he had suddenly started volunteering to stay. She couldn't have been over eighteen, tiny and cute, big black eyes, high cheekbones, delicate features, and a pink uniform.

"Jimmy and me be havin' a couple classes together over at da college. We been studyin' together while he be here and I been beatin' him in cribbage," she said, eyes twinkling. "How about a game?"

"Love to," I said.

"Great." She pulled up a table and chair and put pegs in the board while I shuffled the cards. Forty-five minutes later, I'd learned she was working on her degree in biology and wanted to become a physician's assistant. She lived at home, had two brothers and a sister. She was the oldest. Her father owned a barbershop over on Challwell Street and her mother was a seamstress.

By the time the game ended, she'd outpegged me on every hand. The girl was a shark. Poor Jimmy. He'd have to scramble to keep up with this one.

"I be at the nurse's station if you be needin' anything,"

she said, packing up the board and gently closing the door when she left.

I positioned the pillow in the chair and curled up under the blankets. No raspy mechanical breaths echoed off the walls now that Elyse was no longer on a respirator. She simply breathed peacefully. I sat there, trying to figure out who to whisper thanks to that Elyse would live. Lots of people would thank God, but I tend to avoid anything that smacks of religion.

I'd spent my grade school years being taught by women in black habits and kneeling in church every Sunday morning. I didn't mind it, didn't question it. That's what my family did. I still miss the tradition sometimes and the sense of belonging. But I'd given up any notion of redemption one sunny Saturday morning when I'd watched a little girl die on the sidewalk, chalk still in hand, her blood spilling over the outline of the yellow tulip she'd drawn. I just couldn't see how a God could let that happen.

I fell asleep thinking that the best concept of God that I could muster was one that resided smack in the middle of each of us, and then dreaming about Sister Edina, my seventh grade teacher. She'd slapped me on the wrist with a ruler and left a welt.

I don't know what woke me. The dream? A noise? A change in Elyse's breathing? My eyes shot open. I was alert but confused. The room was pitch black, only a slice of light at the bottom of the closed door. Then I heard it. Someone moving in the room. As my mind cleared and my vision focused, I could just barely make out a figure standing beside Elyse's bed. Too big to be the petite nurse's aid. A man's build.

He hadn't registered my presence. I probably looked like a pile of blankets on the chair in the dark corner. I remained motionless, waiting to see what was happening, who this was. He just stood there, looking down at Elyse. What the hell was he doing? It was clear this was no doctor or nurse bending over Elyse, checking her pulse or listening to her vitals. I was out of the chair in one swift motion, grabbing him from behind. He reacted quickly, shoving me backward into the wall, hard. A sharp pain shot up my rib cage and the air rushed out of my lungs. Then he slammed a fist in my face, and I felt reality slipping away.

I don't know how long I'd been unconscious. When I opened my eyes it was black. I was stunned and confused. Then I heard shuffling, and I realized I was sitting in that vinyl chair, my hand in something sticky, my body covered with the blanket.

I yanked the blanket off just as the man headed out the door.

"Elyse!" I leapt to her bedside and flipped on the light. Her breathing was labored, raspy, hardly there at all. I jammed my thumb on the call button, and waited, it seemed like hours. Finally, they came, two nurses bursting into the room followed by a doctor.

Now I was just in the way. A nurse ushered me out, banishing me to the other side of the door. I knew Elyse was fighting for her life in that room. Hell, I wasn't going to just stand there.

Chapter 21

❧

"D id you see that man?" I asked the young aid, who was
running toward me, looking frightened and confused.

"I heard the noise. I saw him go down the stairs."

"Call the police," I hollered back as I headed to the exit
sign. I half hobbled, half slid down the stairs after him,
barely registering the fact that the stickiness in the chair had
been blood—my blood—and probably accounted for the
severe pain at the back of my skull. All that was important
was that I could still move. I wanted this guy. A sickening
dread filled my chest, an image of Elyse upstairs barely
alive.

I raced out the door into the hot night. I heard an engine
roar to life, then tires squealing on the pavement. I ran
across the lawn to the lot and caught a glimpse of a taillight
through the trees as the car disappeared.

But this wasn't the big city. There were only so many
roads this guy could go down. He was headed up the main
road west toward Frenchman's Cay and the west end of the
island. I fumbled in my pocket for my car keys, grateful they
were there, then jumped into the Rambler and went after
him.

I took the sharp turn out of the parking lot, the car fish-
tailing on loose gravel. Once on the highway, I pulled my
.38 out of the glove compartment and placed it on the seat
beside me.

I pushed the pedal to the floor and sped down along the waterfront, the Rambler maxed out at about eighty-two, the speedometer needle quivering. I was gaining though and finally the taillights appeared, a dim glow up ahead. At Sea Cow Bay, the car took a hard right and started up into the hills, the road twisting and rutted. And dark.

By the time I took the turn, the lights had disappeared around the next bend. I was climbing toward the ridge and the high point of the island. Once at the top, the guy could drop down to Cane Garden Bay on the other side of the island or continue along the ridge to the east. He could also decide to pull onto any one of the dirt turnoffs that led to people's houses or just dead-ended to nowhere.

The Rambler was no match for the car in front of me. The lights were getting farther and farther away and when I made it around the next curve, he was gone. I kept going, hoping to catch a glimpse of the car. At the top I stopped, pulled onto the overlook, and stepped into the gravel. I could see the harbor lights on the south side of the island twinkling below and the soft glow of lights through the trees of the occasional village or home that dotted the hillsides. But I couldn't see any headlights moving down the other side, and nothing on the straight road to the east.

Where the hell had the guy gone? He had to have pulled off somewhere. I had probably driven right past him. I jumped back in the Rambler and started back the way I'd come. Either the guy had pulled off and was hiding down one of the gravel driveways, or he was speeding back down to the main road. If that were the case, he was probably all the way to Road Town by now. I drove slowly, shining my flashlight down each of the driveways as I went and turning down several that seemed more suspicious. I knew that at this point, finding him was a long shot, but it was the only one I had.

Each drive was as deserted as the last. An occasional dog barked in the distance, and eyes glared yellow in my headlights—cats, mongooses, creatures of the night. I saw a light down the next drive and drove to the house, where a man stood on the porch in his robe. I got out of the car and identified myself as a police officer. He was not pleased. He said he'd been awakened by the neighbor's dog and come out.

I took the next turn and headed up another driveway. When I got to the end, there was no house, no dog barking, and no car. I turned the Rambler around and headed back to the road. Just as I pulled out, a car screeched out from under a stand of thick trees not ten feet back. He came up fast, lights blinding in my mirror, and slammed into the back of the Rambler. My first thought was Jergens, swerving past me the other day. I braked and wrapped my fingers around the .38.

This was a game of chicken that the driver had every intention of winning. He cut into the other lane and slammed the car into the side of the Rambler, hard. I never got a shot off as the .38 skittered to the floor. I managed one quick glance at the car, an indistinguishable figure at the wheel, as my tires left the road and the car sped past. I held on for the ride. It was short. The Rambler slowed in all the thick undergrowth, then came to an abrupt halt against a gumbo-limbo tree.

I made one attempt to restart the Rambler. When I turned the key, the engine made a grinding sound and gave up. I grabbed my gun and scurried back up to the road, praying that the guy would come back.

My foot had barely struck the pavement when I saw lights bounce off a nearby hillside—car lights coming up the road and just about to appear around the bend. I scrambled back into the ditch, stretched out on my stomach, and propped my gun between my hands, my elbows firmly planted in the dirt. I took careful aim at the driver's side and waited, intent on taking my best shot. I had every intention of killing this guy.

I could feel the muscles in my forearms cramping, my fingers tightening around the trigger. The car was moving way too slowly. It was still several yards away when a light flicked on from the driver's side, a focused beam that swept across the terrain and directly above my head. The perfect target. I took aim and waited.

Milliseconds before my finger pressed the trigger, I recognized the car and its driver. Dunn.

I climbed to my feet and stood by the side of the road, the tension draining from my body. Dunn unfolded his huge frame from behind the wheel, stepped to the pavement, and walked toward me, his face contorted, eyes troubled. I pressed my palms against my ears.

"Don't say it, Chief."

Chapter 22

❧

"She's not going to make it, Hannah."

"Noooooo," I wailed. "No, it can't be. Please God, don't let that be." My legs gave out and I felt my body crumple. Dunn grabbed me right before I hit the pavement. I could hear myself keening, but one part of me was assessing the whole thing, trying to remove myself from this horrible pain.

"God, don't let it be, don't let it be," I cried, over and over.

Dunn was holding me, rocking with me, the pain so overwhelming I wanted to die. I don't know how long he held me there, my face buried in his chest, his shirt drenched in my tears.

Finally, it ended. I had nothing left. I was exhausted and numb. Dunn pulled me to my feet, guided me to the car, and helped me into the passenger seat. The ride to the hospital was a blur. The next thing I knew we were sitting in the lot and I was staring blankly out the window.

"Come on, Hannah. You need to try to pull yourself together. The doc said there's a chance Elyse will regain consciousness for a minute or two."

Elyse's room was dim when I walked in, just a soft light glowing in the corner. All the life support had been removed, abandoned in the corner. She lay quietly, eyes closed. Mary was sitting beside her and rose when she saw me. We embraced and I tried to swallow the pain only to have it come out in gasps that turned to choking cries.

Mary didn't say anything, just led me to a chair. We sat together in the room, the minutes ticking by. Every once in a while, a nurse opened the door a crack and glanced in, then closed it quietly, leaving us to our painful vigil. Mary sat on one side of the bed. I was sitting on the other side, holding Elyse's hand, my head resting on the mattress, when I felt the gentle pressure of her fingers wrap around mine.

I sat up, immediately alert. Elyse was looking right at me; her soft eyes had a light in them I'd never seen before. She turned and smiled at Mary and back at me. Then she squeezed my hand, and died.

I dropped my head onto the bed and sobbed. I didn't care who saw or heard.

Finally, Mary put her arm around on my shoulders. "Come on, Hannah, she's somewhere else now."

We walked out of the room together. O'Brien, Stark, Dunn, and Snyder were all waiting in the hall. I didn't want to face them, share my pain. I could see their awkwardness and discomfort. Each of them was suffering and each of them knew there was absolutely nothing to be said. Then O'Brien came to me and wrapped me in his arms. I folded into him and buried my head in his chest.

"Come on, Hannah. Hall wants you to stay here tonight. You're hurt and exhausted."

I didn't protest, didn't have it in me. I needed someone else to tell me what to do next. Otherwise, I would have ended up staring at a wall in the waiting room all night or wandering around Road Town in a daze.

A nurse led me to a room, handed me a hospital gown, and left. I stood in the dark room, the damned gown draped over my arm, trying to think about what to do next. Slowly I pulled off my clothes, hardly aware of the damage I'd incurred fighting with Elyse's killer, still out there somewhere. I didn't have the energy for anger.

Finally, I went into the bathroom, turned on the shower,

and stepped in. The hot stream pounded my body, the burns, the bruises, but I was grateful for it because the physical pain distracted me for a moment—until I thought about Elyse just down the hall. I curled in, wrapped my arms around myself, sobbing into my belly as the water splattered across my back. I watched it swirl down the drain mixed with dirt and a tinge of my blood.

I was sitting on the bed when Hall came in, clipboard in hand. He sat beside me for a minute, then got down to business, shining a light in my eyes, examining my pupils, checking reflexes.

"The head injury is superficial," he said. "We'll clean and bandage it. But you are on the verge of shock, Hannah. I want you to stay for the rest of the night. You need rest above anything else."

A nurse came in and handed me some pills and water. I was only vaguely aware of O'Brien coming in. Then nothing.

When I woke, the sun was shining through the open window and I could hear birds twittering in a nearby tree. A glorious day. Then recollection took hold. I buried my head in the pillow, trying to push it all away, find relief back in unconscious sleep.

I was prevented the escape by a nurse who came in with a stethoscope dangling around her neck. "You're awake. Good. I'll take your vitals and then you can have some breakfast. It's almost ten."

The last thing I wanted was breakfast. The woman took my blood pressure and pulse as she talked. "Peter O'Brien just left. The man spent all night sleeping in that chair. He went home to shower only after I promised that if you woke up, I'd keep an eye on you until he got back." She went on and on about what a wonderful man he was and how sorry she was that my friend had died, and how God had his reasons. I wanted to slap her.

She left and returned a minute later with a tray. Propping the pillows up, she placed it across my lap. "I'll be back to check on you in a little while," she said, closing the door.

I took one look at the stuff on the tray and nearly lost it. Christ, I needed to get out of there. I moved the tray to the end of the bed, swung my legs over the side, and stood. Just a little tipsy, probably from the sedative that had put me out last night. I waited for the room to stabilize, found my dirty clothes still on the floor in the bathroom, and pulled them on, though they were stiff with dirt.

I swigged the coffee on the tray—probably decaf—and then got the hell out of there. At the curb in front, I found a cab. I wanted to go home to the *Sea Bird* and Sadie, bury my face in her fur and hear the water lapping at the side of the boat.

When I got to the marina, no one was around. I was relieved that I didn't have to see Calvin, Tilda, or the girls. The last thing the girls needed was to see me in the shape I was in right now. I needed to be alone.

Sadie was waiting at the end of the dock, stock-still except for her tail sweeping back and forth. I knelt and draped my arms around her, stifling sobs. She nuzzled her nose under my chin and whined.

"Come on, girl. Let's get out of here." I stepped aboard the *Sea Bird*, started the engine, freed her from the dock and headed her out of the bay and into open water ignoring the throbbing in my temples. Once past the reef and shallows, I managed to raise the mainsail, set my course with the wind off the beam, and cut the engine. Then I hauled out the jib and let the wind take us.

I sat behind the wheel and breathed in the warm sea air, felt the sun penetrate my body, and tried to find some comfort. A couple hours later, I was pulling in the sails at the secluded little harbor on Norman Island where O'Brien and I had gone skinny-dipping. It was too small for more than one boat and only a few locals ever anchored there. It wasn't even labeled on the charts. Here was one of the few places I was almost guaranteed privacy.

I dropped the anchor and allowed the wind to carry the boat back as I let out enough chain to hold her. Then I put the engine in reverse and gave a tug to set the anchor firmly in the sand. I wasn't going anywhere—not tonight.

All the activity had kept me from thinking. But now I could feel the damned catch in my throat, the stinging in my eyes. I went up to the bow, left my dirty clothes in a heap on deck, and dove into the water, the rush of bubbles and foam sweeping down my body. Sadie was right beside me as I headed to shore. I swam hard, stretching my arms out, kicking seawater high into the air, and welcoming the sting of salt in my wounds, the strain on bruised muscles. By the time I got to shore, I was breathless. I sat on the beach, watching the *Sea Bird* rock gently in the water as Sadie occupied herself chasing ghost crabs into their burrows.

For the first time since I'd come awake to see the dark figure standing over Elyse in the hospital did I think. Somewhere in my mental maze after she had died, Dunn told me that Elyse had been injected with what was probably potassium chloride. Hall could do nothing to save her. If I hadn't been in the room and seen the murderer, her death would have been determined an unexpected complication and in the end ruled accidental.

I didn't find any comfort in the thought that I'd been there to verify the murder. I'd failed Elyse. If I'd only been able to stop the guy. I knew he'd done his work after he'd knocked me out, pushing the liquid into her vein as I lay nearby, stunned. If I'd only been quicker, stronger, more alert. My life seemed to be full of "if onlys", mistakes, and death.

I didn't want to think anymore. I stood, ran back into the sea, and plunged under the surface. I wanted to stay down in the peace of the underworld, but buoyancy forced me off the bottom. I bobbed back to the surface and swam back to the *Sea Bird*. I intended to get plastered.

I climbed into the boat, pulled Sadie up behind me and went looking for a bottle of something—anything. I found one, a nearly full bottle of brandy. I grabbed the bottle and a plastic glass, wrapped a towel around me, and climbed back up to the cockpit.

By the time the sun set, I was completely wasted. I was lying on the bow looking up at the stars when a boat bumped against the side of the *Sea Bird*. I barely noticed and didn't care. Then O'Brien appeared in the dark, two O'Briens actually, both out of focus.

"Hannah, I've been looking everywhere for you. I saw the *Sea Bird* gone. I've been worried."

"Hey, O'Brien. How about a drink?" I slurred, holding up the empty bottle.

"Come on, Hannah. I'm putting you in bed."

I felt him lift me and carry me below. Things spun and twirled around me. I'd feel like hell in the morning but it was well worth another night of oblivion.

Chapter 23

O'Brien was awake and sipping coffee when I stumbled up to the cockpit the next morning. I felt like an army was marching through my head. O'Brien handed me a couple of aspirin and a glass of water, then filled a cup with coffee.

"How am I going to get through this, O'Brien?" I hoped he wasn't going to give me a bunch of shit like "It just takes time, Elyse is at peace," all the rest of the crap that people spouted. I couldn't take hearing it from O'Brien.

"Like you get through everything else, Hannah. You'll walk around pretending you're okay and try to put Elyse way back in the corner of your psyche, same place you put Jake. You'll blame yourself, bury the pain somewhere deep, and try not to let it happen again."

"Jeez, O'Brien. Thanks." I found myself preferring the crap.

"I don't want to lose you because of this, Hannah, don't want you to pull away."

"Come on, O'Brien. I can't talk about *us* right now."

"It's not just us, Hannah. It's you and how you choose to live with this."

"Yeah, maybe."

"No maybe. You need to let others in," he said.

"Fine," I said, and O'Brien saw the futility in further conversation.

"Dunn wants you back in the office when you're up to it. Believe me, he feels as much to blame for this as you do. He realizes you've been right all along about Elyse."

"If only I'd been able to prove it. Find the one responsible before he got to Elyse." As O'Brien so accurately predicted, I was trying hard to hide my utter despair. "What the hell am I going to do?"

"It's pretty obvious to me what you'll do, Hannah. I just hope you don't get hurt tracking this guy down."

By noon I was sitting at my desk at the police station, staring at a blank yellow legal pad and nervously flicking a pencil back and forth in my hand. The office wasn't a comfortable place to be. Every once in a while someone stepped in to offer sympathy. The outer area was subdued, with people tiptoeing and speaking in hushed tones.

"Hannah, I'm glad you came in." I turned to see Dunn standing in the doorway. He looked tired. I was sure he'd been up all night, working with Stark on any evidence that might tell us who had killed Elyse.

"You were right about Elyse, Hannah. I blame myself." I could see how hard this was for him.

"Lots of that going around," I said. "It wasn't your fault, Chief. You did what you thought was right, given the circumstances. Let's face it, I just wasn't good enough to prove someone had sabotaged Elyse's boat, and not fast enough to stop him from killing her."

"Well, I should have paid more attention to your instincts," he said.

"Do you really think it would have made a difference? Whoever killed Elyse was able to get to her with me in the damned room."

"Maybe," he said, and handed me my badge and my pistol. "What have you uncovered so far?" he asked. Dunn knew that my suspension had not kept me from investigating.

"Jillian was not the only one on the *Caribbe* the night it

blew up. According to the Pickerings' daughter, Daisy, there was a man, too."

"And you think he's the one who rigged the stove?"

"Absolutely."

"So who are you looking at? What about Jillian's father?"

"I considered him. I just can't see him being that premeditated about it. If he'd gotten angry at Elyse about her involvement with Jilli he might have threatened her, but I don't see him developing an elaborate plan to blow up the boat."

"Who else?"

"Elyse had been hassling Amos Porter about sediment runoff, but he was making an attempt to rectify the problems at the gravel pit. And if Freeman is elected, Porter probably doesn't have that much to worry about. Besides, Daisy said the man she saw was a white man. That lets Porter out."

"Anyone else?"

"Jergens. The attempt on Elyse fits his affinity to explode and burn things up."

"We've never tied any of the fires on those charter boats or at the dive shop to Jergens."

"Yeah, but I know you tried and if it's Jergens, he's bound to make a mistake. Did anything turn up in Elyse's hospital room?"

"No prints. The guy must have been wearing gloves, and he evidently took the needle with him. He was hoping to slip in, kill Elyse, and get out with no one the wiser. Hall himself admitted that no one would have suspected foul play."

"Where does someone get ahold of potassium chloride?" I asked.

"Looks like it came from the chemistry department over at the college. Someone broke into a lab and grabbed several vials. We got a call about the break-in this morning. Did you get a look at the guy at all?"

"Just a shape in the dark." I leaned an elbow on my desk and pressed my fingers into my skull, trying to ward off the pain and the image of the guy standing over Elyse. "Surely someone at the hospital saw him on the unit?" I said.

"That time of night the place was deserted except for the young lady at the desk." I could hear the frustration in Dunn's voice. "She'd gone to check on a call light down at the far end of the hall. She said she thought it was odd at the time—because when she got into the room, the patient was sound asleep. That's when she heard the commotion. By the time she got back to the front desk, all she saw was the door to the stairs closing."

"What about at the chase scene?" I asked.

"Nothing except the damage to the Rambler. One side is completely smashed in and embedded with red paint."

"Daisy's red car," I mumbled, mostly to myself.

"The Rambler's in the shop. It will be ready this afternoon."

"Fast work," I said.

"Yeah, well, Stark insisted. Not too many folks are willing to refuse him. Look, Hannah, if you need more time, take it. You don't need to jump right back into the middle of this," Dunn said.

"The last thing I need is time off, Chief."

"Okay, but try to keep some perspective. I know how close you were to Elyse. I don't want you hurt too," Dunn said before he went out.

Dunn knew he was wasting his breath. I planned to find Elyse's killer. I wanted the guy dead.

I couldn't figure out what the hell I was missing.

I opened my desk drawer and pulled out the shopping bag with the stuff I'd collected from Elyse's office that first day: the report on the sediment runoff from the gravel pit, the stuff about black urchins and coral bleaching, the rat eradication project. What could any of this have to do with her death?

The appointment book was buried at the bottom. I thumbed through the days surrounding the explosion till I found Elyse's notation to meet LaPlante, the scientist who was conducting the eradication project. It was a loose end.

When I called LaPlante, she said she'd be working over at Hermit Cay all day. I told her I'd meet her out there in an hour. I walked down to the dock, hoping to find a boat so I could head out to Hermit Cay. I knew that Snyder had taken the *Wahoo* to Cooper Island in response to a call about another theft.

I found Liam and Tom at the next dock, hosing down their boat and organizing their equipment.

"Hannah, we are so sorry about Elyse," Tom said giving me a hug. Liam came up behind enveloping both of us. If I hadn't found myself fighting against despair, I would have laughed at the idea of the three of us in a group embrace on a damned boat dock.

"How can such a thing happen?" Liam asked as we disengaged.

"That's what I intend to find out," I said.

Fifteen minutes later, we were heading over to see LaPlante. Liam and Tom had been happy to ferry me, anxious to do anything they could to help me find out why Elyse had been murdered.

We anchored in about thirty feet of water over a sandy bottom and took the dinghy to shore. Several other boats were there, folks onshore and swimming in the turquoise water. A pod of dolphins was out in deeper water, leaping in twos and threes out of the waves, twisting and somersaulting in midair.

"This little piece of land is remarkably diverse for its size," Liam said. "Rocky shorelines, mangroves, dry forests."

The island was all of about ten acres and designated as a preserve. We started down the only trail that led inland. LaPlante had said we'd find her back in the trees. Lizards scurried into hiding places as we approached and the ground literally moved, dried leaves taking on life as dozens of hermit crabs crawled around underneath them. I could hear waves crashing onto the rocks along the exposed shoreline on the other side of the island.

We found LaPlante and one of her assistants, sitting on rocks with clipboards perched on their knees. They stood as we approached.

LaPlante was a stocky woman with a dishwater blond braid hanging down her back, her head covered with a canvas bush hat. She wore old shorts, a long-sleeved work shirt, and running shoes.

"Hello, you'd be Hannah Sampson?"

"I am, and this is Tom Shields and Liam Richards."

"Yes, I've heard you're doing the turtle survey. Great to meet you." She removed a heavy pair of work gloves, held out a surprisingly tiny hand, and smiled warmly. Then she introduced us to her assistant, one of the people from the Park Service who would be maintaining the project when LaPlante left.

"We're in the process of removing the baiting stations. Why don't you come along and we can talk as we work," LaPlante suggested.

"Tell us about the project," Liam said as we headed down the trail. He was like a kid about to hear the story of Peter Pan for the first time.

"We've been eradicating the rats. We've conducted similar programs elsewhere in the Caribbean. Rats are not indigenous to this region so the native species have never developed defenses against them. LaPlante stopped, picked up a fallen coconut, and handed it to me.

"Rat's teeth," she said pointing to the scars on the fruit. "One year, only a couple of rats were seen on this island. A year later, ten were captured in a single night. They're highly omnivorous but exploit a wide range of food sources. They were eating lizards, birds' eggs and young, the edible parts of plants, seeds, and flowers. You name it. They'll chew on crab shells, even trees if there are beetle larvae in the bark."

"How do you get rid of them?" Tom asked.

"We use a rodenticide bait, which contains brodifacoum. It is an anticoagulant that causes hemorrhaging."

"What's to prevent other animals from eating it?" Liam said, obviously concerned.

"There aren't any native mammals on the island, so that's not a problem. Birds and lizards are susceptible to the poison so it has been formulated into wax blocks and pebbles that they aren't likely to consume.

"Most of the rats die underground in their burrows. To minimize the small risk of scavengers, especially laughing gulls, feeding on a rat that may die aboveground, we comb the island every day, remove the carcasses we find and burn them. Invertebrates like the hermit crabs are unaffected by the poison, though we do take measures to keep it out of their reach."

I'd been listening intently, looking for a connection. But at some point I tuned out, my thoughts drifting to Elyse. She would have walked this very trail. What had gone through her mind? I wondered. Did anything LaPlante was saying connect to Elyse's murder, or was this just a huge waste of time?

"What about other vertebrates like turtles?" Tom was asking. "The poison would certainly affect them. Have you seen signs of any nesting here?"

"No, but as you know, the nesting turtle doesn't feed out of the water."

"What about this stuff getting into the water and threatening sea life?"

"No freshwater streams or ponds exist on the island. The poison could get into seawater through crabs but the amount would be minimal."

"Elyse was out here working with you for a while, wasn't she?" I interjected. I knew she had been and I was getting impatient. I wanted to get to the reason I had come.

"Yes, like Liam and Tom here, she was very concerned about the impact of the poison on nontargeted species. I went through the entire protocol with her. We had a team camping out during the three weeks of the project to monitor the site. Elyse spent a week with them. She ended up working side by side with the others, setting bait, taking data."

I remembered when Elyse had been gone last month. I'd kept an eye on the *Caribbe* and watered her plants. She'd come home feeling that the project was accomplishing what it needed to for the protection of the habitat.

"Elyse was really a big help on the project. But that guy she was dating was kind of a pain. He came out to spend the night with Elyse. He actually brought a gourmet meal for two and a couple bottles of wine from his restaurant. Elyse was embarrassed and insisted on incorporating it with our meal—ours being stew heated over a gas stove. One of the guys started kidding about it being rat stew. Reidman laughed along with us but I never saw him take a bite. I have to admit that the team really enjoyed the wine. It was unbelievably good and no doubt expensive."

"Was Elyse drinking?" I asked.

"No, I got the impression that Elyse never drank. The only thing I ever saw her with was her tea. Reidman had quite a bit of wine though. I'm sure it helped him make it through the night, sleeping in the tent with Elyse. He's definitely not the outdoors type. He came out a couple of other times that week and actually helped a bit. Guess his heart's in the right place."

"Why did Elyse make an appointment to meet with you on Monday?" I insisted.

"All she said was that she had something she wanted me to look at. She seemed anxious about it."

"When did she call you?" A disturbing twist in my gut said *this is what you missed, Sampson.*

"It was late Sunday afternoon."

"You remember what time?"

"Yes. I'd just walked in the door. It must have been around five. She said she'd been up at Virgin Gorda all day and had found something."

"But she didn't say what?"

"No. She said it was better for me to see it. We were supposed to meet at the Seaman's Café on Jost Van Dyke first thing Monday morning. I waited for an hour. I didn't hear about the accident until that afternoon."

What the hell had Elyse found? I wondered. And had it been destroyed with the *Caribbe*?

"Thanks for your help, Dr. LaPlante," I said.

"It's Deb," she said, shaking my hand. "I know that you and Elyse were close. She talked about you. I can't tell you how sorry I am. She was so full of life and enthusiasm. Please let me know if I can help in any other way."

"Thanks," I said, my voice catching.

Chapter 24

 ❧

"**D**o you think Elyse would have been satisfied about the safety of the project?" I asked as we walked down the beach and back to the boat.

"Yes," Tom said. "LaPlante is a specialist on invasive species and she seems to have taken every precaution. I'm convinced that the risks are minimal compared to the destruction the rats were doing. If turtles did nest here, the damn rats would be consuming the eggs and hatchlings before they ever made it to the sea."

Tom and Liam insisted on taking me to lunch at the Soggy Dollar Bar, a ramshackle restaurant on the beach in White Harbor on Jost Van Dyke. I knew they were looking for a way to help me escape for a while.

The entrance to the shallow harbor was well marked. We kept the red buoy to our right, the green to our left, motoring into the channel, reef on either side and anchored in seven feet over a sandy bottom. The water was smooth jade and sparkled with sunlight. A few dinghies were pulled up on the sand, a white strip pressed against the sea.

We motored to shore and walked down the beach to the Soggy Dollar. It had gotten its name from the sailors who swam to shore, wet money in their pockets, for a cold beer or an infamous "Painkiller" composed mainly of high test rum. Tom and Liam had heard about the bar's excellent flying fish sandwiches.

The structure was just a roof held up by posts, with a bar and a few tables and chairs scattered underneath. Few of the patrons wore shoes, and most were in swimsuits. A hammock was slung in the shade between coconut palms, a couple stretched out in it sipping something pink.

I was surprised to see Alex Reidman and Neville Freeman sitting at a table in the corner in this isolated harbor bar. I never expected to see Freeman eating anywhere that he couldn't shake hands with at least a couple dozen voters between bites. The two men were in an animated and what looked like angry discussion. Reidman saw us first. He waved us over, but Tom and Liam headed to the bar to order.

"Hannah, what are you doing way over here?"

"We were on Hermit Cay visiting Deborah LaPlante, the specialist in charge of the rat eradication."

"That's a good thing they did over there. Just the kind of activity I'm in favor of. Protecting our native species." Freeman was on his bandwagon.

"What are you two doing here?" I asked. I wondered why Reidman was socializing when he'd just lost Elyse. But then I guess he could be asking me the same question. I hadn't seen him at all since that afternoon at the hospital when Hall had told us Elyse would pull through. Hours later, she was dead. Had it been just two days ago?

"Neville and I needed a quiet place to work and I needed to get out of Road Town for the day. This thing with Elyse, well, I'm having a hard time with it." Reidman didn't look like he was suffering. In fact, he looked relaxed, and his appetite clearly hadn't waned. The waitress had just put a huge steak in front of him.

"As you know, Alex is helping me with my campaign," Freeman said. "I am so sorry about your friend's death. Are there any leads?"

"A few."

"Do you think that LaPlante knows something about the murder?" Reidman asked.

"Elyse was supposed to meet LaPlante on Monday. I

thought I'd try to find out why. LaPlante said Elyse was anxious to show her something. Did Elyse mention anything to you about it?"

"Probably had some material to include in the final report. Elyse was very involved in monitoring the project," Reidman said. "Surely, that had nothing to do with her death?"

About then Tom walked over balancing a couple of plates, Liam following with cold beers. Introductions made, we talked about their turtle survey as they munched on bony bites of flying fish. I wasn't eating.

"With your permission, we'd like to survey Flower," Liam said to Freeman.

"I'm not too crazy about that idea, fellas. You won't find any turtles nesting over there. I've lived on that island off and on for years and there have never been turtles. I'm just not keen on having people traipsing around up there. I'm sure you understand." Freeman turned to Reidman, effectively cutting off any further discussion. Liam simply shrugged, but knowing these two, they wouldn't let it go for long.

I left Tom and Liam on the dock and walked up into town to pick up the Rambler. It was a mess, the grill twisted and askew, the door held in place by a bungee cord, but the engine only hesitated once, then turned over. The mechanic gave me a halfhearted apology and told me to bring it back when I could leave it for a week. I wondered if it was worth it, told him I'd think about it, and headed up to Elyse's office. I was hoping that she'd left whatever it was she'd wanted to show LaPlante there.

By the time I turned onto Main Street and pulled up in front of Elyse's office, the back of my shirt was damp and salty and sticking to the seat. Beads of sweat stung the laceration on my head and dripped into my eyes.

I walked around to the back of the building. I intended to jimmy the door that Reidman had made such a point of lock-

ing. It turned out I didn't need to—the latch was broken, the
door ajar. And damned if I hadn't left my gun locked in the
glove box of the Rambler. I didn't take the time to go back
for it. The intruder could still be inside.

I grabbed a two-by-four that was lying in a pile of debris
and stepped back to the door, listening. A Bequia-sweet sang
from its perch high in a tree and I heard a coconut thump to
earth from a nearby palm. But there wasn't a sound from the
other side of the door. I eased it open with my fingertips,
slipped inside, and stood with my back against the wall.

Elyse's bike was still propped against the far wall, her
microscope on the table, but test tubes were scattered and
broken all over the floor. I moved quietly toward the front
room, stepping carefully around shards of glass. At the doorway, I took a quick look around the corner, then slipped into
the front office. Whoever had done this was gone.

I unlocked the front door, ran out, and scanned the street.
The only people on the sidewalk were a couple of little girls
ambling along, backpacks bouncing from their shoulders.

I intercepted the kids at the corner, trying not to act too
desperate. They were clearly sisters, dressed alike in shorts
with starched and spotless shirts, hair neatly braided in cornrows. They were trying to be polite as they'd been taught,
but I was scaring them.

"No, ma'am, we not be seein' anyone," the oldest said,
draping a protective arm around her sister.

I headed back down the sidewalk, retrieved my evidence
kit from the Rambler, and went inside to call Dunn. He was
out, but his secretary said she'd send Dickson, the lab guy,
right over.

Elyse's office was a mess. Drawers had been pulled out
and dumped on the floor. Papers were scattered all over the
place. The specimen refrigerator in the back room had been
ransacked; waxy-looking pellets and broken vials lay on the
floor in a puddle of chemicals. I pulled on a pair of latex
gloves, scooped the liquid and pellets into an evidence vial,
and labeled it.

About then Gilbert Dickson walked in the front door. He got right to it, dusting every potential surface, applying the lifting tape, and carefully affixing the tape to a card. Then he labeled each card with the location from which the print had come.

"Got some good clean prints from Elyse's desk, the file cabinet, and that refrigerator handle," he said. "I'll run them through the system. Most of them are probably Elyse's but something might come up."

"Do me a favor, Gill," I said, as I handed him the Baggie with the gunk I'd collected off the floor for analysis.

"Sure, Hannah, anything for you," he said. If I didn't know better, I'd say he was flirting.

"Some of the prints you found on the stuff Carr and I collected when we dove the *Caribbe* weren't Elyse's and didn't match anything in the database. How about comparing them to the prints you just lifted in here?"

"No problem. I'll let you know as soon as I have something," he said, closing his kit. "See you back at the office."

After he left, I wandered aimlessly around Elyse's office trying to think. Whoever had broken in had been looking for something. But what? Could it possibly have to do with Elyse's call to LaPlante or the project on the cay? Was the intruder looking for whatever Elyse had wanted to show La-Plante? What the hell could that be? The dots were just not connecting.

I knelt and picked up a photo that had been tossed on the floor, the frame broken. It was Elyse and me standing on the *Caribbe* in dive gear. O'Brien had taken it. I pulled the photo out of the frame, slipped it in my pocket, and headed back to the office.

Stark was at his desk when I got back. He gave me a quick smile.

"How you holding up, Hannah?" he asked.

"I'm okay," I lied.

"Right," he said, and left it at that. He was as unwilling to talk about Elyse as I.

"What's going on?" I asked.

"I was out in the *Wahoo* all morning with Snyder checking on the recent thefts on those boats. My nervous system can't take much more," he said. "It's bad enough being out on the water with you, much less with Snyder. He's a damned speed demon. You know he almost ran the *Wahoo* into a dive boat that was pulling out of the harbor at Cooper? Kid's a maniac."

"It will build your character, Stark. Besides, I hate to admit it but Snyder knows what he's doing behind the wheel. If his testosterone levels ever drop from 'raging' to 'normal,' maybe he'll learn to slow down."

"Except that I might not survive that long. Kid probably needs a good lay. Maybe I ought to fix him up with one of the ladies down at the Doubloon."

"Don't be corrupting him, Stark."

"Hey, I consider it part of his education," he said with a grin.

"Anything new turn up over at Cooper Island?"

"Same story as the others. The boats were broken into while people were onshore at the restaurant. A couple of people saw the *Libation* in the area. Snyder tracked down the record of ownership—Lynn and Geoff Cooper. When I sat down to analyze the pattern of robberies, things started to fall into place. The *Libation* was in every one of those anchorages on the days the thefts occurred. Chief wants us to hang back and keep an eye on them. Mahler and Snyder are on it. As soon as they have something concrete, they'll bring them in for questioning."

"Wait—there is one other thing." I realized I'd never told Stark about seeing Jergens at the Doubloon yesterday afternoon. I'd been too distracted by everything else that had happened. I explained that Jergens had been with the couple that ran the *Libation* and that Mona thought they were involved in some sort of business dealings.

"If Jergens is connected to these thefts, Mahler and Snyder will run him down. Chief has reassigned me to help with your investigation into Elyse's murder. What do you have so far?"

I went through it all with Stark—my initial suspicions about Jillian, her prints on the Ambien bottle, her early denial that she'd been on Elyse's boat that night, and Amos Porter, whom Elyse had been hassling over the runoff into the bay. But I'd written them both off and Stark agreed.

My money was still on Jergens. All along I'd been thinking that the explosion had to do with Elyse confronting Jergens about his failure to protect the reef by educating his charterers. Was there something more involved than a simple matter of revenge on Jergens's part?

"Do you see this as enough motive for the kind of violence we're talking about?" I asked Stark.

"Maybe. We know that Jergens is ruthless," Stark said.

"Yeah, but it was a huge risk to go into that hospital room after Elyse. Would he do that for simple revenge? There has to be something bigger at stake. Maybe Elyse found out about the thefts on the boats and Jergens's involvement," I said.

"We still don't know that he is involved," Stark said. "A conversation in the Doubloon doesn't prove much."

I told Stark about my meeting with LaPlante and that Elyse had arranged to meet with her about something she'd found, more than likely that afternoon when she'd been up near Virgin Gorda.

"You think whoever ransacked Elyse's office was looking for whatever it was Elyse found?" Stark asked.

"I do. But what the hell was it, and did he find it? And how does it connect to Jergens or the boat thefts? None of it makes any sense. My gut says it has nothing to do with the damned thefts, but if not, then what the hell would Elyse have found up at Virgin Gorda?"

"We're spinning our wheels here. Let's put it to rest until tomorrow. Get some sleep and see what Dickson comes up with on the stuff he's analyzing from Elyse's office," Stark said. "We need to get some perspective on all this."

I knew by "we" he meant me, and he was right. Ever since the explosion on Elyse's boat, I'd let anger rule logic. Now I had a killer headache and the grief was getting the best of me.

Chapter 25

❧

It was barely light when I heard clambering on the deck of the *Sea Bird* and the boat started rocking. Sadie dashed up top to find out who was here to visit.

"Sampson! You down there? Hey Sadie." Then a bunch of expletives peppered the air. It was Stark. He never failed to hit his head on the hatch every time he came down the steps into the cabin.

"Stark, what are you doing here? Did Dickson find something in Elyse's office?" I felt my heart rate jump a notch.

"No, it's not about Elyse," he said.

I lay back on the pillow, disappointed and pulled the covers up over my head. "Come on, Stark, I'm still in bed, for chrissakes."

"I can see that," he said. He was standing at my cabin door rubbing his head. "I'll put the coffee on while you get dressed."

"I don't want to get dressed. I want to sleep." I'd slept badly, awakened with nightmares about Elyse. By the time I'd gotten back to sleep, it was three a.m. and now Stark was on my case to get up.

"Come on, Hannah, we need your help."

I reached over my head and slammed my cabin door shut, then slid out of bed and pulled on a pair of shorts and a tank.

Stark was banging around in the galley when I stumbled into the salon.

"Coffee's ready," he said, holding a couple of mugs and a thermos. "Let's go."

"Go? How about filling me in first?"

"We can talk on the way. I've already fed your critters. You need to grab your dive gear, camera, anything else you need."

I packed my gear, knowing full well that diving today was nuts. In the past 48 hours, I'd been beaten, gotten drunk, and lost my best friend. Not to mention the three hours of sleep I'd managed last night. It was a cocktail for disaster. But Dunn wouldn't have asked if there was anyone else qualified. I threw my bag over my shoulder, followed Stark to my car, and tossed him the keys.

He talked as I tried to get some caffeine in my bloodstream. Evidently a boat had been reported on fire and sinking sometime around three in the morning up at the north end of Virgin Gorda. Someone onshore had seen it going down and called the police station in Spanish Town. By the time a rescue boat arrived, the craft had disappeared under the water.

"They've been out searching for bodies," Stark said. "No sign of anyone."

"Why does Dunn think he needs me? Sounds like this was an accident, not a police matter."

"The folks who reported it saw a motorboat speeding away from the scene right after they saw flames and smoke coming from the boat."

"Did you call Carr?"

"Yeah, he's already out there. Don't know how he got wind of it so fast. Guess the fire department radioed BVI Search and Rescue."

Stark helped me load all the gear into the *Wahoo* but he wasn't happy about stepping into the boat himself.

"Come on, Stark. At least Snyder's not driving," I said, gunning the engine.

"Some comfort," he said, strapping on a life jacket.

We had no problem finding the scene. A huddle of boats

already bobbed out there in the water. The fireboat from Virgin Gorda was just pulling away, heading back to shore. I spotted Dunn, his huge black frame silhouetted against the morning sky. The man was unmistakable; no one else held himself the way Dunn did.

Several people were standing around on their boats, smoking and drinking coffee. No one was doing much except staring into the water at nothing. Other boaters were beginning to gather around the edges. It's the same on the water as on the roads—onlookers wanting to get a glimpse of blood and gore. Dunn picked up the loudspeaker mike and warned them away.

I maneuvered the *Wahoo* through the outer ring of boats and tied up alongside Dunn.

"Hannah, I appreciate your coming under the circumstances. I know you want to stay focused on your investigation into Elyse's death, but you're the only one who can do this dive."

"No problem, Chief. Stark filled me in. Does anyone know what boat it was?"

"No. It wasn't a sailboat. People who saw it said it looked like an old fishing boat of some kind, one with a cabin on deck. Sounds more like a local than a charter craft. Don't know what anyone would be doing out here at three in the morning."

"Any idea whether anyone was on board?" I asked.

"Seems pretty likely. No one was pulled out of the water. We have retrieved some debris—life preserver, plastic mug, that kind of thing. Nothing that identifies the boat."

"Stark said there were reports of another craft in the area last night."

"Yes, but descriptions are a bit vague. The people who saw it were out on the veranda of that house up there." Dunn pointed to a white stucco that was spread across the hillside, surrounded by orange blossoms.

"Let me guess. They weren't exactly sober."

"That's right. There were six or seven of them partying

up there. They've rented the place for a couple of weeks. Each of them tells it a little differently. The only consensus is that they saw a fire on the boat and then it slowly sank beneath the surface. They all saw the other boat, which they say sped up Drake Channel and disappeared. No navigation lights."

"Has anyone gone down yet?" I asked, worried about the scene. A couple of dive masters from a local dive shop hovered on a nearby boat and looked like they were dying to get into the action. I knew they were good, but they didn't know anything about crime scenes. It was a problem that Dunn had brought me onto the force to rectify. He assured me that he'd secured the scene and that no one had entered the water.

"I guess we better see what's down there. What's the depth?"

"It's about seventy to eighty feet," Carr said. He was sitting in the back of the boat, studying the dive tables that gave us time limits at various depths and how long we would be required to remain on the surface between each dive to avoid decompression stops. "We've got plenty of full tanks. I figure three dives, twenty-five minutes max each. If we watch our time and depth, we won't need to decompress on our way back up."

"Good." I believed in avoiding decompression dives whenever possible. They always meant more risk. I'd done plenty of them and sometimes thought I was pushing my luck. They involved ascending to designated depths for specified periods that are determined using Navy Decompression Tables. If our dives took us too deep for too long, we'd need to do decompression stops on our way back up to allow the nitrogen, which accumulates in tissues when a diver breathes air at depth for extended periods, to dissipate from our systems before surfacing.

Otherwise we risked the bends, caused by bubbles forming in the bloodstream. A severe case can cause paralysis, loss of consciousness, and death. The pain is excruciating and many divers suffer long-term disability.

I'd known divers who had panicked, miscalculated, or run out of air and surfaced before they'd had a chance to complete the necessary stops. They'd been rushed to recompression chambers. Some recovered, a couple could never dive again, one was in a wheelchair, one died.

We were close to the edge with these dives but if we stayed inside the limits, we'd be fine.

"Okay," I said. "We'll get the general picture on the first dive, check for victims, and evaluate the overall scene. I'll take as many photos as I can. Then we'll surface and decide what's next based on what we find."

I sat next to Carr, pulled on my wet suit and booties, attached my BC to the tank, hooked up the hoses, checked my air (3400 psi), and breathed through the regulator. Everything was fine. I kept my equipment in top condition. I knew one of the biggest dangers in diving was equipment failure. Divers got bad air, their regulators malfunctioned, their gauges failed. There were plenty of other things that could happen underwater and the only tie to survival was the tank on your back. I tried to keep the odds in my favor.

I hefted my equipment to the platform on the back of the boat, buckled on my weight belt, then sat down and pulled on my fins. Dunn helped me into my BC and tank while Stark assisted Carr. I spit in my mask to keep it from fogging, swirled it in seawater and snugged it into place. I grabbed the underwater camera and tumbled into the water. Carr was right behind me.

We descended slowly. Every few feet, I pinched my nose and blew to equalize the pressure in my ears. Carr was doing the same. Visibility was about twenty feet, with a slight current. The deeper we got, the darker it became. At fifty feet, I could see the outline of the wreck. The boat was completely intact and lying on its side right at the edge of a precipice that dropped into nothingness. There was no indication from this vantage that there had been a fire.

I stopped and shot photos. Then we continued to the bottom. I checked my depth gauge: seventy-six feet. Both Carr and I spent a second adjusting the air in our buoyancy compensator vests, just enough so that we were hovering above the bottom. Then we headed for the wreck, our lights on. As we moved in, I shot pictures from every angle, making sure to place the boat in context. Then we moved in closer. We would not touch anything on this first dive, just get an idea of what we were up against. Carr knew that he should stay behind me and follow my lead.

The thing about being under the water is that your world becomes multidimensional. Up, down, behind, ahead. You think you're completely aware of your surroundings and then suddenly something appears out of the blue. That's what happened now. I felt something brush against my fin, was sure that it was Carr. It wasn't. A hammerhead, followed by two more, swam right above me, circling. Logic told me they were not going to bother me, but no matter how much logic I drew on in these times, the fight-or-flight response coursed through me. It was all I could do to talk myself through it. Seconds later and with a few slight flicks of their tails, they disappeared into the deep.

We swam along the port side to the forward section of the boat. I could see the name on the side—*Lila B*. The cabin windows arched around the wheelhouse. I made my way across the bow and around the exterior, straining to see inside, my face mask inches from the glass, tilting my flashlight back and forth through the glass and into the gloom. Things floated inside: paper, pencils, a Styrofoam cup. Fish were nibbling on something that looked like a sandwich.

I could see the wooden spindled wheel, a compass attached to the helm, and behind it a swiveling stool that was bolted into the floor. Someone was sitting in it, ragged arms dangling from the chair. I couldn't see the face. I banged my mask against the window, trying to get a better look. I almost expected the guy to move, react to the clatter. Nothing. I inched along the window, peering into the water-filled room, trying for a better vantage point. With a new perspective, I realized that it was an illusion conjured from nerves—no man, just a jacket that was knotted through the back of the stool.

I kept moving along the glass, trying to pick out signs that anyone was in the boat. I had my mask glued to the last window on the starboard side, focusing my light on the interior side of the door when a face drifted into the window. This time the man was real—grinning at me, eyes open, teeth bared. I lurched backward, the weight of my tanks pulling me down onto the bow of the boat.

Jeez, that was not cool. *Very professional, Sampson.* By the time Carr swam to my side, I was sitting on my knees on the bow. I gave him the okay and signaled him to follow. The face was still there, peering out of the window. I recognized the guy from somewhere.

I nodded to Carr and we continued to swim around the other side of the boat, both of us examining the hull as I continued to shoot photos. Toward the back section of the hull, Carr shone his light over several holes, all charred. It looked as if the fire started in the hold and burned through quickly. I moved in close and shot pictures from every angle. Then I swam up to the deck, continuing to photograph.

I checked my watch and found that we'd already been down for twenty-five minutes. We needed to surface. I signaled to Carr and we headed up.

When we surfaced I saw that the crowd of boats had dispersed but O'Brien had come out with James Carmichael, the owner of Underwater Adventures. Carmichael was a top-notch diver and one to have by your side in extreme conditions. He and O'Brien would be good backups if we needed them.

I sat on the side of the *Wahoo*, resting and swigging water. The day was brilliant, cumulus drifting in a deep blue sky. The reef at the entrance to North Sound reflected teal, turquoise, and crystalline as the water shallowed to the shore. Out here, though, the water was deep indigo.

I described the scene to Dunn and Stark—the body in the cabin and the charred holes in the hull.

"Not much question about why the boat went down. Looks like the fire was extremely hot and burned through the hull before it could be consumed by flames. It would have filled with water fast," I said, taking a long swallow from my water bottle.

"What about the body? Did you recognize the guy?" Stark asked.

"I've seen him somewhere, maybe at the fund-raiser."

I turned to O'Brien who was sitting at the wheel of the *Wahoo*.

"What was that guy's name? The one that Freeman had hauled out of there. The caretaker that he fired."

O'Brien thought about it for a minute before speaking. "Freeman mentioned his name once. I'm pretty sure it's Billings—Theodore Billings."

"Looked a lot like the guy who was glaring at me through the window down there," I said, the horrible grin still vivid in my mind.

"Could you see any injuries?" Dunn asked.

"Nothing apparent." I knew Dunn dreaded having another murder on his hands.

I looked at my watch. Carr and I had been sitting up top for almost an hour, drinking water and munching on cookies—a safe margin of surface time to allow our bodies to dispel the nitrogen in our tissue and keep our nitrogen absorption within the limits for no decompression.

"Guess we'd better get down there and find out." I stood, and stretched. I can't say I was looking forward to going back in. I'd been tense on the first dive and now it was just one of those feelings. I knew every diver in the world felt this way from time to time: jinxed, maybe pushing his luck. Some divers were smart enough to call it a day and head to shore. Others always pushed the limits. For me, there was rarely a choice, like today. We needed to bring that body up.

I gathered a couple of evidence containers and the yellow underwater body bag from the hold on the *Wahoo*. O'Brien helped Carr heft the fresh tanks from Carr's boat and ready our equipment for the second dive.

Carr and I went over our dive plan. This time we would descend directly to the boat and enter the wheelhouse. Once I'd taken interior photos, we'd bag the body and bring it up. I'd done it all before—dozens of times.

We suited up, stepped off the side into the water, and headed back down. Once at the boat, I again took the lead, swimming to the cabin door. There were no apparent intrusion marks on the door, nothing to indicate forced entry. Still I took photos from several angles before Carr pried the door open with a crowbar, avoiding any contact with the door handle. Before going inside, I took wide-angle shots of the interior. It was pretty hard to tell whether there had been any violence inside since everything in there that could float, did.

The body was still up against the window, held in place by the shirt, which had gotten tangled in the window latch. The corpse wore dark brown pants stained with grease, work boots, and a yellow bandana tied around its neck.

I moved in for close-ups, competing with a few fish that thought Billings would make a good lunch. The body had a huge gash in the back of the head and a wound in its side. It looked like Billings had put up a fight before what I was sure was the final blow to the head.

Fortunately, only a few saltwater shrimp had found the wounds as yet. They are voracious feeders. Given time, they would be joined by others—crabs, lobster, and thousands of sea lice, small whitish brown creatures which you'd never know were in the water until they congregate en masse on a dead body. Their first point of attack is the wound. Eventually these scavengers can obliterate tissue and other important evidence.

Recovery in those circumstances required a lot of experience and a strong psyche. I'd once done a recovery with a novice team member who had been on the verge of panic when we encountered a victim blanketed in sea lice. When we moved the body, they swarmed in a cloud around us. When a couple swam under his neoprene hood, the guy freaked out and headed for the surface. Fortunately, we'd only been diving at thirty feet, shallow enough that he'd not gotten into trouble with a fast ascent.

Right now, the few scavengers that were feeding on this victim had done little damage, and they scattered when I lifted the head and enclosed it in a plastic bag. Carr handed me a couple more bags, one for each of the hands. Given the apparent struggle with the assailant, there was a good chance that the coroner would find something under the nails. That done, we zipped the body into a bag and took it to the surface.

"Well?" Dunn asked when we climbed aboard.

"It's Billings. No one else was in the boat. It looks like he was clobbered from behind." I pulled the top portion of my wet suit off and let it hang around my waist. I took a deep breath of fresh sea air, closed my eyes, and lifted my face to the sun. Carr went to the front of the boat and stretched out on the bow. We needed the light, the warmth and time to recharge.

Dunn unzipped the bag and took a quick look. "Damn," he muttered. I knew he'd been hoping for some better news, like maybe that Billings had just drowned.

Finally, we suited back up, got fresh tanks and gathered our evidence containers for the last dive. We'd spent almost an hour down there already. This dive would be short. We knew what we needed to collect and divided the tasks. Each of us carried a couple of water-tight containers in mesh bags so the evidence could be preserved in sea water to prevent corosion.

When we got to the bottom, Carr headed to the wheel-house to remove the knobs from the cabin door. Maybe we'd get lucky and find prints. I swam back to the hull. There I pulled out my dive knife and chipped some charred pieces into an evidence bag. From these, the lab should be able to determine whether an accelerant had been used.

When I got back to the cabin door, Carr and I swam inside looking for a murder weapon and a motive. All the electronics seemed intact—no dangling wires where instruments might have been pulled out. Whoever had killed Billings hadn't been interested in his GPS, radio, or radar equipment. Theft was obviously not the motive here.

A huge toolbox was bolted down alongside one wall. I was about to open it when I was confronted by a threatening set of teeth—a moray eel. It snaked out from behind the box and wriggled off to find a better place to curl. I collected anything that could have been used to crush Billings's skull—a hammer, big pair of cutting pliers, a level. I gathered the tools into a PVC-type tube long enough to contain the items, careful not to smear any prints that might be on them, and then snapped a lid in place on each end of the tube.

Carr was opening lockers and cupboards for any indication of contraband, especially drugs. We collected a few bags of stuff that were probably just flour and sugar. Each piece of evidence was captured in a jar, the lid screwed tightly in place, and dropped into our mesh bags. I collected a cigarette butt, a couple of coffee mugs, and anything else that might contain prints and wasn't bolted down. That was the trouble with an underwater crime scene. You couldn't just dust every surface at the scene as could be done in a dry environment.

We'd pretty much scoured the wheelhouse. I took a final swim around. Under the chart table I found a heavy wrench. Carr swam over with a container and we placed it inside. This could very well be the murder weapon. I shone my light back into the recesses under the chart table, the beam illuminating what at first looked like a piece of rubber matting. Then I realized it was a flipper. I grabbed and pulled.

Damned if it wasn't a dead hawksbill turtle. Had Billings been poaching?

I decided to bag it and take it to the surface. It was possible that it related to Billings's death somehow. Maybe Billings had been interfering in some other poacher's territory or gotten crossways with a colleague. Seemed a stretch—murder over a turtle. But I'd ask Liam and Tom to take a look at it.

Carr swam up behind me. I pointed to the turtle and indicated that I wanted to collect it. I could tell he thought I was nuts. He shrugged and signaled that he was going to head back up with the containers of evidence that we'd filled. He was pretty well weighted down with stuff. I gave him the okay signal and indicated I'd be right behind him.

It was a struggle getting the turtle into the bag, as it kept getting caught in the mesh fabric. Finally I managed to get the thing contained. I looped the ties of the bag over my arm and snugged it up over one shoulder, my camera strap over the other. I shone my light ahead and started out of the wheelhouse cabin. I was three feet from the doorway when the boat rocked slightly, then began a slow tip.

I kicked my fins hard, but before I made it to the door, the boat was tumbling sideways. It flipped on its side, then onto the roof, and started to slide. A sickening feeling of dread twisted in my belly.

Chapter 26

❦

The boat picked up momentum as it slid down the embankment on its roof. I'd lost my flashlight when the boat had flipped over; now I was surrounded by utter blackness and completely disoriented. I was pretty sure I was upside down on the ceiling of the wheelhouse. When I tried to right myself I couldn't move. I was tangled in a mass of loose lines. God knows how far it was to the seafloor—too far to make it to the bottom alive.

I could feel the mounting pressure as the boat went deeper. I kept my fingers pressed into my nose, struggling to keep my ears clear. I could hear joists creaking as the boat bumped the side of the precipice and kept going down. I had to get out, but every time I tried to move, I was pulled up short from behind. I knew my tank valve was caught on something. I twisted in the blackness, trying to get loose.

My fingers grabbed only empty water. I had to release my vest. It was the only way to free myself. I unsnapped the clip that held it around my chest and tried to slip my arm out of the shoulder harness. No go. I finally realized that my arm was wrapped up in my camera strap. I fumbled in the dark, working my fingers from the case to the buckle. I pushed the release and felt the camera fall away. I slipped out of the vest and brought my tank around in front of me, one arm still in the vest, my regulator clasped tight between my teeth. I found a coil of rope tangled around the valve and pulled on it until it fell away.

Just at the edge of my vision, I could see blue lights dancing through the blackness. Then they turned into golden fairies, with the most beautiful translucent wings. I heard myself laughing into my regulator and knew I was hallucinating. Nitrogen narcosis was setting in big-time. If I didn't get out of the boat soon, I'd be thinking it was a good idea to ride it all the way to the bottom.

I groped through the darkness, my arms outstretched, sweeping nothing but black watery emptiness. Finally, my fingers found the wheel. I grasped one of the spokes, and crashed my tank hard against the windows I knew were right in front of the wheel. I felt one give. One more hard blow and my tank broke through. I pulled the tank back to me, wrapped one arm around it, grabbed the edge of the window frame, unconcerned about the shards that tore through my gloves. I kicked hard and pulled myself out of the boat. Water swirled around me. I was being sucked down, tumbling helplessly out of control, in the grasp of the powerful eddies created by the sinking boat.

Finally, the boat fell away and I was left hovering in the vast empty ocean. That's all I could comprehend. My mind would not function. I was disoriented and on the verge of losing consciousness. Darkness was building around the edges of my brain. I wondered how deep I'd been pulled. I knew I should check my gauges for depth and air supply, but it all seemed like way too much effort.

My body did what was natural: It headed up. As I rose from the depths, the water turned indigo; some basic thinking skills returned and I kicked toward the growing circle of light above me. Finally, I checked my gauges. I was at two hundred feet. My air supply registered pretty close to zero. The maximum depth on my gauge showed I'd been at almost three hundred feet. I was stunned and scared. I knew what being that deep could mean.

How long had I been down there? It felt like hours but it

had probably only been minutes. Still, it was long enough and deep enough that I'd be consumed by the bends when I surfaced. I had no choice though but to keep going up. At fifty feet, I felt the first stab of pain shoot through my back and under my rib cage, a sure sign that nitrogen was moving out of my tissue and forming bubbles in my bloodstream. I needed to stay at that depth to allow them to dissipate, but without air that was impossible.

Where the hell were the others? Carr should have seen the boat going over the edge. I scanned the water above me, hoping to see someone, anyone, coming for me. That's when I saw the light, coming close. At first, I thought I was still hallucinating. Then two divers took shape in the indigo water.

Carmichael reached me first with an extra tank. O'Brien was right behind. He grabbed me and took a long hard look into my eyes. I nodded, indicating I was coherent, and let them take over. They got the other tank attached and they took me down. I felt the pain subside. Carmichael checked my gauge to see how deep I had been, then wrote *dive tables* on his slate. I knew what he meant. He was going to the surface to calculate decompression time. O'Brien stayed down with me, his arm wrapped around my waist. We drifted there, waiting for Carmichael to return.

I was amazed to find the mesh bag with the turtle still draped over my shoulder. O'Brien gave me this look like, *what the hell are you doing with a dead turtle on your back?* I could hardly remember myself. If I hadn't taken the time to bag it, I'd have been out of the boat before it started its trip to the deep.

Finally Carmichael returned with a bunch of numbers written on his slate. He'd had to do a lot of estimating. I could see by the numbers on the slate that Carmichael was playing it safe. He wanted me to decompress at sixty feet for ten minutes, then do successive decompression stops at continuing shallower depths for a total of more than two hours, a long, waterlogging procedure. O'Brien and Carmichael took shifts along with some of the other rescue divers who had been alerted and come out, bringing extra tanks. Hours later, I broke the surface into the sunlight.

Stark had stayed. He was reclining under the bimini on Carmichael's boat when I surfaced.

"It's about time you got back up here." He lifted his head and smiled, then walked to the transom and waited while I unbuckled my weights and BC and handed them up. He offered me his hand and pulled me into the boat. He still had his damned life vest on.

I dropped onto a seat in the boat, exhausted and thirsty.

"Are you okay, Hannah?" O'Brien asked, concern etching his face. He handed me a bottle of water and an orange.

"Yeah, I'm all right," I said, taking a long swig of water. My throat was raw, my chest sore, and I had a headache. The water was performing its magic though; some of the fatigue was slowly vanishing, the pounding in my temples subsiding to a throb.

"What happened down there?" O'Brien asked. "When Carr surfaced, he said he looked back and saw the boat sliding down the embankment."

"I tried to swim back fast enough to get to you," Carr interjected. "But I saw it was hopeless. I headed for the surface for help."

"It's okay, Ed. There wasn't anything else for you to do," I said, pulling the orange apart. "I was bagging that stupid turtle when I felt the boat rock and then start to slide. I just couldn't get to the door fast enough. It rolled onto its roof and started down. I was finally able to break out a window." I chewed on the orange and replayed the scene in the boat. The ocean air never smelled so sweet, an orange taste so delicious.

"As soon as Carr told us what had happened, Carmichael and I threw our gear on, grabbed extra tanks, and went down," O'Brien said. "We didn't know what to expect but we were fully prepared for a long, deep dive to get you out of that boat. When we got to the edge of the embankment, we could see your bubbles and then you appeared. Best thing I ever saw." O'Brien sat down beside me and handed me more water. I could see how scared he'd been.

"Thanks for coming after me," I said, squeezing O'Brien's hand and smiling at James Carmichael.

"Hey, no problem." James gave me a thumbs-up. "Shoulda known you'd find your way outta dat boat. All we did was bring you a little air."

"As soon as we knew you were okay down there, Dunn went back into town with the body," Stark said. "You up to a visit to the coroner's?"

"Sure. I'll meet you there," I said.

Carr and Stark headed back in the rescue boat and I rode back with O'Brien and Carmichael. On the way, I thought about Elyse and how similar the sinking of the *Lila B* was to the explosion and fire on the *Caribbe*. And two unrelated murders, two boats sunk within a week in these islands, seemed pretty unlikely. I was anxious to meet up with Stark and find out what the hell had happened here.

By the time we pulled into Road Town Harbor, I'd consumed a gallon of water, a peanut butter and jelly sandwich, and another orange. I was feeling amazingly well. Nothing like surviving.

O'Brien and I wrapped the turtle in ice and loaded it in the Rambler. After nearly dying getting the thing out of the wreck, I wasn't about to let it rot. I'd have Liam and Tom take a look at it.

Chapter 27

❦

The coroner had already removed Billings's clothes and was just beginning to examine the body when we got there. He showed us the shirt. It had a hole in it, along with what he said was probably blood in the fibers—which wasn't too surprising, because there was a matching tear in Billings's flesh, on the right side of his abdomen.

"It's a good-sized wound," the coroner said, probing it with his scalpel. "Don't think it's a knife wound. Too big, too jagged. Lots of trauma around the edges. See this?" He was pointing to the bruises that encircled the wound.

"Yeah," Stark said, bending over for a closer look. Stark might be afraid of water, but nothing about the dead bothered him in the least.

"It's not what killed him though." The coroner tipped the body over on its side. "This is what did it," he said, pointing at the deep wound at the back of the head. "Skull was crushed."

He continued to examine the body from head to toe before he spoke again, his eyeglasses perched on the end of his nose.

"The man sure put up a fight. Quite a few defensive wounds—look at all the bruising on his arms. I'd say he had them up to deflect the blows. At some point, he must have been knocked to the floor on his face. That would have been when the final blow came."

"What about a weapon?" I asked. "Any guesses?" I was leaning against a nearby table, close enough to see all that I needed to see.

"From the looks of the wounds and the bruising, I'd say something the size and heft of a crowbar."

"We retrieved some tools—a wrench, hammer, pliers. Could the wound be from something like that?" I asked.

"As soon as the lab examines the tools for blood and fibers, I'll take a look at them, see if the pattern of the wound matches, but I'm putting my money on a crowbar. I've seen the damage one does before. People seem to prefer them when it comes to killing, you know?"

"Yeah." If he was right, we hadn't found the murder weapon. Whoever had killed Billings had taken it with him—maybe dumped it out in deeper water, or else stashed it in the boat that had sped out of there after the *Lila B* started burning.

"I'll be checking the air passages and lungs for smoke inhalation, but I'm betting this guy was dead long before he could breathe any fumes."

We'd seen enough to have a pretty good idea what had happened on that boat. Whoever had started the fire was trying to cover up any evidence of murder. It hardly ever worked. There were always signs. Even when a body had been badly burned, the bones would tell the story. In this case, the boat had gone down before fire did its damage to the corpse.

"Call us when you have a complete report?" Stark asked.

"Will do." The coroner had removed his glasses and was holding a magnifying glass and probing the head wound with tweezers when we left.

Back at the office, Stark and I filled Dunn in on the coroner's initial findings. I tried to convince him that we should be picking up Jergens.

"Why Jergens?" he asked.

"Come on, Chief. It's Jergens's M.O. He sets fires. I think

he set Billings's boat on fire after crushing his skull. I'm betting he was responsible for the explosion on Elyse's boat as well."

"Maybe, Hannah, but we don't have enough to hold him. Right now, we don't have a shred of evidence against him in either murder. And what possible relationship could he have with Billings? We need more. You two go talk to the wife. She's already been told about her husband's death."

Eleanor Billings lived over at East End on the second floor of a whitewashed house. The yard was trimmed and raked; heliconia, hibiscus, bougainvillea, and oleander flowered under a canopy of palm trees. An emaciated island dog lay in the shade, oblivious to our approach.

Stark knocked at the door and we stood waiting. It was a long time before an old woman with white hair and a housedress that hung from her huge frame answered the door. She didn't exactly welcome us to step inside.

"Whatcha be wantin'?" she asked, her face set in a frown.

"I'm Detective Stark, this is Detective Sampson. Is this the home of Eleanor Billings?" he asked.

"That's right, but she don't need no visitors right now," she said, moving to close the door.

"Who is it, Mama?" a voice called from the back.

"Coupla detectives, honey. They got no call to disturb you now."

"It's okay, Mama." A younger, slimmer version appeared behind the big woman. "Come in," she said.

The apartment was small and neat but overflowing: a living room couch, a couple of overstuffed chairs, a threadbare rug, vases filled with flowers from the garden and hundreds of china figurines most of kittens and angels. One of them looked just like the fairy I'd been convinced I saw drifting in the *Lila B.* Kind of made me wonder.

The old woman headed to the kitchen and started putting dishes in the sink, making as much noise as possible.

"I guess you be here about Teddy." Eleanor cast a hopeless glance toward the kitchen. "Please sit down." She'd obviously been crying. Her eyes were red, and she held a balled-up mass of tissues in her fist.

Stark took a seat on the couch while I perched on the arm of one of the chairs, hoping to avoid contact with any of the fragile glass creatures.

"We're sorry to bother you at a time like this," I said. "But we would like to find out what happened to your husband."

"I be wantin' to know da same thing."

"What has Teddy been doing since you left Flower?" Stark asked.

"We got an old fishing boat, been sitting in storage for ten years. 'Bout the only thing Teddy's dad left him, named after Teddy's mama. Teddy was fixing it up. Had an idea about takin' tourists out to do some sportfishing. Teddy thought he could be makin' a good business. Had dreams 'bout what that 'ole boat would look like when he finished. 'Course, he was putting all dat modern equipment on her. Went down every day to work on it. His brothers be loanin' him some money and we be havin' a little saved."

"Do you know what he was doing up at the north end of Virgin Gorda?" Stark asked.

"Teddy been tryin' to make a little extra money doin' some fishing. Had a few fish traps down. Maybe he don put some up dat way. Sometimes he be out testin' the boat engine, that kind of thing. He could get caught up in dat boat and spend all day out der but he always be home by nine. I knew something be wrong when he be gone all night. I was 'bout to call da police when one came knockin' on my door dis mornin'." Her face contorted, her eyes teared as she recalled the moment that she had heard her husband was dead. She covered her face with the palms of her hands.

"Was there anything of value on the boat?" I asked when she regained her composure.

"Jus dat new equipment. Like I said, boat was old. Teddy rebuilt the engine, put in a GPS, bought a new radio, dat kinda thing. He was doing a lot of woodworking. Had da in-side pretty tore up."

"All the equipment was intact when I went into it," I said, immediately realizing my mistake.

"You be on dat boat? You be the one who found Teddy? Was he hurt bad?"

"I don't think he suffered," I lied. From what we'd seen at the coroner's, Teddy had suffered plenty.

"I hate to have to ask you this," I said, "but was Teddy in-volved in anything illegal?"

"No way," she said, anger replacing the sadness for an in-stant.

"Anything you tell us now can't hurt Teddy," Stark said. "But it could help us find out who killed him. Maybe he was trying to keep food on the table and got involved with the wrong people. You couldn't blame him, out of work and scraping by." Stark was trying to give her an opening to talk.

"I said no."

I wondered whether she was covering for her husband or simply clueless. Instincts told me neither.

"Do you think he went out there to meet someone?"

"I just can't imagine who dat would be. He never tole me about meetin' nobody."

"What kind of work did Teddy do for Freeman?" Stark said.

"Me and Teddy both worked out on Flower Island. We lived in da little cottage behind da big mansion out there. Tended to the house and da land. Teddy worked real hard on dat place, nailing and pounding. He be real handy with a hammer. He don keep things in perfect shape. Took a lot of hard work. Da house be real old. I kept up da inside, polish-ing and cleaning, and also tended da gardens. Freemans, dey be staying dar 'bout two times a month—weekends mostly. Less since he be busy with dat election."

"Why did Freeman fire Teddy?"

I remembered how Billings had lashed out at Freeman at the fund-raiser yesterday.

"Accused Teddy of stealing. We be workin' for da man for two years. Never no problem. Den that. Teddy never stole nothin' from nobody. He was real angry 'bout it."

"Did your husband know Fred Jergens or a couple named Cooper who own the *Libation*?" I asked.

"I not be knowin' dos names at all. Teddy never mentioned none of dos folks."

"Maybe Teddy was working with them, owed them money, didn't want you to know about it," I suggested.

"I just don know. Teddy might have tried to keep something like dat from me," she admitted. "He be real proud and real worried about money. Ever since he lost the job on Flower, he not be himself."

"One other thing, Mrs. Billings," I said. "Did Teddy smoke?"

"No, never did," she said, surprised by the question.

"Anybody helping him work on the boat smoke?"

"No. Teddy didn't want nobody else on da boat. He was real particular about dat boat and how things were done."

"We'll let you be, Mrs. Billings," Stark said, lifting his huge frame off the sofa.

"What do you think?" I asked when we got out to the car.

"Man, I don't know," he said, rubbing a hand over his skull.

"I think that Billings found out the same thing that Elyse did," I insisted. I knew he'd think I was stretching it. He did.

"It all sounds pretty sketchy."

"You got any better hypothesis?" I snapped. I was tired, short-tempered, and frustrated.

"No, but that doesn't mean I'm going to invent one."

"Maybe it's all connected to the robberies," I said, trying to reason with him.

"If Jergens is involved in those thefts, we'll find out about it," Stark said. "But stealing from boaters doesn't make him guilty of killing Elyse or Billings."

Chapter 28

Mary had left a message on my office phone, insisting I meet her for dinner at the Callilou.

"Hannah, I know you're suffering. So am I," she'd said. "It will help us both to talk." Nothing like having a psychiatrist as a friend. She hadn't given me an option, simply told me to be there.

By the time I arrived, Mary had already gotten a table.

"Hannah, I'm glad you made it," she said, standing and giving me a hug. I could see the strain in her face, and the sorrow.

I hadn't realized how good it would be to see her. She was the strongest connection I had to Elyse.

"Let's order drinks," she said. "I think we both could use one."

About then Alex Reidman walked up to the table with a bottle of wine.

"My compliments," he said. "This is the best merlot in the house, and my favorite."

I recognized the bottle. It had the same label as the one I'd found when I dived the *Caribbe*. I mentioned it to Reidman.

"Yes," he said. "Elyse and I had dinner on the *Caribbe* last week, must have been Wednesday. I brought the wine. We had a wonderful evening. I still can't believe we won't have another."

Why the hell did his attitude piss me off? I guess it was because I knew that Elyse had not been close to Reidman.

He opened the wine, smelled the cork, and poured a tiny bit into a glass he'd brought with him, swirled it, drank, and smiled approvingly. Obviously, he thought he was the only one capable of the evaluation.

"I think you will like this," he said, filling our glasses.

"Thank you, Alex," Mary said, taking a sip of wine. "It's excellent." I simply nodded.

"Enjoy," he said, placing the bottle on the table and then heading to the kitchen.

"I don't like that man, Mary."

"I know. But let's not worry about him. How are you doing?"

I gave her the short version of my dive, avoiding the gory details, like the fact I'd nearly drowned. Then we talked for a long time, mostly about all the good times we'd had with Elyse.

She filled me in on Jilli as well. The girl had taken Elyse's death hard, but thankfully Jilli's mother had stepped up. Jilli told her parents about the abuse at school.

Her father was furious. Rita was the rational one and made arrangements to keep Jilli in school and at home.

"I know Jilli wants to see you," Mary said.

"I'll see her, but I need to wait till I know I won't break down in front of her."

"It would be okay if you did," Mary said.

"Not for me," I whispered.

About then Reidman joined us with snifters of brandy to accompany our coffee. Last thing I wanted was brandy after consuming a bottle of it on the *Sea Bird* two nights ago.

"Heard you had some difficult diving today," he said.

"I'm always amazed at the speed of news on this island," I said. "How did you hear about the dive, Alex?"

"Ran into Edmund Carr in town. He told me you recovered Billings. Said you'd been in the wreck bagging a dead turtle when the boat let loose."

"A turtle? For goodness sakes, Hannah, why would you do that?" Mary asked.

"Seemed important at the time." I was amazed that the turtle had been the topic of conversation between Carr and Reidman.

"Well, thank God you got out," Mary said. I knew what she was thinking—two friends lost in a matter of days.

Mary and I said goodbye in the parking lot. I unlocked the car and headed home. The night was dark, the sky dotted with thousands of stars. It was past nine and the road was deserted. A lizard absorbing the remaining warmth of the concrete scurried off into the weeds as I approached, and insects swirled in my headlights. As I turned into Pickering's Landing a car came out of nowhere and sped past, the brake lights glowing once before it took the next bend and disappeared.

Once I stepped aboard the *Sea Bird* exhaustion took over. I fell into bed and into a deep dreamless sleep. Sometime in the middle of the night I was awakened by the sound of Sadie growling. Then she raced up the steps. When I got out on deck, she was on the dock, fur ruffled, barking at something onshore.

"What is it, Sadie?" She turned and whined at me, then directed her attention back to shore.

I went below, threw on my sweats and running shoes, grabbed a flashlight and the .38 and headed down the dock with Sadie by my side. I couldn't see or hear anything, but Sadie seemed determined that something was there and I didn't think it was just a mongoose out hunting in the bush. When we got to the marina parking lot, she stopped and bared her teeth. I flipped off the light. I didn't feel like turning into a target.

"It's okay, girl," I whispered. I walked slowly into the lot scanning the deep shadows, trying to see anything at all. I crept to the front of Calvin's old pickup, took a quick look underneath and then stepped around in a crouch, gun raised.

Nothing. Tilda's car was parked alongside. I was moving along the passenger side when I heard a sound, a footstep in gravel. About that time the lights came on in the marina.

"What's going on?" Calvin hollered from the doorway.

A shape materialized from the passenger side of the Rambler and took off into the trees. I went after it, racing through the bougainvillea and frangipani in the Pickerings' yard and out to the highway. By the time I got there, I heard a car around the bend laying rubber.

Calvin came up behind me breathless, brandishing a wrench.

"I heard Sadie barking. Figured there was trouble," he said. "Did you see who it was?"

"No, just a black shape."

Tilda and the girls were standing in the doorway when we got back. Rebecca had a tight grip on Sadie. I wasn't sure who was comforting whom.

Calvin grabbed another flashlight and we took a look around. The Rambler was the only victim. The passenger door was wide open. No problem getting into it with only a damned bungee cord holding it closed. God knows what anyone would want. The only thing inside were still in a heap in the backseat, the black cocktail dress, and red heels I'd worn to distract the guy at the gravel pit. The intruder clearly had no sense of fashion. I opened the glove compartment. Everything was intact.

"This be a mess." Calvin had made his way around to the back of the car.

I slid out of the front seat and went to see what Calvin was looking at.

"Looks like he was trying to get into the trunk." Calvin shone the light on the lock, now twisted and misshapen.

I put my key into the lock, held my mouth just right, and turned. The trunk popped open and we were assaulted with the unmistakable odor of sea life. The turtle still lay on the tarp in a melting pile of ice and dirty salt water. The only

other object in the trunk was the evidence kit that I'd shoved
to the back when I'd loaded the turtle.

"Not much in here dat anyone woulda wanted," Calvin
said, referring to the turtle. "My truck be filled with tools. If
Sadie hadn't started barking, da guy probably woulda broken into it and gotten something of value."

"Maybe, but maybe he was after the turtle."

"How would anyone know it was in dar?"

"I wasn't making it a secret. Everyone down at the docks
this morning saw O'Brien and the crazy American woman
loading the turtle corpse into the trunk."

"Well, I guess that tortoiseshell would be worth some
money."

We filled a couple of buckets with ice from the marina
machine, dumped it over the turtle, and slammed the trunk.

"Don't think dat fella be back, but I be leaving da outside
light on da resta da night just in case."

"Thanks, Calvin."

Sadie and I walked down to the *Sea Bird* and went back
to bed. My dreams were filled with horror—vivid images of
Elyse floating in the sea surrounded by hundreds of dead
turtles and empty turtle shells.

Chapter 29

❧

The next morning I sat on the deck of the *Sea Bird*, sipping coffee and shaking off the nightmares. The sun was just hitting the tops of the palms on the western side of the cove, tinging the fronds with a pinkish hue. Sadie and Rebecca were romping on the beach, the dog's yips and the child's laughter breaking the silent morning. Nomad lay beside me, purring as I stroked her head.

The caffeine was beginning its work, helping brain cells to fire. I hadn't had any real sleep in the past week, and the intensity and physical exertion of yesterday's dive had sapped my energy. My chest felt tight from all the compressed air I'd breathed and my calves were rebelling after the intense finning I'd done inside the boat as it plunged into the abyss.

When the sun blasted over the horizon and into my eyes, I hobbled to my feet, every muscle protesting. Nomad escaped to the shade by the mast and curled up. I knew that when I came home, she'd still be up there, on the other side, following the shade around the mast. Nomad rarely left the boat unless it was to follow me out to the sandy shore. As long as she was on the *Sea Bird*, she felt secure. She considered the boat hers. I was merely a guest.

I left Sadie playing in the water with Rebecca and drove into town. Tom and Liam were waiting for me in the marina parking lot.

"What happened to the trunk?" Liam asked as he watched me wiggling the key in the lock and popping open the lid.

I told them about the intruder while I struggled to get the turtle out and into the cart that they'd brought up from the dock.

"Maybe they thought you had something valuable in the trunk, like a shotgun or pistols. Lots of people know the Rambler belongs to a police officer," Tom said, trying to come up with a reason why someone would want to get into my car.

"I think the guy was after the turtle. The question is, why? Maybe you two can figure out what killed it."

We wheeled the turtle out to Tom and Liam's boat and they went to work examining it and taking measurements.

"She's an adult female, thirty-five inches long," Liam said, retracting the tape measure. We hoisted the turtle onto their scale and Tom recorded the figure on his data sheet—eighty-six pounds.

They removed a very old tag that they found still attached to the scutes. Tom cut it off.

"I'm pretty sure this turtle was tagged when they did the last survey. I can still make out the numbers. Liam, where's that report?"

Liam went below and came back up with a bound manuscript, dog-eared and torn. He opened it to the section on coding and ran his finger down a row of numbers.

"Yeah, this turtle was tagged right here in the BVI. Probably been returning to nest for the last fifteen years. What a shame. She should have had another ten years at least. Hawksbills can live fifty years or more. Unfortunately, many don't make it that long these days."

They found no apparent wounds, but identified a couple of old injuries. Tom outlined the scars, one across the shell—a jagged line that looked like it had cut all the way through to the flesh.

"Probably a propeller," Liam said. "This old girl was

lucky to survive that. The scar in the flipper is most likely from a shark."

They collected their instruments from the hold, placing them in a row on the deck—a scalpel, hemostats, forceps—then began their dissection. Thirty minutes later, they knew why the turtle had died: It had bled to death, internal hemorrhage.

Neither of them had seen anything like it.

"Why would Billings have this turtle on his boat?" Tom asked, baffled.

"Maybe he saw it washed up onshore and figured it was worth collecting. He'd know the shell was worth some money. You said the boat sank up near the north end of Virgin Gorda?" Liam said.

"That's right. Any guesses about why this turtle bled to death?" I asked them.

"Sure looks like it got into something," Tom said. "The question is, what, and where did it come from? These turtles will eat a wide variety of debris—plastic and Styrofoam pieces, tar balls, plastic pellets. These substances interfere with metabolism but I've never seen this kind of excessive internal hemorrhage. I suppose it's possible that it ate something with an accumulation of toxins in it. But I can't imagine what."

"This could be a real problem," Liam said. "Where there is one poisoned turtle, there are likely to be more. Damn, these sea turtles are being hit from every direction. Sometimes I wonder if there is any chance of saving them."

"Come on, Liam. Let's not give up on them now. Let's just figure out what happened here," Tom said.

We agreed that Deb LaPlante should examine the turtle. She was an expert in the effects of toxins.

I used the phone up at the marina. LaPlante picked up right away.

"I was just on my way to a meeting with the staff, but I'd really like to take a look at it," she said. "It could be any number of things, but I can tell a lot by examining it. Look,

I'll be back at my lab by two. Can you bring the turtle up then?"

I told her we'd be there.

With time to kill, I wanted to check out the area where the *Lila B* had gone down. While I maneuvered their boat out of the harbor, Tom and Liam wrapped the turtle with stuff that looked a lot like shrink-wrap, then covered it with more ice and a tarp. They'd insisted on coming along to talk to LaPlante about the turtle.

A half hour later, I cut the engine and let the boat drift over the spot where the *Lila B* lay. It was just around the point at the far end of Virgin Gorda.

I could see the white house from which the witnesses had seen the boat on fire. It was nestled in green shrubs and blossoms. The people on that veranda would have had a ringside view. Farther around the point was Flower Island, Freeman's little paradise, then another bay and the inlet through Eustatia Sound and into North Sound.

I headed over to the white house and we tied the boat up at the dock. A long set of wooden steps led to the house. Tom and Liam stayed behind, poking around onshore while I started up the steps to see if anyone was home. When I got to the top, the entire territory spread out in the distance— Tortola, St. John, and St. Thomas a gray shape in the distance.

Down on the shore, I could see Tom peering under a rock, nudging something with a stick. Liam had waded into the water and was investigating the underside of the dock. Fascinating stuff for these two. I'm sure they'd be content to spend an entire day studying that little part of the world. Hell, maybe they'd find something that would explain what that turtle had gotten into.

At the house, a man in his early thirties, barefoot and shirtless, answered the door. I told him I was with the Tortola Police Department and followed him to the veranda, where the rest of the houseguests were lounging in various stages of dress. Some had turned a brilliant red and had re-treated to the shade of the awning.

The man who had answered the door explained that the group was composed of four couples escaping children, work, and the cold for a while. They'd been on the island a week now.

"I know that you've already spoken with one of my colleagues, but I'd like to go over it with you again just to make sure."

"Well, like we told the police officer, we were out here late, listening to music, dancing. We'd all had plenty to drink. Julie's the one that saw the spark." By now those who had been sprawled in the sun had gathered under the awning to listen in.

"At first, I wasn't sure what it was," Julie chimed in. "There was another boat pulled alongside. Then the spark turned to a flame. We were all thinking the other boat was there to help. But then it sped away, leaving the boat to burn."

By the time the group figured out who to call, the boat was sinking. No one had gotten a good look at the other boat. All they knew was that it was low in the water and fast. They all agreed there were two people, the driver and an-other, both big enough to be men.

"Did you see anyone on the boat that sank?" I asked.

"Never saw anyone on it at all. In fact, we thought maybe once the fire started, the guy was rescued by the one in the other boat. 'Course, we heard different later. The divers pulled up a body. Nasty job," he said, shaking his head.

"Yeah." I didn't admit to being the one who'd had to do it. "Had you seen the boat around before?"

"As a matter of fact, I'd seen it a couple of times this past week when I was out walking," the woman named Julie said. I had the feeling that Julie was the one most aware of her surroundings. She paid attention.

"Really? When?"

"Three or four times since we've been here. I think he came up the channel from Tortola."

Seemingly, Billings had been in the area all week with the *Lila B.*

"Did you notice where he went or what he was doing?" I asked.

"Well, every time I saw him he was kind of drifting in the inlet there. I thought he was probably fishing. There are those buoys bobbing out there that mark the fish traps."

I knew what she meant. The local fisherman tied anything that would float, mostly empty plastic bottles, to the lines that went to the bottom where they'd place their traps.

"Did you ever see him pulling the traps up?"

"No, I never did. A couple of times, I was out on the point with my binoculars. I'd see him sitting on the deck of his boat with a pair of binoculars of his own directed at the shore."

"Do you remember seeing him Friday afternoon before the boat caught fire?" I asked.

"Yes. I was taking a walk around the point. I saw him anchored just off the entrance to the bay. I didn't see anyone on board. But on my way back, I saw a man rowing across in a little dinghy and climbing onto the boat."

"What did he look like?"

She described Billings perfectly, all the way down to the yellow bandana he'd had tied around his neck.

"Could you tell where he was coming from?"

"Sure, I saw the dinghy pulled up on the beach over there in the trees," she said, pointing at Flower Island. "He was coming from there."

When I got back to the shore, Liam and Tom were sitting on the beach under a tree. I filled them in about what I'd learned. Then I untied the line from the cleat and Tom turned the boat toward Flower. They'd been dying to get a closer look at the island and this gave them just the excuse they needed. Evidently Freeman had continued to refuse them access. He did not want people tramping onshore or snorkeling in the shallows and disturbing the habitat.

We anchored in a sandy area in about ten feet of water next to a fifty-foot wooden sailboat that had to be Freeman's. There were a couple of other moorings, one with a dinghy tied to it and the other empty. These waters were too shallow to bring anything but a little boat in close to shore. There was one other boat tied to the dock, which meant someone else was probably on the island.

Flower was a flat piece of land, rising only a matter of feet toward the center. The white sandy beach stretched for at least a half mile in each direction and was lined with coconut palms. If this had been St. Thomas or Miami Beach, the island would already boast a luxury resort with swimming pool, beach umbrellas and lounge chairs littering the sand. I had to give Freeman credit for protecting this unspoiled piece of paradise. It had to be worth a fortune.

"Can't believe there aren't any turtles nesting here," Tom said. "It's a perfect place for hawksbills and greens. They like to nest in the sand under bushes like those." He pointed to the low shrubs that skirted the edge of the trees. "A shame. Fifty years ago this island would have been a haven for hatchlings."

We rowed their little dinghy to shore and tied it to the dock. Before we could even step foot in the sand, a man came up the beach, a nightstick hanging from his belt.

"Nobody be allowed on dis here island," he said, resting his hand on his stick. "This be private property."

"Detective Sampson," I said. "I'd like to speak with the Freemans." The guard hesitated, unsure about what to do. He was green, had no skill in terms of menace.

"You been working here long?" I asked.

"Less'n a week. Dey be worried about folks comin' here when dey be away, breaking in. Some trouble with da ole caretaker, I guess."

"Are the Freemans here?"

"Just da missus. Follow me, but you got to stay on da trail."

The house was back in the trees—a stunning place, some sort of mixture of Southern landowner and Caribbean, huge columns on the front. In the back I could see a couple of small wooden structures where the house servants would have lived.

There was a woman kneeling in the garden digging in the dirt. She wore a pair of loose-fitting pants and a wide-brimmed straw hat. Her bare feet were white on the soles blending to dark brown around the edges. She startled when she heard our approach, and stood.

It was Sylvia Freeman. I'd never seen her in anything less formal than a suit. She looked a lot more at home in her current garb, relaxed and happy, until she saw us. Then her whole body tensed, ready for defense.

"What are you doing here?" she asked. "This is private property." I could tell she was embarrassed to have been caught digging through the dirt in old pants rolled at the ankles.

"Dat what I be tellin' dem," the guard said. "But dis lady say she be police."

"We're sorry to invade, Sylvia."

"Neville isn't here, he's down in Road Town."

"Can we talk with you? We just came from that white rental on the point and one of the people there said she saw Teddy Billings over here on Friday."

"You might as well come in out of the heat." She stood and brushed sand off her pants, then led the way up the front stairs and opened the door. Inside was amazingly cool. We settled in a glass-enclosed porch at the back of the house, filled with rattan furniture and plants. A ceiling fan circled slowly above our heads.

A maid appeared from the back, carrying a tray with a pitcher and glasses. She placed it on a table and served.

"Thank you, Sara." Sylvia smiled at the maid.

"This is a stunning place," Tom said. "It must be well over a hundred years old."

"Yes, my great-great-grandfather helped build it," she said, "for his white master. I love it here. I try to come out whenever I can. Unfortunately, it is not often enough since Neville's gotten so involved back in Road Town. Now with the campaign . . ." She trailed off, a look of regret crossing her face.

"Were you here Friday when Billings came ashore?" I asked.

"Actually, when we got here, we saw his dinghy over on the far end of the beach. Neville was really angry. Told me to go in the house and went stomping down the beach looking for him. When he fired Teddy, he told him he never wanted to see him on Flower again."

"What was the problem?"

"Neville said he caught Teddy stealing."

"What did he steal?"

"Well, we gave Teddy a free rein at the building supply outfits in Road Town. He would just sign for materials. Neville discovered that Teddy was charging material for his own use and even selling some of the goods to friends. I couldn't believe Teddy would do such a thing. I was sorry to see them go. Eleanor and I were friends."

"Do you know why Teddy was here the other day?"

"Neville said he'd come to pick up an old dinghy motor that he'd left in the shed. He said he let Teddy get it and told him not to come back again. I could hear them arguing all the way up here. Neville was accusing Teddy of putting his nose in things that didn't concern him."

"What things?" I asked.

"I don't know. When Neville came back to the house he said that Teddy was drunk. Neville was worried about Teddy coming to the island when we were gone."

"You know Teddy's boat went down out past the point Friday night?"

"Yes, I can't believe it. I don't know how Eleanor will survive." She seemed genuinely concerned.

"What do you think he was doing out there?"

"I don't know. And that boat on fire. Horrible. Neville says he probably left a kerosene light burning and then passed out on the boat. Funny, I never knew Teddy to drink much."

I was surprised that she didn't know he'd been murdered. When I told her, she was confused, then horrified.

"Why would anyone kill Teddy?" she asked.

About then Neville walked in.

"Ms. Sampson, Tom, Liam! What are you folks doing here?" He held out his hand and smiled, but I could see he wasn't pleased to have visitors.

I told him we were just doing some checking on Billings.

"Tom and Liam on the police force now?" he asked, sarcasm filling his voice.

I ignored it. "Can you tell me why Billings came back out here after you fired him?" I asked.

"He said he came to get a motor he'd left, but I'm sure he hoped to make away with other valuables too. The shed is full of expensive tools. I let him get the old motor, and told him I didn't want to see him out here again."

"Sylvia said you accused him of snooping," I said.

"My wife was hearing things," he said, giving Sylvia an angry look. "Now, if there's anything more that you need, you can phone my secretary for an appointment at my office."

Without another word, he walked us out the door and all the way back down to our boat. The guard was leaning against a nearby palm. Freeman gave him a warning glare and the guy straightened.

"I'm sorry if I seem rude," he said, finally, "but this island is a place to escape. You understand. With all the campaigning, Sylvia and I need a place to get away to now and then."

Chapter 30

❧

We found Deborah LaPlante in her makeshift lab, packing up boxes. Her assistant was nearby analyzing data on the computer.

"Looks like you're getting ready to leave," Tom said.

"Yes, the people who will take over the monitoring of the project and maintain the bait stations are up to speed. I'll be going at the end of the week. I have another project on an island down near Costa Rica."

"You've done a real service here," Liam said. "It would have been a shame if the rats had decimated every species on the island."

"Thanks, Liam," LaPlante said. "But it was the islanders who made it happen, and they'll keep things on track."

"Let's see this turtle you called me about," LaPlante said.

Tom and Liam hefted it up to LaPlante's exam table and pulled off the plastic. George, her assistant immediately lost interest in his numbers and came over to help.

He and LaPlante went straight to work, pulling back the incision to expose the body cavity. She spent several minutes probing one organ after the other.

"The internal hemorrhaging is very apparent," she said.

"Ya mon, it looks just like the inside of one of our rats," George agreed.

"It is certainly consistent with poisoning. There's blood

pooled in the abdominal cavity and the muscles have a gray tinge due to lack of blood."

"Can you tell what kind of poison it might be?" I asked.

"It has to be an anticoagulant. The brodifacoum that we've been using in the rat eradication would certainly be a possibility. But other wildlife are usually affected only if they prey on a rodent that has eaten the poison. Accidental poisoning has occurred in areas where the poison has been used irresponsibly for rodent control in agriculture and industry. It has caused death in raptor species—hawks, owls, and eagles.

"Currently, its use is recommended for only those who are licensed. As I explained when we met last, we've immediately removed any rats that died aboveground to ensure that predators cannot get to the dead animal. But even if they did, birds are the ones that are usually affected. Certainly not sea life."

"What if the poison got into the water?" I asked.

"Well, it is highly toxic to aquatic organisms, but it has an extremely low solubility. Even if some had run into the sea, it would not create a hazard."

"How would this turtle have ingested it then?" Tom asked.

"I just can't imagine. I don't see how the poison that we've been using here could threaten any sea life at all. In fact, I'd say it was impossible," she said.

"What about from another source?" Tom asked.

"I don't know of anyone else using the poison in the islands and I think I would have heard about it. As I said, there are controls."

"What does the poison look like?" I asked.

"Come on into the back. I'll show you." We followed her to a small storage room that was stacked with boxes marked with a skull and crossbones. She opened one of the boxes and pulled out a sealed plastic bag full of pellets. It looked like a bag of dried cat food with a waxy covering.

"This is how we get it. The pellets contain a minute percentage of brodifacoum. As I said, this poison is very effective in small doses."

"Do you keep records of the shipments and usage?" I asked. I was sure that these pellets were the same as the ones I'd found in Elyse's office. They'd been soggy and mixed in with the spilled chemicals on the floor.

"Sure, it's a fairly simple procedure," she said, pulling a clipboard off a nail. "Every time poison is taken to the site, it's recorded on this sheet—the date, amount, and initials. Of course all the poison is targeted for the project, so it's fairly straightforward.

"No lock on the storage room door or controls in terms of access?"

"Not really. The only people who use the lab are those working on the project. Last one out locks everything up."

"Have you ever noticed any sign of forced entry or something out of place?"

"Never," she said, then hesitated.

"Wait a minute." LaPlante stood there gazing at the boxes then started shoving several aside and checking behind others. "That can't be right," she said, picking up the clipboard and running her fingers down the page. "This isn't adding up."

"George," she called to her assistant, who sauntered in with coffee cup in hand.

"Has any poison gone out to the site without being recorded?" she asked.

"No way. We filled the stations last week. Should all be recorded there. We won't be doing any filling for another couple of weeks. What's the problem?"

"The tally doesn't match." She showed him the clipboard.

"What do you mean?" he asked, studying it. "Yeah, that's my entry. The last shipment came in a month ago. I went through and checked the boxes then. Everything was accounted for."

"There are four boxes missing, George. That's a lot of

poison. Check with Marty and Bill, would you? Maybe they took them out to the site and forgot to record them."

"Will do."

"I'm sure this is a simple clerical error," she said.

"Did Elyse have access to the poison when she worked on the project?" I asked.

"Yes, but surely you don't think Elyse would have taken any out of the lab?"

"No, I don't. But I did find a few of these pellets in her office. I wonder if that's what she wanted to show you."

"That's odd. Why would she have any of it? And why would she want me to see them? She'd have known what they were."

"Maybe she found them somewhere, maybe the same place this turtle got into them, and wanted to talk with you about it. I'd like to take a few of these pellets with me if that's okay and compare them to the ones I found in Elyse's office."

LaPlante scooped some into a plastic bag and sealed the top. "Just don't mix these in with your cereal by mistake," she said.

"Thanks." I took the Baggie and stuffed it in my pocket. "Would you let me know what you find out about those missing boxes?" I asked.

We left the turtle with LaPlante. She would send tissue samples over to a lab in St. Thomas to confirm the presence of the poison. Those results could take weeks.

I left Liam and Tom at the dock and headed over to the hospital. I'd finally worked up enough gumption to go see Jillian. I knew I couldn't ignore the kid. Damned if on the way, the Rambler didn't begin to sound like a bunch of maracas were shaking under the hood. By the time I limped it into the shop, the noise emanating from the engine was more like a steel band. I left it there, wondering if it was long for this world. It had been through a rough few days. The mechanic was upbeat about it though.

"Hey, no problem. I be havin' her running like a top in no time." But this was the same guy who had worked on the car earlier in the week. He'd called it good after he'd pulled the grill out, done some minimal engine work, and looped a bungee cord through the open driver's window and around the back window to hold the door closed. I told him to fix everything—the engine, the body damage—whatever it took, I'd pay. It was a stupid expense for the old car, but I wasn't about to let it go to the junkyard. I left it sitting there in the lot, looking forlorn, the grill in a lopsided grin, and walked the remaining three blocks to the hospital.

Jilli and Rita were in the lounge, heads together, talking, when I got to the unit. I thought about turning right around and heading out the way I came. I didn't want to interrupt, I rationalized. About then Jilli saw me and a tear trickled down her cheek. There was no turning back now. I went over and sat beside her. Rita gave me a quick smile, said she'd let us talk alone, hugged Jilli, and left.

"I'm so sorry about Elyse," Jilli cried, throwing her arms around me.

"I know," I said, fighting back the tears that were building. I did not want to break down. I'd had enough of it—the damned tightening in my throat, the hollowness in my chest. No stopping it though. The two of us sat with our arms around each other in complete meltdown until Jilli lifted her head.

"Are you going to be okay?" I asked her.

"Yeah. How about you Hannah?"

"I'll get through it," I said. We talked a while about her staying home and getting counseling.

In the lobby on my way out, I found Rita waiting for me.

"You know, Ms. Sampson, I owe you my apology—and my thanks," she said. "I know you were the one who asked Mary to check on Jilli that day after you visited. At the time, I was upset about your interference, and Mary's. But the two of you and Elyse saved her. I wish I could thank Elyse. I can't believe I was so blind. I almost lost my daughter."

Chapter 31

❧

At seven-thirty the next morning Stark and I were on our way into the office. He'd come by to pick me up at Pickering's Landing since I was again without a car.

"Did you get the coroner's report on Billings?" I asked him. He was holding a jelly donut with one hand and steering his car with the other.

"Yeah," he said, munching. "He died from the head wound. No surprises there."

"What about the wrench, the other items we brought up from the scene?" I sipped the coffee that Stark had picked up for me.

"Like the coroner said. None of them fit the pattern of the wound. We got partials on the wrench but they were Billings's. Coroner is still saying crowbar."

"What about drugs or alcohol?"

"Neither turned up," Stark said as he put the rest of the donut in his mouth.

"No alcohol?"

"Nope," he mumbled through crumbs.

"Freeman told his wife that Billings was drunk the afternoon when he'd been out on Flower."

"Couldn't have been. It would have shown up in the blood test."

"Yeah." I wondered why Freeman would lie about it.

"Lab could have mixed up the results. It's been known to

happen. I'll check it out. That white stuff you collected was just what you thought—flour and sugar. Cigarette was American, Marlboro. Lab sent it for DNA, but you know how that will go. Could be weeks before results come back."

"Anything on the charring?"

"Yeah, big surprise—gasoline with a little oil mixed in. Whoever did it probably just dumped a tank of gas from their dinghy engine down into the hull.

"By the way, last night we arrested Jergens and the Coopers, that couple that owns the *Libation*."

"Jeez, Stark. Glad you got around to mentioning it. What happened?"

"Mahler and Snyder followed them to BVI Sail, heard a lot of shouting and scuffling in the office, and busted in. Mr. Cooper was lying on the floor and his wife was on Jergens, scratching the hell out of him. Mahler pulled her off. Damned if Jergens's desk wasn't strewn with a bunch of stolen goods—several expensive watches, credit cards, a diamond bracelet, rings, earrings."

"Jergens say anything about Billings or Elyse?"

"No, but the Coopers say he was with them the night Billings's boat went down."

"You believe them?"

"Can't see why they'd lie about it. Doesn't seem to be much love lost between them and Jergens."

"So where does that leave us?"

"Suppose Jergens could have hired someone else to do his dirty work." Stark was licking jelly off his fingers.

"I don't know. I can't imagine Jergens wanting to miss that kind of fun. It's what gets him off."

"Well, I don't think he was the one on Billings's boat."

I was having a hard time adjusting to the fact. Though I hadn't put together the how or why, I'd been sure Jergens was responsible for the attempt on Elyse and for Billings's death.

"One other thing," Stark said. "I got the results of those

prints that you lifted at Elyse's office. Folder's there in the backseat."

"Did you look at it?" I reached behind me and grabbed a manila folder.

"Yeah. No matches to any prints in the database," Stark said. He honked at the car in front of us then swerved around it, waving at the guy.

I opened the file and examined the two thin sheets of paper. It was just as he said, no matches, which meant no one who had left a print had ever been caught in a crime. There was one thing though. The print that Dickson had lifted off the refrigerator matched the prints on the wine bottle that I'd recovered from the *Caribbe*. I was pretty sure that they had to be Reidman's. He'd told me he'd brought the bottle of wine to the *Caribbe*.

Of course, the fact that Reidman's prints would be in Elyse's office was not really surprising. He'd been in there the day I'd gone to check it out and probably often enough before to see Elyse. But on the handle of her specimen fridge? Why would he ever have a reason to open it? I planned to ask him.

At the office Stark and I began by talking with the couple from the *Libation*. They were young, scared, and willing to spill it all. We separated them. I took Lynn; he interrogated Geoff. They told identical stories. They'd come to the islands two years ago from Britain and never wanted to leave the BVI. They had invested all their savings in buying the *Libation* and had been about to lose it all. They'd been sure they could make the business work, given a little time. They started stealing from yachts a few months back, taking cash and anything they could sell easily. They said it was only until they could get their feet under them and make a go of the business.

Unfortunately, Jergens had found out what they were doing when one of his charterers told him that he'd seen the Coopers boarding a BVI Sail boat. Jergens made an excuse, told the guy the *Libation* often made deliveries in the evenings and that it wasn't a problem. Then he'd gone to the Coopers and said he wanted in and threatened to go to the police if they didn't comply. He'd cased his own charterers and told the Coopers which boats to go after.

Neither one of them admitted to knowing anything about Billings. They'd seen him out in his boat now and then, but never spoken with him. And they had no idea what we were talking about when we asked about Elyse. Or about dead turtles.

"Too bad," I said after Stark and I finished comparing notes. "They really got in over their heads. Stupid."

"Yeah, I don't think they're tied up in anything but theft though," Stark said.

"Dammit, everything leads to dead ends." I was frustrated. "Let's go see what Jergens has to say."

He was sitting in the interrogation room, with his arms crossed over his chest, barely containing his anger. His face was set in a stony gaze, eyes blazing.

"Got nothing to say to either one of you assholes. You can just take me back to my cell."

"Fine. Let him rot down there till he finds himself a lawyer stupid enough to represent him," I said to Stark, and opened the door.

"You think you can threaten me?" He was poised for an attack, then thought better of it. Nothing like having Stark leaning against a wall, flexing muscle.

"I wouldn't call it a threat," I said. I was stalling though, hoping he'd start talking.

"I didn't have anything to do with those thefts. That couple came to me trying to sell that stuff. I was about to call the police when those two cops busted into the office."

"That's not the story the Coopers are telling."

"It's my word against theirs."

"Not really. We got a warrant to search your property. Found a lot of stolen goods in that desk of yours and in the storage shed out back."

Jergens was trying to come up with a good reason that these things were on his property. I figured now was the time to really catch him off guard.

"Why did you kill Teddy Billings?" I asked.

"What the hell are you talking about?"

"Teddy find out you were stealing?" Stark asked.

"Damned if you're going to pin a murder on me!" Jergens stood suddenly and threw his chair at Stark. Stark ducked; the thing shattered against the wall. Before Jergens could get his hands on him, Stark had him pinned in the other chair and I'd cuffed him.

"What about Elyse Henry?" I insisted. It was my turn to be pissed.

"You two are crazy. Never heard of this Billings, though I'd have loved to have gotten my hands on Henry. I wouldn't have killed her though, if you know what I mean." He smirked and leaned back, tilting the chair onto its back legs.

The thought of him putting his hands on Elyse made me sick. I lost it. I kicked the chair hard and Jergens went crashing to the floor. I left him lying there and stomped out.

"Well, that was productive," Stark said as he stepped out behind me.

When we got back upstairs, Dunn waved us into his office. Mahler was there. He'd been following up on Jergens and the Coopers, beginning to put the pieces together to make the case against them.

"Jergens was over on St. Thomas trying to pawn some of that jewelry," Mahler said. "We should be able to nail him cold on these thefts."

"The thing is, he left Tortola on Saturday afternoon and wasn't back till midday Monday," Dunn said, turning to me. "Mahler talked to the pawnshop owner and the clerk at the hotel where Jergens stayed. That means he wasn't on the island the night Elyse's boat blew."

More dead ends. I told myself we weren't really starting from scratch, but it sure felt like it.

Chapter 32

❧

When in the dark, ask a reporter. I found Betty Welsh sitting on the edge of her editor's desk, lecturing him about the need to do a more complete coverage of the campaign.

When she saw me, she waved, turned to her boss, tossed him a look, and left him sitting there. Betty did what she wanted, boss or not. No one told her how to do her job. She got away with it because she was the best reporter in town.

I followed her down the hall to her office, which was decorated in muted grays and blues. I figured Betty designed it that way so that nothing competed with her outfits. Today she wore green stretch pants with a long tunic shirt in red paisley. Her earrings looked like clusters of red grapes. She reminded me a lot of a Christmas tree.

"I heard what happened, Hannah," Betty said, closing her office door. "I'm so sorry about Elyse. If there's anything I can do, please let me know."

"As a matter of fact, there is. I saw you talking with Teddy Billings outside the Callilou. I'm sure you heard he was killed. Did you know him?"

"Never saw him before that morning, but I wanted to know what his ranting at the fund-raiser was all about. It was obvious he had been on the verge of accusing Freeman of something."

"What did he tell you?" I asked. I knew if anyone could wring information out of a source, it was Betty.

"Not much. He said Freeman fired him because he wanted him off of Flower. He said something was going on out there that Freeman didn't want him or anyone else knowing about."

"I don't suppose he said what?"

"No. He wanted to make sure he was right first. He promised he'd get back to me about it," she shrugged, resigned. "Guess that's one story I won't be writing."

"You'll have a story," I told her. "When I figure out the ending."

Talk then turned to the election, and by the time I left Betty's office, I'd gotten an earful about dirty island politics. She'd gone on for a good half hour about the anonymous calls that the paper had received implicating Abernathy, the candidate running against Freeman, in everything from homosexual affairs to jaywalking. She'd been the one to check the stories out.

"Nothing to any of it. Abernathy's a good man. He doesn't stand a chance against Freeman though. He doesn't have the money to throw at this campaign that Freeman does. Don't know how Freeman pulls it off—sure he has money, but most of it is tied up. Must have a big piggy bank somewhere. 'Course, I'm checking it out. And if Billings knew something that got him killed and it's connected to Freeman . . . jeez."

Betty was putting a fresh coat of hot pink polish on her nails when I left. I stopped at Abe's Lumber Company and tracked down Abe in the back of the lumberyard. He was running a forklift filled with bundles of plywood. When he saw me, he turned off the engine and jumped down off the machine.

"No one but employees allowed back here," he said. "Don't want nobody gettin' flattened under a load of wood."

"Police," I said. That's all it took. We went back to his office and he pulled out the accounts for Freeman while I looked over his shoulder. He fingered through the bills. There were no unusual charges or purchases with Billings's signature. When I asked him whether Freeman had ever questioned any of the charges, Abe told me that neither Neville nor his accountant had come in to go over the account. So, Freeman had lied about why he fired Billings.

I went back to the station and managed to talk Stark into going out to Flower with me. I had to promise to avoid all wakes, keep the speed down, and to buy Caribs and calamari down at the docks when we got back.

I pulled the *Wahoo* up to one of the moorings out in the bay at Flower and Stark and I motored to shore in the dinghy. Stark wore one of those orange life preservers that went over the head and hung around the neck—one of the most cumbersome and uncomfortable lifesaving devices known to man, especially when the thermometer was topping a hundred. He tried to look nonchalant as he held fast to the ropes that ran along the sides of the dinghy.

The boat dock on Flower was deserted. I wondered where Freeman's guard was. Stark pulled the life jacket off and threw it in the dinghy, his demeanor now restored to hard-assed. We ignored the no trespassing signs and walked straight through the trees to the main house. No one responded when we knocked. I tried the door. Locked. Stark and I agreed that it would be foolhardy to break in. Dunn would have a hard time explaining what the hell we'd been doing, especially to someone like Freeman. We walked around the grounds, checking the outbuildings. They too were locked.

"What would possibly be in a shed worth locking up and putting a guard on the island, no less?" I wondered aloud. We still hadn't seen the guy. Maybe Freeman had let him go.

"Could be tools, boat engine, all sorts of valuable stuff."

"Yeah, maybe."

We found nothing at all on the grounds that indicated why Freeman would have wanted Teddy Billings off the island, or why Teddy had been out here on several occasions watching from his boat through binoculars and sometimes coming ashore.

We walked back to the beach and along the shoreline. Neither one of us knew what we were looking for. But there had to be something. Billings had told Betty Welsh that there was something going on out here that Freeman didn't want anyone to know about.

"Look at this." Stark bent down to examine a stake that had been pounded into the sand. "It's a survey stake."

When we examined the area, we found more, an entire layout for a large structure. It was an ideal spot, backed against the trees and facing the beach. It looked too big to be a house, but then Freeman might be in for opulence and an image once he got elected.

Along the back edge of the staked area I stumbled across a disturbed turtle nest. Hundreds of broken eggshells were scattered in the sand.

"What the hell?" I squatted and examined the area with a stick.

"Musta been rodents, maybe birds, got to the nest," Stark said.

"Freeman told Liam and Tom that there weren't any turtles nesting out here."

"Maybe he never saw this nest."

"Well, someone spread poison around it." I pointed the stick to a few pellets that were mixed into the sand. "This is the same stuff they're using over at the project on Hermit."

When we got back to the *Wahoo*, I pulled out my dive gear and began suiting up.

"What do you think you're doing, Sampson?" Stark said.

"LaPlante said that dead turtles on Billings's boat could very well have ingested rat poison. I've only seen the poison at the project site, in Elyse's office, and now on Flower. But the thing is, that female turtle couldn't have ingested it while nesting. According to Liam and Tom, turtles forage in the water, not onshore. They go to shore for only one reason and that's to lay eggs. If the dead turtle on Billings's boat got into this poison, it wouldn't have been while nesting."

I pulled my mask over my face and rolled into the water. It was shallow here in the bay, no more than thirty feet, and absolutely clear. The bottom was sandy from the shore all the way out past the moorings, with patches of turtle grass—long slender green blades, sprinkled with sand. Farther out were coral formations.

I skimmed over the turtle grass, hovering just off the bottom and keeping my fins from stirring up sand. It's amazing what one can encounter in turtle grass. Sea cucumbers, conch, starfish lay in the sand among the blades. But what was really amazing were all of the wax pellets scattered among them. I pulled a plastic bag out of one of my vest pockets and was filling it with pellets from the ocean floor when I heard a boat approaching. When I surfaced, a dinghy had pulled alongside the *Wahoo*.

Stark was arguing with the driver, Freeman's guard. I removed my fins and weight belt and threw them in the *Wahoo*, then climbed up on the back transom, pulling off my mask and dive vest.

When the guy saw I'd been diving, he went ballistic.

"Can't be divin' out here. Mr. Freeman finds out, he have my hide."

"How come you weren't keeping an eye on the place?" I already knew the answer to that question. He had a welt forming on the side of his neck and a slash of frosty orange lipstick on his chin.

Chapter 33

❧

Back in Road Harbor, Stark and I stopped at the Calamari Cart, a dockside vendor that mimicked a city hot-dog stand, except this one sold fried calamari in those red-and-white checkered cardboard containers. I inhaled half a basket of fried calamari and a beer. Stark had already consumed three overflowing baskets of the stuff and was starting on his fourth when I left. Once he filled up, he was going back to question Eleanor Billings about the poison out at Flower. I was going to talk to Neville Freeman.

Freeman's office was in a new, three-story building down on Nibbs Street. The building was typically island—bright pink, pink roof, lush with hibiscus and bougainvilleas. A gold plaque on the front exterior was labeled "The Freeman Building." I went inside and checked the directory. Neville's offices occupied the entire second floor.

A receptionist was sitting at a desk in the waiting room that opened up at the top of the stairs. Freeman was just coming out of his office—with O'Brien, of all people. I didn't like it.

"Guess you're here to see me, not Peter," Freeman said, with lecherousness in his tone. "Why don't you have a seat in my office while I walk Peter out?"

"Great. I'll talk to you later, O'Brien," I said. I walked to the window and saw the two of them emerge from the building. I went over to Freeman's desk and, with the eraser end of a pencil, nonchalantly pushed around the papers that layered the desktop. Most appeared to be campaign material.

I took another quick peek out the window. O'Brien and Freeman were standing on the sidewalk and it looked like they were arguing. I could hear Freeman's receptionist down the hall shooting the breeze with another woman. I hurried back and started shuffling through the stack of paper in the basket on the corner of the desk. At the bottom, I found a contract. It was for the transfer of Flower Island to a company called ASR Associates.

I slipped it back in place when I heard Freeman's angry voice directed at his receptionist. He was giving her grief about the length of her coffee breaks. I was standing at the window admiring the view when he walked in.

"Have a seat, Detective Sampson. I hope this is a social call and not business." Freeman was too intent on studying my legs to look me in the eyes. I knew he was wishing my shorts were a whole lot shorter. I, however, wished they were a whole lot longer. I got right to the point.

"Detective Stark and I were out on Flower today."

"What were you doing out there? You don't have any right to go on the island without my permission," Freeman said, his lust quickly turning to anger.

"We went out looking for you," I lied. "I was hoping to ask you a few more questions about Teddy Billings."

"I told you to make an appointment. Besides, there's nothing else I can tell you."

"Well, he did work for you and some things have come up since we last spoke."

"'Did' is the operative word here." He stood behind his desk, knuckles on the surface in a pose that was meant to intimidate.

"I'd just like to confirm a few things," I said. "He'd been with you for how long?"

"A couple of years, but I didn't know him except in terms of his work on Flower. He and his wife lived in the cottage in back. I rarely saw him, except in passing. He knew what needed to be done around the place without a lot of guidance from me."

"You said that he'd been charging huge sums on your account, but I talked with Abe down at the lumberyard. He says no one from your office ever checked on the account and there was no indication of a problem with Billings doing any excessive charging. Why did you think he was stealing?"

"I'm afraid you'd have to ask my accountant, but don't expect access to my private finances, Ms. Sampson."

"Billings told Betty Welsh that he thought something was going on out at Flower. Want to explain what?"

"Nothing but Billings looking for a way to get even. What better way than to have Welsh print some dirt about me in the island newspaper and threaten my candidacy." He was leaning over his desk now, eyes glaring. "In terms of his murder," he went on, "I have no idea, but it's pretty obvious Billings had a temper. And it's also obvious to me at least that he was a thief. Maybe he stole from the wrong person."

When I asked him why Billings was hanging out around the island, Freeman shrugged and said he wouldn't be surprised if Teddy was looking for the chance to come ashore when they were gone and get even, maybe vandalize the place.

"Sylvia told me he was drunk when he was out there the last time, but the coroner didn't find a trace of alcohol in his system," I said.

"Don't know where she got that idea."

"She said you told her."

"She's mistaken. And there is nothing more I can tell you about Billings."

"One other thing," I said before he had a chance to end the conversation. "We came across some rat poison out there. What's that all about?"

"I hired a fellow to get rid of the rats. They've become a real problem." Freeman didn't miss a beat.

"Did you think about asking for assistance from the woman doing the eradication on Hermit Cay?"

"My guy knows what he's doing."

"Why are the pellets scattered all over the bottom of the bay then?"

He hesitated for just a split second. "Evidently, one of the boxes broke on the deck of the boat and the pellets were swept into the water."

Freeman acted surprised when I told him about the disturbed turtle nest.

"In the fifty years I have lived on that island, I have never seen a turtle nesting and I'm sure there will never be another. It was a fluke. I imagine rats got into it. You can see why I want to get rid of them." God, Freeman had a quick answer for everything. Perfect politician.

"I hear you're selling the island?"

"I don't know where you heard that, but it's rubbish."

I didn't think it was wise to tell him I'd been rifling through his desk. Freeman was getting really pissed, red splotches surfacing under his dark skin.

"Now, Detective, if you don't mind, I have a meeting." He'd finally had enough. He stood and ushered me to the door.

"You know I can offer you a very lucrative position on the police force, once I'm elected," he said, his tone shifting from indignation to something worse—a damned purr. "But I need to know that you are a team player." He was standing with his hand on the doorknob. He actually put the other arm around my waist. I pushed him away and glared.

"Don't cross me, Detective," he said, and opened the door.

"Is that a threat, Neville?"

"Just a friendly suggestion."

O'Brien was sitting in the shade waiting for me when I came out of Freeman's building.

"How about a walk?" he said as he stood and took my arm, not giving me a choice.

"I don't know why you are supporting that asshole," I said. "He's a womanizer and he's corrupt. He actually offered me a better position on the force if I would be a 'team player,' as he put it."

"I agree. In fact that's why I was up at his office. I told him that I had decided against endorsing him. I've heard him talking out of both sides of his mouth during meetings with various constituents. He's trying to appease everyone, but once he's in office, it's going to be his agenda."

We headed down to the waterfront and walked along the sidewalk. A breeze was blowing in off the sea.

"Perfect sailing conditions," O'Brien said.

I waited for him to get to the point. He hadn't been sitting in front of Freeman's office waiting for me to talk about the weather.

"I get the feeling you're avoiding me," he finally said.

"Come on, Peter. You know I've been tied up in this thing with Elyse."

"So much so that you can't return my call? I left a message on your machine at the office."

I'd gotten it but didn't admit that to O'Brien.

The last time I'd seen Peter was when I'd dived out at Billings's boat a couple days ago, and we hadn't really talked since that morning on the *Sea Bird*. I wasn't avoiding him but I hadn't made a point of seeing him either. I didn't want to be pressured about our relationship.

"Admit it, Hannah—you're just plain scared. When are you going to get past your fear of getting too close? Instead of letting me help you through Elyse's death, you're pushing me away. You need to let the people who care about you, help you."

"Let's not have this conversation now, okay?"

"Never the right time is it, Hannah?"

"Look, I know you're concerned about me and I appreciate it, but I just need some space. Can't we just leave it at that for a while?"

"Okay. The ball's in your court. You call me when you're ready to talk." O'Brien stormed off and left me standing there.

Goddammit, why couldn't he let things be?

When I got back to the office, I called LaPlante. I needed to know whether they had figured out what had happened to the missing boxes of poison. Her assistant, George, answered. He told me that no one had taken those boxes to the site. They were just plain unaccounted for. I queried him again about who had access. Same story. Everyone who worked at the site had a key to the lab.

"How many people would that be?"

"Let's see. There's the three regular volunteers—Brian, Liz, and me. A couple of temporary volunteers also had keys while they were working for us. That would be Elyse Henry and two Parks Service people who came over from St. John for a week."

"Do you have records of all those keys being returned?" I asked.

"Let me check." I could hear him rummaging through a drawer. Finally he came back on the line. "Looks like there's only three here but I had four extras made."

Obviously, the record system involved throwing the key in the drawer. "Do you remember anyone else being in the lab besides the authorized volunteers?"

"Just the fellow who visited Elyse. He was here with her and Brian helping load some boxes on the boat to take out to the cay."

"That would be Alex Reidman?"

"Yeah, that's his name."

Chapter 34

I headed up to the Callilou to talk to Reidman. He'd been like a gnat buzzing around my ear that I brushed away. I knew it was because I didn't want to believe Elyse could misjudge anyone so completely. Now the gnat was evolving into a swarm. His anger when he'd found me at Elyse's office that morning, then going to Dunn and complaining that I'd been trespassing, the break-in and his prints on the refrigerator . . . And he'd been the one to bring up the dead turtle that night Mary and I had eaten at the Callilou. He'd probably heard it was in the Rambler's trunk.

I drove down along the waterfront. Dozens of brilliantly painted fishing boats were pulled up on the beach and nets were spread out in the sand to dry. Several fish traps were stacked up near one of the sheds. I could see a sailboat out in the channel, mainsail flopping from side to side in the wind—someone having trouble getting the boat pointed just right.

It was almost three when I got to the Callilou. There was only one car in the lot, an old brown Plymouth. The "Closed" sign hung on the front of the restaurant but the door was open. I went in and hollered a couple times, but the music in the kitchen was blasting. Jimmy Cliff, if I wasn't mistaken.

I made my way through the dining room and past the swinging doors into the kitchen. The chef was standing near the stove deftly chopping scallions with a huge knife. He threw them in a pan of butter, swinging his hips and singing. He wore a jacket that was as starkly white as his skin was black.

"Hello," I shouted over the music.

"You got a delivery, you can drive round da back," he hollered, still bent over his task.

"Actually, I'm looking for Alex Reidman."

"Oh, sorry dar, ma'am," he said, turning and reducing the volume. "What dat you be sayin'?"

"Alex Reidman? Is he here?"

"Naw, ain't seen him around at all dis fine day. Can I be helpin' you?"

"You know when he'll be back?"

"No. Da man weren't here when I got in. Usually he be back in time for da dinner crowd."

"Thanks." I headed out the door as he cranked the volume up to deafening levels.

I went back through the dining room and stopped at the hostess stand. The steps up to Reidman's apartment were behind it, carpeted in deep red plush. What the hell. The chef would never hear me up there, that's for sure.

At the top of the stairs, artificial ferns stood sentry on either side of double doors, a brass knocker on each, especially made with Reidman's monogram, ASR. Same initials as on the contract in Freeman's office.

I lifted one of the knockers and let it drop, the sound echoing down the steps. I waited for a couple minutes, then tried the door. It was unlocked. I eased it open slowly and called out, then stepped inside.

The apartment was just as Elyse had described. I found myself standing in one expansive room. The ceiling towered above and angled off to a peak at a stone wall from which water trickled down into a pool. The remaining walls were glass, with a panoramic view of ocean. Reidman's apartment and the restaurant below had been built right out on the point in the rocky outcropping, the terrain dropping straight down to the shore, where waves crashed off the rocks.

The interior was done in angles and lines, strictly modern, wood floor polished to a fine hue. He'd decorated the place in black and white, accented with chrome, marble, and glass. I didn't know much about art, but the stuff he had scattered around looked expensive—some abstract oils and several stone sculptures. The place was a completely closed environment, air-conditioned and sterile. Not a balcony or deck opened to the outside. It felt a little like a fishbowl. I'd have gone nuts living here, unable to open a window or step outside to the ocean air.

I wandered through the place, looking for anything that might tell me more about Reidman. There wasn't much— tables spotless and uncluttered, a couple of *Architectural Digest*s strategically placed on the glass coffee table in front of a black leather couch.

The entire apartment seemed more like a showroom than a place to live.

There was a door off to the right. I turned the knob. Damned if it wasn't locked. Odd, a locked door in an apartment where the front door was left unlocked. Reidman obviously didn't want anyone wandering into that room—clearly I needed to get in there. I knelt and examined the lock. Pretty basic. I carried a set of tools on my key chain for just such occasions and had the door open in a matter of seconds.

This was Reidman's office and den, the only place that really looked lived in. There was a stereo, a TV, and a couple of lounge chairs in one area. The other corner held a high-tech complex of computer equipment, fax machine, copier, you name it. A coffee machine in the corner was still on, the pot half full—a reminder that Reidman could be back any minute.

I took a quick look around his desk: bills from purveyors, several marked overdue; a business checkbook for the restaurant; daily deposits; employee check stubs. I opened the desk drawers, thumbed through bank statements. In the bottom drawer under a stack of restaurant stationery was a separate set of bank statements for ASR Associates. The last deposit had been a nice round $100,000. The account balance was close to $750,000, but had been down to almost zero the month before. Where was that kind of money coming from and what the hell was Reidman doing with it?

I opened a nearby file cabinet, oak and antique. I was about to pull out a file labeled *Deeds* when the music from the kitchen quit and I heard voices. It sounded like Reidman was giving the chef grief.

I eased the file drawer closed, stuffed the bank statements back under the stationery, took a look around the room to make sure I'd left it the way I'd found it, and pulled the door closed and locked behind me. I had just settled on the leather couch and opened a *Fortune* magazine when Reidman walked in.

"Alex," I said, putting on the most innocent smile I could muster, "I hope you don't mind. The door was open. Your chef said you wouldn't mind if I waited for you."

"No problem," he said, but I could tell he was not pleased to see me. I set the magazine down and gave him another one of my winning smiles.

"What are you doing here, Hannah?"

"I thought you could help me figure a few things out."

"I can try," he said.

"Do you know if Elyse had any reason to bring any rat poison back from Hermit Cay?" I asked.

"That's a funny question. I don't see why she would. What makes you ask?"

"They found several boxes missing. When I found her office trashed on Thursday, there were a few of the pellets scattered on the floor. Didn't know what they were till I saw them at LaPlante's lab."

"Maybe she had rats at the office," he suggested.

All of a sudden everyone had rats. "Did you ever go into her specimen refrigerator for anything?"

"Why would I do that?"

"We took prints after the break-in. Got a nice clean one

off the refrigerator handle that matched the one on the wine bottle I pulled out of the *Caribbe* wreckage. Was thinking it might be yours."

"Hell, I guess I opened the fridge. I stopped by one afternoon when Elyse was working at the microscope. She asked me to pull out a sample for her."

Nothing like the miracle of recall at the appropriate prodding. I supposed it could be true.

"So Elyse never talked to you at all about what she did on Sunday?"

"I told you. I didn't see Elyse on Sunday. Last time we'd been together was for dinner on Friday night."

"One other thing, Alex," I said standing. "I was wondering about ASR Associates. I didn't know you had another business."

"My other business is just that—my business. Come on, I'll walk you out." He took a quick glance at his office door and then opened the front door and locked it behind him.

I wanted to know what was in the file labeled *Deeds* that I'd found in Reidman's office.

If I hurried, I could get to the island clerk and recorders office before they closed. I knew any property transfers would be filed there.

The clerk glanced at his watch and gave me a dirty look when I walked in. "We be closin' in twenty minutes," he said.

"I'd like to look through the land transactions that have occurred in the past, say, six months," I said.

"That will take me at least a half hour to pull and you got to be lookin' at it here. I think you better come back in da mornin'."

I flashed my badge and a fifty. "How about you stay long enough to pull the records and I'll lock the door when I leave? I'm a police officer and this is urgent."

He plucked the bill out of my hand and headed to the back. While he was collecting the materials, I used the phone to call Stark. He'd spoken with Eleanor Billings. She said she'd seen turtles nesting on Flower many times in the years she'd worked there—wasn't anything she gave much thought to. When Stark asked her about the poison, she remembered Teddy telling her he'd seen some boxes marked hazardous in one of the sheds and that he'd intended to ask Freeman about it.

"So much for Freeman's story that there were no turtles nesting on Flower. Why lie about it?" Stark asked.

"I've got some ideas. I'll call you back." I hung up as the clerk returned balancing a twelve-inch stack of bound printouts. He dropped them on the desk behind the counter.

"You can work here. I don mad a fresh pot a'coffee. Just be sure to turn it off when you leave and lock da door."

"Hey, thanks."

"No problem. I can be usin' dis money." He pulled on his cap and left.

I poured myself a cup of coffee, then settled in. The printouts were organized by dates. I started with the most recent transactions. There were records of stores being bought and sold, building permits being applied for and approved, records of parents transferring their home to a child.

By the time I got to the bottom of the stack, I'd found four entries with ASR Associates as the new owner, including Flower. Officers were listed as Neville Freeman, president; Alex Reidman, vice president and treasurer; and Sylvia Freeman, secretary. ASR had gotten the other properties for amazingly little, and Flower had simply been transferred. All of them were up near North Sound and made a nice ring around the sheltered bay.

At least some of the money moving in and out of the account had to be going toward these properties. Where the hell was Reidman getting that kind of money? Elyse had said he'd left a lucrative business in finance in the States. He probably had made a bundle, more than Elyse had ever suspected. And he'd have made contacts. He may have brought in a few investors.

I could think of only one reason that Freeman would agree to turn Flower over to a corporation and then buy up the surrounding property. That would be for development. They planned to turn the gorgeous bay into something less beautiful but more lucrative. Those stakes that Stark and I had found were probably the layout for the first structure.

I knew that the current administration in the BVI had written a set of policies about development in response to the islanders' concerns. Few wanted to see the islands turned into another St. Thomas, teeming with visitors in three-thousand-room hotels, beaches littered with umbrellas under which tourists sipped rum punch. Getting Freeman elected would ensure that would change. With political power and favors brokered, policies could be manipulated or just plain ignored.

But the law was another matter, and destroying habitat of the sea turtle was against the law. Freeman had managed to keep people off the island for years, but he would have known that he'd have to eliminate the turtles before he could start building. He couldn't hide them from every construction worker who set foot on the island and he couldn't pay everyone off. When Liam and Tom arrived to begin the survey of nesting grounds he must have realized that he had to eliminate the turtles before someone discovered them. No wonder he'd hired a guard and been so insistent that no one was allowed on the island.

Freeman would have wanted Eleanor and Teddy Billings off Flower when he decided to eliminate the turtles. Accusing him of stealing was a good way to get rid of him. But Billings wasn't about to let it go. He'd realized something was going on and he'd been determined to find out what it was. When he snuck ashore he'd found that dead turtle. More than likely he'd also found the ruined nests and broken into the shed to discover the poison. He may have actually been stupid enough to tell Freeman he was going to talk with Betty Welsh. Freeman and Reidman had to kill him or lose everything.

But what about Elyse? She'd been up at Flower that Sunday to take water samples. She'd found something—poison pellets, a dead turtle, something. Unfortunately she'd probably told Reidman about it. So he'd dropped sleeping pills in her tea, rigged the boat, and took off, crushing Daisy's sand castle as he hurried across the beach.

The trouble was, this was all speculation. The land transactions were there in black and white, but there was no law against buying property or setting up a corporation. With some investigation though, the kind that Betty was so good at, their plans would be exposed. All she'd need to do was discover what firm had done the surveying on the island. The poisoning of the turtles would also come out.

It would mean the loss of the election and the fortune they would have made on the development, fines, maybe even short jail time because of the turtles. It wasn't enough. They had killed to protect their investment. I wanted these guys in jail for life for killing Elyse, but I didn't have a shred of evidence. They had covered their tracks well. No weapons, prints, or witnesses could identify them.

Chapter 35

❧

It was dark by the time I pulled the door to the records office closed, stepping from icy air-conditioning into a blanket of mugginess. Businesses were shut down tight, lights off, the sidewalk deserted. Across the street in the alley, a trash can suddenly clattered to the ground and rolled to a halt. I overreacted, pulling my .38 as a scrawny gray cat darted out of the darkness and scurried down the sidewalk, tail pointed to the sky.

I holstered the gun and headed past the alley toward Main, hoping to find a cab. A fleeting gust of wind swirled through the vacant street, blowing dust and paper across my shoes. By the time I felt his presence, it was too late. The man emerged from the shadows of the doorway, gun raised.

"Don't try it," he said, as I reached for my weapon. "I won't hesitate to shoot."

"Carr? What the hell?"

"Sorry, Hannah. Hand me the gun, real slow," he said, moving into the light.

Edmund Carr, my dive partner? Another piece fell into place. "Guess you were right in the middle of this, huh, Ed? Since you work at the bank you were able to transfer funds and properties."

"That's right. I helped Reidman and Freeman get those properties real cheap, foreclosing on overdue loans."

I remembered the man in his office that day, desperate for an extension that Carr was not about to give him.

"Come on, Ed. You can't get away with this. Just put the gun down." I tried to reason. It didn't work.

"I said I'll shoot," he warned again, pointing the damned gun at my chest.

Staring at Carr, I decided to gamble and grab my gun, hoping that he wouldn't be fast enough to stop me. He was a banker after all, not a cop, and he'd made the mistake of moving in too close. When I moved to unholster my gun with my right hand, his eyes followed. In one quick swipe, my left elbow made contact with his face and I felt the distinctive cracking of bone. I knew I'd broken his nose. His gun went skittering across the walk. I was reaching for my weapon when suddenly I felt hard steel pressed to the back of my head.

"Hold it right there, Sampson. Just drop it." I let the .38 drop from my fingers and turned.

It was Alex Reidman. "Just give me an excuse," he said, jamming the gun into my temple. "Jesus, Carr, can't you do anything right."

Carr stumbled to his feet, pressed his hand against his nose and glared. "Goddammit, Sampson. You'll pay for this," he said, wiping blood away with his shirtsleeve.

"Not now, just go get the damned car," Reidman said.

A couple of minutes later, Carr pulled up to the curb in a classic red BMW convertible, dented and scraped. Daisy's car. I figured the rest of the paint was on my Rambler.

"This your car, Alex?"

"Yep, it's a beauty, huh? I keep it garaged except for occasions like this."

"Yeah, or when you're rigging boats to explode or shoving needles into someone's arm."

"That's right—and I'm not too happy with the dents you put in it. Now just get the hell in."

Reidman opened the back door and shoved me onto the seat. Carr climbed in beside me.

"Thought this was supposed to be a no-brainer," Carr said as Reidman hit the gas and swerved out of the lot.

"Don't worry, you'll survive. Next time, don't get so close to her damned elbow."

"So what are we going to do?" Carr said, glancing nervously out the back window.

"We'll meet Freeman over at Flower as we planned. No one's going to miss Sampson until tomorrow and they certainly won't be looking for her out there."

Reidman pulled into the marina at Road Harbor. "Go down and fire up the boat. I'll bring Sampson."

"Why don't we just shoot her here?" Carr said.

"Not a good idea. Shots will bring the cops to the docks. Besides, we might need her."

I could see the wheels turning. Reidman was working on a scheme to end any investigation into the deaths of Elyse and Billings. It would involve keeping me alive until he could work out the details.

Freeman was standing on the dock on Flower Island when Reidman pulled up and cut the engines. He'd probably heard the cigarette boat's noisy rumble all the way up at the house. He shone his flashlight on the boat, the beam cutting across my face.

"What the hell is she doing with you?" He didn't wait for an answer. "Get her inside," Freeman ordered, and stormed up the path. No doubt who was in charge here. Carr jumped onto the dock and I followed, noticing the keys that he'd left dangling from the ignition. Reidman was right behind me jamming the damned gun in my ribs.

"Hey, take it easy, Alex," I said, glaring at him over my shoulder.

Sylvia was standing at the door when the four of us came up the path.

"Neville?" She was confused when she realized that Reidman had a gun pointed at me. "What is going on? Why is Detective Sampson here? Who is that man?" she asked, referring to Carr. I could hear the fear rising with each question.

"Calm down, Sylvia. This is Edmund Carr. We have a little business with Sampson here. You just go on out to the kitchen, darling."

Jeez, what a condescending jerk. Sylvia wasn't putting up with it either. Freeman had clearly crossed a line.

"Don't think you can dismiss me that way," she said. "What kind of trouble are you in?"

"Seems the detective is upset about the turtles. We need to set her straight."

"I told you poisoning those turtles was a bad idea," she said.

"Worse was killing Billings and going after Elyse," I said before Freeman could stop me. A little discord among this group could only do me good.

"Keep your damned mouth shut." Freeman swung at me, connected, and sent me crashing into a coffee table.

"What is she talking about, Neville?" Obviously, Sylvia hadn't been informed of all her husband's activities.

"Come on, Sylvia," I said, sitting up on my knees and wiping the blood from my bottom lip. "Surely you know that Neville won't let anything stand in the way of his ambition? Or do you just pretend it isn't happening, like you do with his philandering?"

Sylvia dropped into a nearby chair, stunned.

"You need to keep your damned mouth shut or else I'll shut it permanently," Freeman said.

I ignored him. "Alex, you know you'll be the one charged with the attempt on Elyse. I bet Freeman's kept his hands clean when it came to murdering her and Billings. Let me guess—he sent you and Carr out to kill Billings while he was being seen at some campaign event by dozens of people."

"I know what you're doing, Sampson," Reidman said. "It won't work. Freeman and I have been partners for some time now. We need each other. You think I'd come down to this godforsaken place to retire and open a restaurant?

"I met Freeman when he came to New York looking for funding two years ago. He had his plan all worked out—a multimillion dollar resort complex that catered to the wealthy. But he needed a partner, someone who could help bring in financing and ensure his election. This is just the beginning of a very lucrative relationship for both of us. Once Freeman is elected, well, let's just say we'll make millions."

"What if he doesn't win?"

"Oh, he'll win. Paying to make sure of that has taken only chump change. A few payoffs here, a few threats there. We've got the election in our pockets."

I switched my gaze to Carr who was leaning against the far wall, smoking. "How the hell did you get involved in this, Ed?" I said.

Reidman didn't give Carr the chance to respond. "Ed here helped us acquire those properties," he said. "Very convenient having the VP in charge of loans. Half his accounts are in arrears. All he had to do was pressure the owners of the properties we wanted. They were real willing to sell at a reasonable price when he threatened to foreclose."

"Guess Billings's boat didn't just shift in the current and tumble over that embankment when we were diving, did it, Ed?"

"Hey, I'm real sorry about that, but you should never have gone back in there after that turtle. Can't believe you made it out."

"Are you the one who tried to break into my trunk?"

Carr just smirked.

"You know, Ed, I'm beginning to get the picture here. And guess what, you're the one who's expendable—more than expendable. Now that all the land has been acquired, these two don't need your services anymore."

"Shut the fuck up, Sampson," Reidman said. Finally I had hit a nerve.

"Come on, Ed, don't you see it? They're going to pin all of this on you and step away free of any implication that they have done anything. You're the only one we can tie to Billings's boat. I told you to quit smoking—DNA tests came in this morning. They indicate that the cigarette butt I retrieved from the *Lila B* was yours, and we found the crowbar, your prints, Billings's blood. Stark is getting a warrant. He's probably at your apartment as we speak." I could lie with the best of them.

Carr was buying it, getting nervous. He looked at Reidman, then Freeman, and realized I could be right. I kept talking.

"Sure, they shoot me, put the gun in your hand and then kill you. Freeman calls the cops afterward, says you brought me out here—God knows why, probably thought the island was deserted—and killed me. Freeman says he heard the shot, grabbed the gun he keeps for protection, came running, and shot you—too late to save me though. With the right spin, he could turn it all his way. Make himself a hero. After all, he got the guy who killed me and Teddy Billings, probably Elyse too.

"How will you lay all the blame on Carr though?" I said, turning to Freeman. "I mean, what's his motive?"

I was making it up as I went, but I could tell I wasn't too far off. So could Carr. He had lifted his gun and pointed it at Neville's chest.

"Come on, Ed," Freeman said, holding his hands in front of him. "You're letting her get to you."

Suddenly a shot reverberated through the room from behind me. Carr put his hand to his chest and looked amazed when it came away bloody. Seconds later Reidman fired again, this time a direct shot to the head. Carr went down hard and didn't move.

"You've got a big mouth, Sampson," Reidman said, pointing the gun at me. "But hell, that's done. Just like you said, Carr had served his purpose. We have the properties we need. We've set it up just as you've suggested. We've already planted a needle and some potassium chloride in his apartment."

"Dunn won't buy it. Neither will Stark. They will want to know why," I said. "Why Elyse? Why Billings? And why me?"

"Don't worry about it, Sampson. We'll figure it out. Maybe Elyse and Billings both saw Carr doing something illegal, like poaching turtles. Hell, maybe it was a love triangle—Elyse and Billings involved and Carr a jealous former lover. I like that idea."

"Yeah, you would, having been in similar situations yourself," I said. "But you'll never convince anyone with those stories."

"I'll make sure there aren't a lot of questions. And why would there be? Everything will be tied up in a neat little package, law and order restored."

"Stark and Dunn aren't fools. Not a chance you can get away with this."

"Oh, I'm not too worried about Stark and Dunn. Elections are only a week away. Once I'm in office, I'll be shaking things up in the police department. It will mean going along or getting out."

I glanced at Sylvia. She'd been practically catatonic, observing it all from her chair in the corner. Carr's gun had skittered across the floor and lay at her feet. Now she bent over and picked it up, examined it, and then pointed it at her husband. Her expression said it all: she'd put up with this asshole long enough.

"Sylvia, give me the gun, honey, before you get hurt," Freeman cooed. Reidman had moved from behind me and was quietly making his way around for a clear shot at Sylvia.

It happened fast. I saw Freeman give Reidman the nod. Sylvia saw it too. Understanding flashed across her face just before the bullet struck.

I had little doubt about who would be next.

Chapter 36

❧

I was out the front door before Sylvia hit the floor and halfway down the trail by the time they got out to the porch.

"Get her!" Freeman yelled.

It was black in the trees, the path littered with rocks and brush. Somehow I'd managed to stay on the trail and was just about out of the trees when I caught my foot on a root and went down hard, something sharp slashing into my knee. I ignored the pain, stumbled to my feet, ran across the beach and down the dock. If those keys weren't still in the ignition, I'd be up shit creek, trapped. I jumped into the boat and found them right where Carr had left them. I had just released the line when I heard Reidman stomping down the dock.

"Stop!" he shouted, raising the gun.

Right. I threw the boat into gear and was away from the dock when he fired. When I looked back, I could see him and Freeman clambering into the other boat that had been tied up to the dock. I could tell by the sound of the engines that they would have no trouble keeping up with me.

I headed out toward the tip of Virgin Gorda, a barely visible lump on the dark horizon. The swells were high, at least eight feet, with whitecaps breaking. I was taking them straight on, the boat blasting through the water, sending spray over the windshield and drenching me in salt water.

When I rounded the point and turned into the channel to-ward Tortola, the ocean flattened out and the boat lifted to plane over the surface, picking up speed.

I glanced behind me and damned if they weren't gaining on me fast, just yards off my stern. Reidman emptied his gun at me, the bullets pinging into the back of the boat. He was still too far to do any damage, but they'd be on top of me in minutes. I presumed the break in gunfire meant he was re-loading. I turned the boat hard to the left, then back, hoping to slow them in the wake I was creating. Engines whining, their boat went blasting over one wave, then the next, flying through the air, then slamming back on the water.

I was running close to shore when Reidman's aim got better. A bullet smashed the windshield six inches from my head. The next couple hit the hull, and seconds later the en-gine sputtered, then smoothed out again. I knew it was only a matter of time before it quit.

I turned hard into shore. The last thing I wanted was to be caught out here in the water. There would be no escaping. At this distance, it was too dark to make out the shoreline, but I knew I was at the western end of Virgin Gorda, close to the Baths. This was a popular day anchorage for boaters. The white expanse of beach ended where boulder formations towered some three stories high into the water. I'd either end up smashing the boat into one of the rocks on my way in or I'd get lucky and find the sand. Freeman had sped right past me when I turned in and was now coming around. I could hear him cut back on the throttle.

I peered into the blackness, trying to pick out shapes. I'd had to reduce my speed. I barely missed a pile of rocks just under the surface, apparent only by the disturbed water that swirled around them. Then the dim white line of the beach took shape, a small patch nestled among the granite mon-sters. I maneuvered the boat in through the boulders. Once I had a clear shot at the beach, I gunned it. The engine sput-tered once, then caught, and the boat blasted through the shallow water and scraped the sandy bottom. I braced myself as it shot up onto the shore and came to an abrupt halt on the beach.

The shore was deserted at this time of night; the vendors' stalls, usually overflowing with sarongs and T-shirts, were empty skeletal shapes. I jumped out of the boat and ran straight for the boulders. O'Brien and I had climbed through these rocks many times. The sandy trail wound its way among the boulders, through watery caverns, past caves, and up steep rock faces, eventually coming out the other side to one of the most spectacular little coves on the entire island.

I knew there were plenty of places to hide. I heard the boat circling, Freeman and Reidman talking. Then they motored in slowly and cut the engines.

I left my shoes under a bush at the entrance to the trail, just obvious enough so that they'd see them. I wanted to make sure they knew I'd come in this way. I crouched low and crept spiderlike between two huge boulders that leaned into one another, forming a triangle opening at the bottom and marking the way into the boulder field.

Once through, a narrow trail between the towering rock walls led to a cavernous room. Though I couldn't see the watery pools inside, I could hear the water rushing into them from the sea just beyond. A ladder that had been installed for hikers went up to the top of a boulder and then down the other side.

I could hear Reidman and Freeman out on the beach. They were shining their lights into the boulders. Every once in a while a beam bounced across a rock wall. Then Freeman spotted my shoes.

"She's gone into the boulders on the main trail. She won't be hard to find."

I knew I'd have a much better chance at them one at a time. They were both armed. If I could take one down quickly, I'd be evening the odds. But how the hell was I going to separate them?

"You go around and come in from the other end of the trail," Freeman said. "I'll go in the front."

That was easy. I'd go for Freeman first. He would be within a couple of feet in a matter of minutes, and he'd be the easiest to take. He was out of shape—too many high calorie fund-raisers.

I climbed the ladder and eased my way along a narrow ledge above the room, back pressed against the rock wall, fingers feeling their way along the granite surface. I knew there was a crevice big enough to hide in maybe ten feet away. I'd noticed it every time I hiked through, thinking about what a perfect nook it would be from which to observe the cavern and not be seen. I never thought I'd really end up climbing into it. I had to assume that Freeman knew it was there too. I wouldn't be able to give him enough time to think about it.

I saw his light shining down the narrow passageway. Christ, I needed to find that hole before he walked into the room. Otherwise I'd be a sitting duck, standing on that ledge in full view. Finally my fingers came to the opening. I eased back into the dark just as Freeman stepped into the cavern.

He scanned the interior, his light skipping over the rock walls. Stray beams crossed the opening where I hid. Then he moved toward the pools and searched around rocky edges. I waited.

Then he started along the walls, shining the light in every possible crevice big enough to hide me. He was moving so damned slow. Finally, he stopped right below me.

I scurried out to the ledge, took a second to aim, and jumped. I came down right on top of Freeman and we tumbled to the floor. His light flew out of his hands and the gun went off, the bullet ricocheting off rock. He used his weight to roll on top of me with the gun still held tight. But Freeman was completely out of his league. He wasn't familiar with the ungentlemanly rules of engagement. I jammed my fingers in his eyes, and at the same time brought my knee up into his groin. He yelled and rolled off me. He was trying to scramble to his feet, the gun now dangling from his hand, when I grabbed the flashlight and smashed it into his skull. I knew by the sound that he'd be out for a while.

It wouldn't be that easy with Reidman. He would have heard the shot, and when Freeman didn't return his call, he'd know what the situation was. He'd be coming my way.

I grabbed Freeman's gun and ejected the clip. Only three rounds. I searched his pockets. Nothing. What the hell was he thinking, coming in after me without more ammunition?

I stood for a moment trying to figure out what my next move should be. I knew it was a mistake to head out of the protection of the boulders and back to the open beach. The boat I'd run up onto the sand wasn't going anywhere. And Reidman wouldn't have made the mistake of leaving the keys in their boat this time.

I'd have to wing it. A lot depended on Reidman. He would expect me to be between him and Freeman or else making my way out onto the beach and to the boat. I needed to find a way to get behind him. I headed into the dark interior of the boulder field in the direction I figured Reidman would be coming. He'd have his flashlight on and his finger on the trigger. This time, though, I had a weapon. Three bullets were better than an empty clip.

I was feeling my way up the boulder when I heard him coming up the other side. I slid back down it and darted onto a side trail as he jumped off the rock and planted his feet in the sand. He stood there listening and shining his flashlight down the trail. I waited in the dark. Something with sharp pointy claws crawled over my foot, hopefully just a crab. I resisted the urge to shake the damned thing off. Finally Reidman moved past and started down the trail.

I followed, my bare feet silent in the sand, but some instinct made him turn, his light hitting me right in the eyes.

"Hold it, Reidman," I warned when he saw me. I had my gun aimed at his head. He stood for a second, smirking, and flicked off his light. Instantly things went black. Shots echoed, one catching me just below the elbow. Searing pain streaked into my wrist. I ignored it and shot back, aiming for the gun flashes. I heard him moan then run down the trail.

"Shit," I muttered. "Stupid move, Sampson."

I turned on the flashlight I'd grabbed off Freeman and walked up the trail to where Reidman had stood. His light lay in the sand, a patch of which was saturated in red. So we'd both been hit.

The bullet had gone right through my arm and blood dripped off my numb fingertips. From the puddle in the sand though, I could tell that Reidman was in worse shape. I tore a strip of fabric from the bottom of my tank top and wrapped it around my forearm, using one hand and my teeth to tighten it in place.

Then I cut my light and followed the trail, a sandy band of white barely illuminated by a rising moon, that went in the direction Reidman had headed. If I was lucky he'd decided to give the whole thing up, go back to the boat, hightail it out of there, and nurse his wounds. But I knew I was dreaming. Reidman wasn't the type.

More than likely he would be waiting for me along the path just as I had waited for him. He was injured and no longer had a light but I had to assume he had more ammunition than I did, because I had only one bullet left. I'd fired two at him in the dark.

I moved ahead, placing each foot silently in front of the other in the soft sand, every sense alert for the unexpected— a pair of hands coming at me out of the dark, a bullet crashing into my chest.

I stopped and bent to examine the trail in the moonlight. If Reidman had stepped off the path into a side chute, I'd be able to track him. I could see the deep indentations in the wet sand, distinct from all the others. Reidman had on the cowboy boots he was so fond of wearing. I was sure that no self-respecting tourist or islander had been wandering around the Baths in cowboy boots in the past week. He was still on the trail, heading back toward the entrance.

I heard scraping on the rocks ahead. I kept going and seconds later reached the boulder that he had apparently just scaled. Even in the dark, I could see splotches of blood on the rocks. I touched it—sticky and wet.

I scurried up the side of the angled rock and stopped just before the top. I knew that the wall of boulders stretched out before me along the trail, one towering right next to the one I was perched on. Too damned many places to hide. Again I waited, listening, crouching on the boulder, working to ignore the throbbing in my arm and the blood that was seeping from under the makeshift bandage. I was scared shitless, heart pounding against my rib cage. I knew it was going to be him or me. His only hope of salvaging his future was to kill me.

Hell, maybe the best thing to do was go hide somewhere in the rocks until daylight and the ensuing tourist influx. Trouble was, I wanted this guy and I wanted him now. I crept up the remaining two feet to the top of the boulder and peered over.

I heard the distinct sound of the trigger click right before the bullet hit the rock near my left ear and ricocheted into the dark. I tumbled down the other side of the boulder, landed, and rolled as another bullet thunked into the sand where I had just lain.

Reidman kept firing in rapid succession. Finally, the inevitable occurred. He kept pulling the trigger, unwilling to accept the fact that his gun was empty. Clearly, Reidman had crossed over the edge of reason into the confusion of absolute fury. It was his undoing. He hurled the gun at me in the dark, then launched himself off the rock.

He was falling right toward me. I lay on my back, raised my weapon, and fired. My last shot. Dead center to the chest. He landed beside me and didn't move again.

Chapter 37

◦⁓◦

The night was typically Caribbean, filled with the chatter of crickets and tree frogs, the sea breeze perfumed with blossoms. The moon drew shadows in the sand, nine human figures outlined across the expanse of beach.

We were watching hatchlings, a hundred or more, struggling out of their nest. O'Brien, Tilda and Calvin, Daisy and Rebecca, Tom and Liam, Jillian, and me. It was the nest that Elyse and I had watched the turtle lay her eggs in—less than two months ago.

After Freeman's arrest, the election for chief minister had been just an exercise. Freeman's name had remained on the ballot, but a man in jail wasn't likely to win much support. Bertram Abernathy was elected by a landslide. Betty had written her story. Headlines in the *Island News* had filled the paper for weeks. Betty had agreed to the "anonymous source" concept, and I'd given her every sordid detail about Freeman and Reidman.

Freeman had spilled it all after the fiasco at the Baths and his arrest, laying all the blame on Alex Reidman. It became clear why Elyse had been a threat. She'd been out near Flower taking water samples and snorkeling that Sunday afternoon when she'd discovered the pellets in the turtle grass. She'd collected some of them, then swum into shore where she'd discovered a dead hawksbill washed up on the sand.

She took a tissue sample and arranged to meet with La-Plante.

Unfortunately she mentioned her discovery to Reidman that night when he'd gone to the *Caribbe*. After he dropped the pills in her tea, he'd ransacked the boat without finding the samples. He would have realized she'd left them in her office. Before he'd stepped off the *Caribbe* and trampled all over Daisy's sand castle, he'd rigged the stove and left Elyse to die.

The morning that I'd been in Elyse's office, Reidman had come in to find the samples. When he found me there, he'd had to wait for another opportunity. He'd locked the door when we left, and then complained to Dunn about my trespassing. Then he'd come back later, broken in, torn the place apart, and found the samples in the freezer. He'd been careless though, letting a few pellets scatter. He'd been standing right there in the hospital when Dr. Hall said Elyse would recover. He wasn't about to let that happen. I'd been a fool not to see it all from the beginning. I knew part of it was that I didn't think Elyse could have misjudged Reidman so badly herself.

Sylvia had known all along about her husband's plan to get rid of the turtles and had been against it. But she was no match for him. He'd told her to jump and she did, until he'd tried to kill her. Now she was looking forward to testifying against him. She was one angry woman. The bullet wound to her side was healing but she'd not be forgetting the moment that her husband had given Reidman the okay to shoot her.

Sylvia had announced that she was turning the properties that ASR Associates had acquired, including Flower, into a nature preserve. With Freeman in jail and Alex Reidman dead, she'd ended up as chief stockholder. The lesser investors and stockholders that Reidman had solicited in the States had gone along with her when they'd been threatened with exposure—attempts to fix an election, threats to endangered species. She'd already arranged for the removal of the poison from the island and the cleanup of the bay. Tom and Liam had spent weeks out there on damage control.

I was sorry about Edmund Carr. He'd been a good dive partner and I'd trusted him. Carr had gotten involved because of his position at the bank. Not only had he been helping with the purchase of property but he was also filtering money from Reidman into Freeman's campaign account using names of fictitious donors. One thing led to another, and suddenly he was with Reidman on the *Lila B* crushing Billings's head with a crowbar.

He'd have figured it was worth it. Once Freeman was elected, all three stood to make huge profits and God knows what their future plans in the islands would have been. But Carr had always been expendable. He should have known that.

Freeman was denying involvement. His lawyer was arguing that Reidman, along with Carr, had killed Billings and engineered everything from the poisoning of the turtles to the acquisition of the properties, and then had shot Carr and Sylvia. But it would never hold up. Sylvia would testify against him, and the crowbar with blood and hair embedded in the end had been found on his boat. There was plenty on Freeman even though he had never gotten his hands bloody. After all, he'd tried to kill a police officer out at the Baths, not to mention being an accessory to murder.

After Elyse's funeral, O'Brien and I had talked. We had taken a walk down to the waterfront, out to the little point past the SeaSail marina, and found an old cargo ship's anchor that had been embedded in the rocks for years. We sat on the iron hook, encrusted in rust and barnacles. Neither one of us had said a word since we'd left the cemetery. I really didn't know what to say. Finally, I started.

"I don't want to lose you, O'Brien. You know I'm crazy about you."

"So you say, but we've been kind of stuck in this relationship. You know I want more than a couple days a week. I want full time."

"I don't know. I just don't know. Can't you give me some time and space?" I pleaded.

"I've been giving you that. It's been over a year. And I don't really want to simply live together. I want to marry you, Hannah."

"Jeez, O'Brien."

"Look, Hannah. I'm forty-five years old. Every once in a while I think I'd like to have a kid, teach him to sail before I can't raise a mainsail any longer. I'd like to do that with you."

"O'Brien, a kid?" I'd given up on that idea when Jake had died. I'd come to terms with it long before I'd met O'Brien. And a kid at thirty-seven? Jeez. Some women did it, but I didn't think I could be one of them. I was way too scared of failing and way too worried about what I would have to give up.

"What about my job?" I asked him, because all the other stuff was too hard to talk about.

"You know, one of these days, that determination of yours to fix what might not be fixable is going to get you killed. Quit the job, Hannah, before that happens."

"I'm not ready to do that, O'Brien. You're asking me to plunge into a whole new life, one that I'm not at all sure I'll be good at."

"You won't know until you try it. I thought you were a risk taker," he said.

"Well," I said, "there are risks and then there are risks."

Finally though, I'd agreed to try living with him. I knew it was all tied to the loss of Elyse, though for the life of me I didn't know how, and I was still too brittle, my emotions too raw, to think it through.

I had told O'Brien I'd give it a couple of weeks and insisted on keeping the *Sea Bird* just in case. Now it had already been a month and damned, I was feeling comfortable with the arrangement.

O'Brien was standing with his arm around me as we watched the migration of the hatchlings to the sea. I fought the tears, remembering the night Elyse and I huddled on the beach whispering and watching the turtle build its nest and lay its eggs. Never in my worst dreams would I have thought that I'd be standing here now, without Elyse—that she wouldn't have been a part of our efforts to protect the turtles on their dangerous trek.

Jillian was standing right beside me. She looked at me and smiled. Then she ran to help Daisy and Rebecca scoop a wayward hatchling into the foaming waves.